Raves for
DEAD CITY

"A rising star on the horror scene."

—Fearnet.com

"*Dead City* is much more than just another zombie novel. It's got heart and humanity—a merciless, fast-paced, and genuinely scary read that will leave you absolutely breathless. Highly recommended!"

—Brian Keene

"The pace never lets up as McKinney takes us through the zombie apocalypse in real time—every second of terror is explored in depth as the world goes to hell.

—David Wellington, author of *Monster Island*

"*Dead City* is an absolute must-read for zombie lovers, but McKinney's excellent storytelling makes it a great read for anyone who loves the thrill of a gruesomely delicious page-turner."

—Fran Friel, Bram Stoker Award–nominated author of *Mama's Boy* and *Other Dark Tales*

"*Dead City* is a zombie tour de force—the story moves along at breakneck speed and never lets up. Joe McKinney knows how to toy with readers' emotions, masterfully capturing the essence of humanity in the face of unspeakable horror."

—Amy Grech, author of *Apple of My Eye* and *Blanket of White*

"Joe McKinney's DEAD CITY is a tense, thrill-a-page nightmare, written with great passion and authority. Surely one of the best zombie novels ever set down in blood."

—Lisa Morton, two-time Bram Stoker Award winner

"*Dead City* wastes no time jumping straight into mile-a-minute thrills and gruesome action. This seminal zombie novel culminates in a heart-wrenching finale, and I found that as the undead hordes multiplied, so too did my respect and admiration for author Joe McKinney."

—Joel A. Sutherland, Bram Stoker Award–nominated author of *Frozen Blood*

"*Dead City* is an action-packed, pedal-to-the-metal zombie novel that never loses sight of its humanity. McKinney uses his background as a homicide detective to bring a level of realism to a vision of the apocalypse that is both urgent and frightening. A timely nightmare that you will not put down. I can't wait to see where this series leads."

—Gregory Lamberson, author of *Personal Demons* and *Johnny Gruesome*

"McKinney writes zombies like he's been gunning them down all of his life."

—Weston Ochse, author of *Empire of Salt*

"*Dead City* is a full-throttle page-burner that torques up the terror and does not let up. You'll want the shotgun seat for this wild ride. Bring a crash helmet."

—J. L. Comeau, www.countgore.com

"Welcome to Joe McKinney's *Dead City* universe, a relentless thrill ride where real characters do bloody things on nightmare streets. Break out the popcorn, you're in for a real treat.

—Harry Shannon, author of *Dead and Gone*

"*Dead City* is a well-written and compelling first novel. A scary, fast-paced ride, full of hair-raising twists and turns that keep the reader spellbound. Do yourself a favor and snag a copy . . . thank me later.

—Gene O'Neill, author of *Taste of Tenderloin* and *Deathflash*

DEAD CITY

JOE McKINNEY

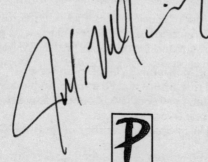

P

PINNACLE BOOKS
Kensington Publishing Corp.
www.kensingtonbooks.com

PINNACLE BOOKS are published by

Kensington Publishing Corp.
119 West 40th Street
New York, NY 10018

All Kensington titles, imprints, and distributed lines are available at special quantity discounts for bulk purchases for sales promotions, premiums, fund-raising, educational, or institutional use.

Special book excerpts or customized printings can also be created to fit specific needs. For details, write or phone the office of the Kensington special sales manager: Kensington Publishing Corp., 119 West 40th Street, New York, NY 10018, attn: Special Sales Department; phone 1-800-221-2647.

ISBN-13: 978-0-7860-2358-5
ISBN-10: 0-7860-2358-9

First printing: November 2006
First printing (with excerpt of *Apocalypse of the Dead*):
    October 2010

10 9 8 7 6 5 4 3

Printed in the United States of America

The new world may be safer, being told
The dangers and diseases of the old.

—John Donne

Chapter 1

There's an empty parking lot near the corner of Seafarer and Rood where I used to go to fight with my wife. Most district cops have some hidden little spot where they go to escape all the crap that comes with working patrol, and that parking lot was mine. From there I was pretty much invisible and I could still make almost any call in my district in less than five minutes.

My wife, April, and I were going at it at least once a week back then. When she'd call with that pissed-off tone in her voice that said I was in for a long one, I'd head straight for Seafarer and Rood. There, I'd pull under the canopy of an enormous oak tree near the back of the lot, and hunker down for an earful of whatever I'd done wrong. I used to watch the curves of its trunk and branches while she yelled at me, and even now, when she grows impatient with some little thing I've done, and the old familiar tone creeps back into her voice, I think of the dry, dusty smell of oak.

Six months before that, she'd given birth to a beautiful baby boy, our first. We named him Andrew James Hudson, after his grandfather. That little guy changed my world. After he was born, I'd tell anybody who'd listen that being his daddy was what I was put on this Earth to do.

Before Andrew, I worked the dogwatch shift, eleven at night till seven in the morning. That was back when April and I were first starting out. It wasn't the best for getting time together, because we only had a few hours during the evening to spend with each other. But I got an extra $300 a month for working at night, and that part was good.

Then, when April got pregnant, we started trying to plan the way things would work, and arguments kept flaring up.

One day she had a long phone conversation with her sister, who had two kids already, and that night she told me, "I'm gonna need you here with me at night. The baby's gonna be waking up every few hours to feed, and I can't do that alone."

So I asked some of the guys at work what I could do and found out I qualified for a hardship transfer. That's how I ended up on the second shift, 3 to 11 pm with Wednesdays and Thursdays off. April wasn't happy about me working on the west side, because it was a rough part of town, but when you put in for a hardship transfer, you have to take what they give you.

And hardships are only good for six months. After that, they move you back to wherever they need you, which is almost always on dogwatch.

On this particular evening, we were fighting about me going back to nights when Chris Tompkins pulled up next to me. He rolled down the window of his patrol car, and I gestured to him that I'd be a minute. I kept on listening. April was doing all the talking.

"Eddie, just tell them you need to stay on second shift," she said. "Why can't you just tell them that?"

"It doesn't work that—"

"What do they think? Now that the baby's born you can just go back to working nights? I need you home now more than ever."

"I know, sweetie."

"The whole reason you got the transfer is so we can take care of Andrew together."

"I know."

"I'm sure you're not the only one with a baby at home. Just go in there and tell them you need more time."

"But, sweetie, it doesn't work that—"

When she started up again, she was so loud I had to pull the phone away from my ear. I looked at Chris and rolled my eyes.

He smiled uncomfortably and gestured, *Do you want me to go?* He was cool that way, a good guy with a wife of his own. I hardly ever saw him outside of work, but if someone had asked I would have told them he was good people.

I shook my head, still listening for April to take a break.

Chris leaned back and turned up the volume on his car's stereo. He was listening to a news station, and I heard the newscaster say something about the flooding down in Houston. Then I heard something about volunteers from the Red Cross being attacked and beaten by the flood victims they were trying to save.

I didn't really catch it, because April was still going strong. Something about how I had had plenty of time to talk to them about staying on second shift, and the fact that I hadn't yet made her wonder if I really cared about how hard this was on her, staying at home with Andrew all the time.

I put my hand over the phone and said, "What in the hell are you listening to?"

April barked at me.

"Not you, sweetie," I said. "The guy next to me is listening to something on the news."

Chris turned it down.

"Thanks," I said. To April I said, "Go ahead, sweetie."

Just as she started up again, the dispatcher interrupted her. "52-70."

Chris sat up, waiting for me to respond. 52-70 was my call sign. Chris was 52-80.

When I didn't answer, the dispatcher called again. "52-70, Officer Hudson."

I said to April, "They're calling me. Hold on a second." April was still talking when I found the mike and said, "Go ahead, 52-70."

"52-70, take 52-80 with you. Make 318 Chatterton, 3-1-8 Chatterton, for seven to ten males fighting. Complainant says they look intoxicated."

Chris dropped his car into gear and waited for me to do the same.

I waved my hand at him and said, "Hold on." To the dispatcher I said, "52-70, ten-four. I've got 52-80 with me."

Chris still had his car in gear. He was looking at me with a mixture of impatience and uncertainty.

"Hang on," I told him.

To April I said, "Sweetie, they gave me a call. I've got to go."

"You weren't even listening to me, were you? When are you going to talk to them about staying on second shift?"

"Soon."

"Your transfer expires next month."

"Come on, hon, I've gotta go."

"Fine." But her tone said it wasn't fine. It was very much not fine, and I was going to hear about it later.

I put the phone down on the passenger seat, leaned back, and covered my face in my hands. She wore me out and I had to take a second to regroup before I left for my call. All I needed was to take that frustration with me and then have it erupt during an argument with some drunken asshole. Officers go to Internal Affairs for stupid mistakes like that.

"You okay?" Chris said, but I knew he meant it was time for us to get moving.

"You're too eager," I told him. "Let them fight it out. By the time we get there, they'll be too tired to fight us."

The newscaster on Chris's car stereo was talking about rioting again. I only half listened to it, though. Like most people, I'd grown numb to the terrible destruction that had been all over the news for the last month.

The city of Houston, not 250 miles to the southeast of us, had been hit with five major hurricanes in the span of four weeks, leaving most of the city wasted beneath flood water and debris. Every morning, after I crawled out of bed and turned on the morning news, there were more images of mud-colored water two- and three-stories deep, moving sluggishly through the streets of Houston, the roofs of houses and buildings looking like rafts floating in sun-dappled, oil-stained sludge, and of course there always seemed to be blackened and swollen corpses drifting through the wreckage.

The news had taken a lot of heat for showing all the dead bodies. They claimed they were trying to be discreet about it, but there always seemed to be corpses just the same.

Some of the guys from our police association had gone down to Houston to help out, and they all said that it was the worst thing they'd ever seen. Sanitation was nonexistent, and the whole place smelled like death. Something like two million people had been forced to evacuate, and most of them had come to San Antonio. All five of our military bases and every out-of-

business shopping center, had been turned into tempo-
rary shelters of some kind, and yet they kept coming. I
heard on the news that FEMA was flying as many as ten
commercial airliners a day into Kelly Air Force Base,
and every single plane was packed with evacuees.

Supposedly, there were still at least a million people
to evacuate from the areas south of Houston, and conditions for those left behind were nightmarish. Listening to Chris's stereo, I figured they were talking about
food riots or something, because there had already
been plenty of those.

"Can you believe this?" he asked me, wrinkling his
nose in disgust at whatever he was listening to now.

"I haven't really been listening," I said. April's voice
was still ringing in my ears.

"It sounds like Houston's gone nuts," he said.
"They're saying the survivors are attacking the boat
crews that are going in to help them. This guy is even
saying people are eating people down there."

"Great," I said. "And those are the same lovely people that FEMA's gonna fly in to our shelters. Can't wait
for that."

"This guy's saying the riots and everything have been
going on since last night. They've only just got word of
it from people that were evacuated this morn—"

"52-70." The dispatcher calling me again.

"Crap." I keyed up the mike. "Go ahead, 52-70."

"52-70, second call. I'm getting it as burglars-in-
action now. You and 52-80 getting close?"

"Ten-four, ma'am," I lied. "Still on the way."

"Ten-four, 52-70. Make it Code Two."

"Ten-four." To Chris I said, "Now we go."

"Roger that. I'll follow you."

Code Two means lights, but no siren. We're allowed
to go ten miles an hour over the speed limit, but we
can't blow stop signs or red lights. That's reserved for
Code Three.

Of course, nobody ever does Code Two. It's either get there when you get there or go balls to the wall. There's no in between.

I hit my lights and Chris and I tore out of the parking lot, leaving long, looping skid marks behind us. We headed south on Seafarer, down to Plath Street, and made a left. From Plath we turned into the Geneva Summits subdivision, went down four blocks, and turned left onto Chatterton.

Chatterton goes up a gradual rise to the left, and then breaks right suddenly and goes downhill all the way to the end where it dead-ends into the back of the Arbor Town Elementary School. That curve can come up on you quick, and if you take it too fast you can end up in somebody's front yard.

I came off the gas as I got to the curve and turned on the car's alley lights.

As we pulled up to the three-hundred block, everything seemed normal. There was a small group of people off to the left who didn't seem too concerned about a pair of police cars lit up like Christmas racing down their street, but otherwise the street seemed quiet.

I took a quick count of four men and two women, and turned my attention back to the houses on the right.

Most of the houses in Geneva Summits are small, two- and three-bedroom one-stories with brick fronts and old, weather-beaten wood siding on the sides and backs of the houses. It was one of the bright spots in my district, with regular folks who had regular jobs. No dope houses. No meth labs. No hookers. Just regular, decent people who did pretty well compared to the rest of the west side. They didn't call the police much.

It was already getting dark and most of the houses had their lights on, their owners settling down to dinner and the TV.

But farther down, as we got closer to the call, the

street seemed different. Something was just a little off, but I noticed it just the same.

I pulled my car up to the curb three houses down from the call in front of a red-brick one-story with long, knee-high hedges running down both sides of the walk.

"52-70," I said to the dispatcher. "Myself and 52-80 are ten-six at the location."

"Ten-four," she answered back. "All officers hold the air until I hear back from 52-70 and 52-80."

I got my radio and my flashlight and Chris and I started toward the house, working our way quickly through the cover of the trees.

We didn't see anybody at first. I could hear dogs barking not far away, but nothing else.

Still, it felt wrong somehow.

Then I saw her. She stumbled out from around the corner of the house and headed toward the street in an aimless, confused sort of way. She was a short, plump, dark-haired Hispanic woman in her mid- to late-twenties, wearing a light blue T-shirt and black pants that were a little too tight for a woman with her kind of figure.

The way she moved, I thought for sure she was drunk.

She didn't seem to notice us.

Chris and I stayed back for a moment, watching her and the house at the same time.

The woman moved closer to the street, and in the soft buttery light of the street lamps it looked like she had spilled something on her shirt. It was wet, with dark splotches on her shoulders and sleeves and a massive tear down her left side.

And then, from the same corner of the house where the woman had come from, more people appeared. They all moved with the same stop and start lurching motion that made me think of the drunks that sleep under the rail bridge behind the homeless shelter downtown. They all had that same kind of career-drunk haze about them.

Chris and I turned our flashlights and guns on them at the same time. The beams from our flashlights raked across their faces and I counted six people.

Chris shouted, "Stop! Police!"

They didn't respond—at first. Then they staggered in our direction.

"Stop! Let me see your hands!"

I keyed my radio. "52-70, we have six at gunpoint!"

"Ten-four," the dispatcher said, her voice glassy smooth and calm. "52-60, 52-62, 52-72, start that way. Make it Code Three."

I heard the melodic *cling clang cling clang* of my radio's emergency tone going off and after that I stopped listening to it. All of my attention was focused on the problem in front of us.

The street lamps threw an uneven light across the yards, creating deep pockets of shadows between the trees. As the group of drunks moved toward us, I kept losing them in the shadows, and it wasn't until they were up close that I really got a good look at them.

Chris and I both backed away, guns and flashlights at the ready. I caught sight of a man as he moved across my beam, and in the split second I had the light on him I could tell his face was all cut up. His cheeks had the swollen, lumpy look of someone who has just lost a fight, and there was a gory mixture of fresh and dry blood on the side of his neck. His eyes were clouded over with a milky white film, like a dead man's.

He moved more quickly than the others, but still with that clumsy, falling gait of someone who seemed to have forgotten how to walk. He didn't register the gun pointed at his face, and he didn't blink or look away or avert his eyes, even though I had my flashlight shining right in his face.

It looked like he didn't even see it.

"Get down on the ground!" I yelled at him, keeping the beam on his face. "Do it now!"

If he heard me at all, he gave no sign of it. I was yelling at a blank slate.

"Spray!" I yelled over my shoulder. That was for Chris's benefit. When the pepper spray gets in the air, you can go down coughing even if you don't get hit by it directly.

I holstered my Glock and came up with my canister of pepper spray.

"Get down on the ground!"

When he kept coming, I squeezed my finger over the trigger and waited for him to get in range. Pepper spray works best inside of three or four yards.

As he got closer he raised his hands to grab me. I pointed the canister at his face and pulled the trigger, giving him a tight, one-second burst and then backing away, just like in training.

Pepper spray takes a split second to do its damage. When people get hit with it, they usually stop, not hurt, but stunned, for just a moment, and then fall to the ground screaming, clawing at their eyes, and yelling like mad because that stuff fucking burns.

But the guy I sprayed didn't even skip a beat. He kept coming, and for a second I wondered if I missed or if he blocked the spray with his hands somehow. I let him get close again and then pumped another short one-second burst at his face.

I got it in his eyes. I was sure I got him in the eyes. But nothing happened. He didn't even blink. He opened his mouth and the skin around his neck tightened, but no sound came out.

There's enough spray in one canister for six one-second bursts. When I hit him with it again, I got in close and emptied the rest of the pepper spray right into his face.

I threw the empty canister to the side as I stepped back and stared at the man in amazement. I was riding a wave of adrenaline, and I had to force myself not to charge him and take him down with my bare hands. The air was thick with spray and I didn't want to get incapacitated by it.

Somewhere in the back of my mind I remembered the pepper spray course they taught us at the Academy. They said three percent of the population is naturally immune to the effects of the spray, but I had never actually seen anybody from that three percent.

The only other people I ever heard of who could shake it off like my guy was doing were meth freaks, and he wasn't moving like a meth freak.

As I backed up I heard Chris yell. I looked over at him and saw that the plump woman in the spandex had somehow managed to get right on top of him. I was surprised to see him go down. He wasn't big or anything, but he was in good shape.

She was clawing at him. Her fingernails raked across his face, cutting him, and then suddenly she knocked the gun out of his hand.

He slapped at her with his flashlight, but couldn't break away completely. Their arms were caught up in each other.

He landed a good jab with the butt of his flashlight and backed away. Then I heard the sharp metal on metal snap of his baton as he extended it and cocked it back over his shoulder.

He swung it down on her knee sharply, and then again, punctuating the second stroke with the sickening crunch of broken bones.

The woman's whole body reeled from his blows, but she didn't cry out and she didn't go down.

He hit her again and again, moving around her, keeping her at arm's length and striking her legs when she got too close, but no matter how hard he hit her, she wouldn't go down.

"What the hell!" he yelled. They were moving around each other in a strange, clumsy type of dance, Chris keeping the beat with his baton on her legs. "Why won't she go down?"

But I couldn't help him. I had my own problems to worry about.

The man I just pepper-sprayed was still reaching for me. He put out a mangled hand and I dodged underneath it. Before he could turn around, I kicked the back of his knee and pushed him down.

He didn't even try to break his fall. Didn't put his hands out or anything.

In the distance I could hear sirens and the uneven rise and fall of the roaring engines, and I knew help was getting close. But there were more people gathering around us now, and as I turned slightly I thought I recognized the people from across the street we had seen as we came in.

That's when Chris went down.

All his attention was focused on the woman, and he never saw the two men who grabbed him from his right side.

I saw one of them bite him and Chris screamed. He spun around frantically, knocking their hands and faces away as he landed on the ground.

They reached for him and he rolled away. He jumped to his feet with his gun in his hand and fired two quick shots at the man who bit him, nailing him squarely in the chest.

The sound broke the air, but I was the only one who flinched. No one else in the yard even registered the shots.

The man he hit staggered backwards, knocked straight up by the force of the impact, but he didn't fall.

I watched him shift his weight from one foot to the other in a clumsy, teetering dance and then start to walk forward again.

Chris fell backwards, clutching his neck, the blood already jetting between his fingers. Even as he fell he kept his gun leveled at the man.

I ran over to him and pulled him back.

"He fucking bit me!" Chris shouted.

I put Chris behind me and yelled at the man he had just shot. "Stop! Don't you fucking move!"

I had my gun barrel trained on his chest and still he kept coming.

I couldn't help but look at his face. There was nothing behind it, like one of those zombies in the movies. His gaze fell on me, but I knew somehow he wasn't looking *at* me. There was no cognition, no intelligence in his eyes. They were clouded over, a mystery.

Chris and I backed into the street, careful to keep our distance.

"Shotguns!" I yelled, and waved Chris toward our cars.

We both scrambled back to the patrol cars, avoiding the people who were coming after us from three sides now.

As we circled around to the trunk of my car I noticed that Chris was having trouble keeping up. He had gone pale, and his breath rattled in his throat, like he was choking on phlegm.

"You won't be able to shoot," I told him.

"I'll cover you. Get the shotgun."

I popped the trunk and pulled out my shotgun case. The Department gives us the Mossberg 500—a standard, tough-as-nails twelve-gauge pump, built to take a beating and fire just about any kind of shell made.

I dumped six green beanbag shells into the magazine tube and another into the breach. We're not allowed to use slugs on patrol, only the less-than-lethal beanbag rounds.

The beanbags are still pretty fierce, though. One or two hits at less than ten yards can put almost anybody on the ground and leave them with a couple of broken ribs, no matter how tough they think they are.

I closed the trunk. "You ready?"

Chris nodded, but he looked very sick. "What's wrong with them? I shot that guy. How come he's still walking?"

"I don't know," I said.

They stumbled closer. Watching them come, I couldn't shake the feeling that I was looking at a crowd of walking corpses. It was like they had stepped right off the screen of some Hollywood horror film.

We moved out, staying on the driver's side of our cars and careful to keep the engine block between our positions and the crowd that was still advancing on us through the grass.

The whole time we were doing that I could hear our cover officers getting closer, and from the way the engines and the squealing tires were starting to drown out the sound of the sirens, I figured they were just outside the subdivision.

Help was less than two minutes away.

I pointed the shotgun at the three men who had just entered the circle of street-lamp light next to our cars.

Chris was still standing, but he was bleeding badly. It was running down the side of the car where he was leaning for support.

I focused the shotgun's ghost ring on a man about ten feet away and yelled, "Get down on the ground!"

The man ignored my order and walked right into the fender of my patrol car. It was like he expected to just walk right through the car.

"Get down on the ground!" I yelled.

He turned and moved around to the front of the car, his hands out in front of him, ready to grab.

When he stepped into the street, I fired.

My first shot went wide of center mass, hitting him in the shoulder. The impact spun him around, and he went down to his knees, but he didn't cry out. He didn't even try to clutch at the spot where the beanbag hit him.

I racked the next shell into the shotgun and raised the barrel, ready for another target.

When the man I had just beanbagged stood up, turned, and faced me again, I felt my heart sink down into my stomach.

People just don't do that.

I've beanbagged people before, and nobody has ever just stood right back up, even from a glancing blow.

I searched his face for some indication that I had hurt him, but there was nothing there. There was no emotion, no expression, no content of any kind. He was empty. The eyes seemed to look through me into nowhere.

"Stay down! I'll hit you again. Stay down!"

I aimed my next shot more carefully. I took my time and centered the ghost ring right in the middle of his chest.

He was less than five feet away when I fired, and he took the full force of what a twelve gauge can do. The blow knocked him backwards, off his feet, and laid him out flat on his back.

At that distance I wouldn't be surprised if I smashed his sternum into dozens of little pieces.

I racked the shotgun again. That noise usually clears every room that hears it, but none of those people seemed to care.

They didn't run, or blink, or look to each other for support. They never paused at all. Their pace never varied, even when they reached out to grab at us. Every move was slow and plodding, like an old woman trying to climb a flight of stairs.

More of them were coming around the front of the car now and I fired two more beanbags as quickly as I could at the first two in line.

The one closest to me went down.

The one behind him staggered back, but didn't fall.

"Stay back!" I yelled. The air around us was filling with gun smoke, and there were so many of them coming at us that, even with the shotgun, I couldn't keep them back.

The first guy I bean-bagged walked into my car again. I jammed the barrel into his chest and fired. I fired again as he fell to the ground.

Chris and I backed up.

We were out of shells and the shotgun was useless without them.

I went for my Glock.

"What are they, Eddie?"

"Move! Move!" I said, and pushed Chris along the side of the car. I almost had to carry him to get him to go because he was having trouble supporting his own weight. He couldn't run at all.

As we reached the back of my car, I froze.

From between my car and Chris's car another man stumbled into our path.

He turned and faced us and in that one moment I lost all composure. His face and his arms were a mess. There was blood everywhere, and his face was so badly shredded that I could barely recognize his features.

What looked back at me wasn't a face at all. There was a massive gash starting just below the left eye. It was blood red and protruding from the socket like a squashed grape. The gash opened downward in a jagged triangle that spread around the jawbone, ending at a flap of skin that was caked over with dirt and hanging uselessly from his neck. Gleaming white pearls of teeth showed through the sinews of what remained of his cheek.

His right arm was just a bloody stump, but he reached for me with it like there was still a hand attached.

I lowered my weapon in confusion and disgust, then snapped it back up. "Stop! Don't move!"

But he kept on moving.

I fired a single shot square into his chest, and he rocked back on his heels, teetering for a moment before regaining his balance.

His gory arm came up again, and he reached for me.

I aimed with both hands.

My gun barked three times, and all three shots slammed into his chest. Again he rocked back, but I couldn't make him fall.

My training told me that it was body armor—nobody can take that kind of pounding unless they're wearing body armor.

When he came at me that last time, I aimed for his face and fired a single shot. The bullet struck him in the cheek, and a gory bloom of blood spray and bits of flesh and bone and teeth spread out across the white hood of the police car behind him.

The man flew backwards, landing on the car's push bumpers. I watched him struggle to regain his feet and more than anything else in the world I wanted to run as fast and as far away as I could. The shock of what I had just seen and the juice pumping through my system made me want to throw up.

I grabbed Chris by the shoulder and pushed our way to his car. I tossed him in the backseat and forced my way back to the driver's seat.

So many people had gathered around us. They were everywhere, hands tugging at my uniform, pulling me away from the car.

I climbed in and slammed it into reverse.

There were people banging on the doors and windows and the trunk, but I didn't bother to avoid them.

I stepped on the gas and peeled out, knocking people to the ground as I shot away from the curb. Swerving like a drunk, I kept the pedal on the floor all the way back up Chatterton.

At the top of the hill I was doing maybe fifty miles per hour and was completely out of control. I glanced off two parked cars and careened across the lanes just as two police cars came up on me.

When I saw their strobes I cut the wheel sharply and went into somebody's front yard. I couldn't keep the car in a straight line and the front end got away from me. The car spun suddenly to the right, and when the wheels caught, the car shot back toward the street.

We finally came to a stop after hitting a brick mailbox and the back end of somebody's parked car.

The last thing I remember was the airbag exploding in my face.

Chapter 2

I don't think I ever totally passed out, but I don't remember being put in the EMS unit either. When I finally came to, there was an oxygen mask on my face and an EMS tech was trying to put a blood-pressure cuff on me.

I recognized him from some of the calls we'd made together, but I didn't remember his name. I think it was Robertson or Robinson or something like that.

I coughed hard and couldn't stop. It felt like I was being ripped apart inside.

"Take it easy, Hudson."

I reached for the oxygen mask and tried to pull it off my face. He grabbed my wrist so I couldn't.

"Leave it there."

"Let me go," I said, though it came out muffled and slurred through the mask, all in one syllable.

I struggled weakly to sit up. My neck and shoulder felt stiff and I thought I was going to throw up.

"You stay there. Your sergeant said for you to stay put."

"I'm gonna throw up."

I got the mask off my face, and this time he didn't try to stop me. I turned my head to one side and coughed again. My face and eyes were burning, and I figured I must have gotten some of that pepper spray after all.

"Where's Tompkins?" I asked.

"I don't know," he said, still trying to fit my arm with the blood-pressure cuff. "They were taking him Code Three to Downtown Methodist, last I heard. He looked pretty bad when they pulled him out of the car."

He raised my arm off the gurney. "Come on, now. I've got to get this thing on you."

"What about the people we shot?"

It was urgent. I had to know. I grabbed his arm and squeezed hard. "Tell me!"

He didn't want to say anything about it, I could tell. He stammered, and when I pressed him even harder he blurted out, "I don't know. Let go of my arm."

"Those people wouldn't go down!" I was almost yelling it at him and I could see him looking at the straps on the gurney next to my arms, wishing now he had put them on me.

"They were zombies!" I said, urgent to get it out. "Like dead people. We shot them, and they wouldn't go down. They just kept coming!"

"Settle down." He pushed my shoulder back down on the gurney and tried to hold me there.

"Let go, damn it! Let me go! Get off!"

He tried to hold my shoulders down but I could tell he didn't want to have to fight me. Firemen don't like fighting people with guns.

He finally backed off and let me sit up. "I'm going to get your sergeant," he said. "You wait here. I'll get him and he can explain it to you. You wait here."

He opened the side door and left me alone in the back of the unit. I leaned back and put my hands over my face, completely exhausted. The adrenaline had carried me that far, but now I was crashing.

All I wanted to do was keep my eyes closed and my mind empty. But even as the tension was leaving my body, my mind was turning circles around itself, still trying to comprehend the violence of the last few minutes.

I had experienced the same sort of letdown a few times before, after being involved in car chases and fist-fights and stuff like that, but never had the feeling been so strong, so unshakeable.

When I opened my eyes, I forced myself to pause over my surroundings, hoping that I could stop replaying the incident in my mind by engaging myself with something mundane.

It was completely dark outside now and the only light came from the cheap, city-improvised track lighting along the roof of the ambulance. The halogen glow gave everything a sterile, institutional atmosphere, and the sickening smell of anesthetic and sweat made me feel hostile and unhealthy.

All ambulances are the same.

I've been in the back of EMS units hundreds of times before, interviewing people about traffic accidents and shootings and attempted suicides. But that was the first time I had ever really paused to take in the way they made me feel. I knew then that I hated it. I hated it all and all I could do was count the rows upon rows of insulin bottles and saline solution and sterile bandages, and I realized I was getting nowhere sitting there thinking about it. I was closed off and claustrophobic, and I wanted out. I had to get out.

I tried to sit up and just as quickly wished I hadn't.

My neck and shoulder were throbbing and my eyes and chest still felt like the pepper spray had settled in to stay. All I could do was cough and spit and wait for the burning to go away.

I put my head back down on the gurney and studied the road map of what the next few hours were going to be like.

I had been at other officer-involved shootings, and I had seen firsthand the crap they had to go through.

The officer at the center of it all was always off in his own little world, with everyone else running around him, trying to be cool about it, but still asking each other what had happened and whispering in those hushed tones that they hoped it was a good shooting— for the officer's sake.

What they meant was they hoped the officer hadn't screwed up.

It made me wonder if maybe I had screwed up. Was I going to lose my job? I kept seeing the scene play over and over in my mind and I wondered where I had gone wrong.

I knew the detectives and evidence technicians and the supervisors were already on the way. Some of them were probably already doing their thing.

They would start by walking around the place, taking pictures, knocking on doors, and talking to people that may or may not have seen anything. The position of every last piece of evidence, from the placement of shell casings to the length of skid marks and the damage to both our cars would be mapped out with surgical precision, bundled together in a thick manila folder and presented to the disciplinary board for administrative review.

And while all that was happening, I was going to have to sit in a windowless little room at headquarters, waiting for some detective to take my statement and wondering what everybody else was saying about what I had done. Was I gonna get sued? Was I gonna be looking for a new job?

It was going to be rough for me, but not nearly as bad as what was happening to Chris. He was going to have to do the same thing I was, except he was going to do it from a hospital bed.

It occurred to me that I didn't even know his wife's name. But whatever her name, she was going to get that call from the sergeant, saying Chris was hurt and he was at whatever hospital he was at.

Yes, she could come see him as soon as she liked.

No, she wouldn't be allowed to talk to him until the detectives got his statement.

And then I thought of April and Andrew, sitting at home and going through the whole bedtime routine, totally unaware of what just happened.

April would put Andrew to bed, make herself a sandwich, and turn on the TV to watch the news.

She would learn about everything from some talking head, and because the investigation was still going on, they wouldn't say the names of the officers involved or how badly the officer at the hospital was hurt.

The news would say something like "His condition is critical" or "He's in stable, but guarded, condition."

But those words don't mean anything when you need to know how your husband is doing. They're meaningless, too full of ambiguity to answer the desperate questions. They're sterile and confusing and totally useless and God! Why did I have to beat myself up over this? Why all the doubts?

I just wanted to sit there and rock myself to sleep. As uncoplike as that sounds, that's all I wanted to do.

I could feel the tears welling up behind my eyes and I thought, *Perfect*.

My sergeant was supposed to be on the way. He would open up the door to the EMS unit and find me there crying my eyes out.

I wondered who was going to have to be the one to come in and talk to me. Stevenson was the junior sergeant, so it would probably be him, even though he wasn't my direct supervisor. They always get the junior man to handle the unpleasant—

Gunfire.

I could hear a roll of pistol shots that sounded like firecrackers through the metal walls of the EMS unit.

They were coming from several different directions at once. Screaming and yelling erupted all over the place, though I couldn't hear what was being said or recognize any of the voices making the noise.

More gunfire.

The shots were coming so fast and so close together that I couldn't count them. I recognized the crack of the Glock—lots of them—and the booming authority of the shotgun punctuating the pistol fire like an exclamation point.

I jumped off the gurney, forced my way out of the EMS unit, and into the street.

The EMS techs had parked with the doors of the unit away from the scene, and when I ran around the side of the ambulance I was bathed in red and blue strobes.

There were people everywhere, running, yelling, fighting with each other.

Two EMS guys had a third man down on the ground. They were struggling to keep his shoulders pinned to the pavement, and he was doing everything he could to bite them.

Another man in a firefighter's uniform was face-down on the running boards of a fire truck. He wasn't moving.

I saw one of the guys from my shift on his hands and knees, swaying back and forth like he was about to fall over. His hands were soaked in blood.

A frantic crowd of civilians were running past me, but there were others walking toward the scene with that same staggering walk I had seen earlier.

I saw several small mobs coming down to the street from nearby lawns.

The red and blue strobes cut through the yellow

glow of the street lamps, giving everything and everyone they touched a strange, pallid cast.

Off in the distance I could hear more sirens, but they seemed to be heading away from us.

Two other officers from my shift were taking cover behind a police car and firing their handguns into an approaching crowd of people.

Even as I reached for my gun and ran over to join them, I couldn't believe we were shooting unarmed people. It went against everything I was trained to do and everything I had been brought up to believe was sacred.

But no matter how I felt about it, I still went down right beside them and pointed my weapon at the approaching crowd.

The officer to my right glanced over at me when I crouched down next to him. "What the hell is going on?" he yelled.

"I don't know."

"What are those things? I shot one in the chest six times and he still kept coming."

He didn't wait for me to respond. He stood up and started firing over the hood of the car. He emptied the entire magazine, ejected it, and dumped in another with such speed I thought there was no way he could be aiming his shots.

The slide dropped back into place on his Glock and then he was firing again. Brass casings went flying through the air, bouncing off the sides of the police car and rolling toward the curb.

"They won't fucking die."

And then they broke through our lines.

Through the smoke and strobe lights I saw shadows move. The shadows turned into badly torn and abused bodies, still moving and still walking.

They came through gaps in the cars and attacked a policeman who was firing at them from behind a car door. They collapsed on top of him in a writhing mass of arms and faces. I could hear him screaming for help even though pistols were going off right next to my ears.

An officer named Flores ran into the open to help him.

Several of the people who had overcome the other officer got up and shambled toward him.

Flores was a wiry, tough little guy and a crack shot—I knew that from shooting next to him during in-service. He could empty an entire magazine into a target the size of a dinner plate at twenty-five yards and make it look like anybody should be able to do it.

He aimed at a man in a sport coat and slacks and fired three times.

I could tell he hit the guy because the impact stood him straight up. But the man kept walking toward him, seemingly unafraid and unconcerned by the bullets smashing into his chest.

Flores stood his ground, though. He raised his gun again and fired three more shots.

When the man kept coming, Flores fired a single shot into his forehead, and that dropped him to the ground.

A moment later, Flores was firing single shot after single shot into the crowd, and bodies were dropping with every trigger pull.

It was disgusting to watch, and beautiful, in a way. His speed and accuracy were unbelievable.

But even as he leveled the crowd in front of him, more and more people were approaching through the darkness and smoke. They didn't make a sound, which was the eeriest thing about them. With the rest of us yelling all around them, the only noise they made came from their shoes dragging on the pavement.

I couldn't tell how many of them there were or even where they were, because our visibility was next to nothing. And the part of the mob we could see wasn't giving us a chance to regroup and organize.

I turned and saw more people walking toward us from the rear.

There were already more people than I could count walking between the cars in front of us and to our right. Flores was still firing like mad, and when he fired his last round, he holstered his gun and began to fight with his nightstick.

He had one of the old-style black hickory batons and he was swinging for their heads.

He knocked one of them over and brought the baton down so hard on the back of the guy's head that the nightstick snapped in half.

He threw away the pieces and reached for his collapsible metal baton.

The crowd closed in around him. There were just too many of them for him to take them all, and they managed to pull him down to the ground.

I didn't see him die. I couldn't stand there and watch that happen.

It was no use shooting anymore. There were so many of them and they were so close to each other and to the other officers that I couldn't fire and be sure I was hitting the right people.

Most of the officers around me had gone to fighting hand-to-hand.

I saw an officer pin a man to the ground and try to handcuff him.

One of the officers who went to help Flores was surrounded by the mob, his back up against a fire truck. He climbed up the side and landed on top of the hoses. The mob reached up to grab him, clawing at the chrome valves and dials just below him, but they couldn't get at him.

Through the smoke several officers and firefighters

came running back up Chatterton. I ran in the same direction, figuring we could regroup and call for more cover.

Getting through the wreckage was like navigating an obstacle course. There had to be more than twenty cruisers up and down the street, and most of them looked damaged—some only a little, others completely torn apart.

I couldn't believe that all that destruction had happened so quickly, that we had lost control so completely and in such a short period of time.

As I scrambled through the cars I could see people everywhere. An officer named Harner was maybe twenty yards off to my left, fighting with a group of three men.

I turned in that direction to help him, but never made it.

There, in front of me, was the man with the torn face, that horrible mud-encrusted flap of skin still dangling from his neck like a thick cut of fabric.

He had a hole in his jawline where I had fired the head shot that took him down. I saw three blackish-red holes in his chest, and I knew I had put those there too.

But I didn't see recognition in his face. His eyes seemed empty. His mouth hung open hungrily.

He grabbed me.

Out of instinct, I knocked his arms away, backed up, and pulled my gun.

"Don't come any closer," I said.

I pointed my Glock at his forehead and squeezed the trigger. In that moment, the world around me slipped away into silence. The only thing I saw was the brass casing tumbling out of my gun and landing somewhere off to my right.

It was a clean shot, right on target.

His head snapped back, and he folded to the ground in a heap.

I was in a daze. Over and over again we practice the shooting drills—keep your weapon up, scan left, scan right—but when it comes right down to it, nothing ever goes like the drill. All the skills the Department taught me melted away and there I was, a bare, exposed nerve, overloaded with shock.

And then there was a rush of activity as the world came crashing back on top of me. The colors, the sounds, the confusion—all of it hit me at once.

The mob kept coming and coming, and as I stood there shaking off my haze they began to close in around me.

I told myself to run, to fight, to do anything but stand still. But my feet were frozen to the ground.

I felt a hand grab my shoulder.

It was like cold water on my skin and, in that instant, I found my feet. There was a hole in the mob in front of me and I took it. I ducked my shoulder and knocked a man in a denim jacket to the ground.

I got through the cars and hit the grass running.

The houses on the north side of Chatterton share a common stone wall that separates their backyards from the neighborhood greenbelt. I went around the side of a house and through the backyard, over the back wall, still running as fast as I could go, and I didn't stop until I was out in the middle of the greenbelt.

Once there I stopped and caught my breath. I hadn't run since I was a cadet at the Academy and I was out of shape.

The cold night air burned my throat. Shots were still being fired out in the street, but there were fewer now, with long pauses in between. Tall oak trees and houses blocked my view, but I could still see the glow of the emergency lights and the smoke rising up into the air.

I needed to get to wherever our shift was going to regroup, but I had no idea where that was. And there was no one around to tell me. I was alone, cut off.

The greenbelt was a mostly flat, open swath of unde-veloped land about forty yards wide where the runoff water from the subdivision collected and channeled away after heavy rains.

Wind whipped through the tall grass. The hurri-canes that had decimated Houston for the last four weeks had brought almost daily rains to San Antonio, and the grass was lush and thick. It buzzed with mosquitoes.

A few months earlier I had chased a couple of kids through that greenbelt, and I had seen wild strawberries growing everywhere. Blackberry bushes clustered around a few large blocks of milky white limestone outcrop-pings. It had been peaceful then, after the chase, and it might have been so while I stood there were it not for the frantic desperation ragging inside me.

I watched as the wind pressed the grass flat, and it looked to me like an enormous piece of glistening black velvet.

I wondered what I was supposed to do.

I knew I had to find a car. Without a car I was a sitting duck, just waiting to be swallowed up by that mob.

But to find a car I would have to go back into the street, and I really didn't want to do that. I had no idea how far this riot had spread and there was no way I was going to rush headlong into something I didn't under-stand.

Being cut off and alone made me intensely aware of how quiet it was. I was so used to the noise and activity of patrol that I had developed the ability to talk on the phone, talk to complainants, and listen to my radio—

I looked down at my radio and realized that was why it was so quiet. I guessed that the EMS guys had turned it off while I was in the unit. In all the commotion I had simply forgotten about it.

When I turned it on I heard something unbeliev-able. The radio was a mass of overlapping voices and emergency tones. Officers were screaming for help, pleading for backup, and it seemed like all twenty dispatchers were trying to talk at once.

Nothing made any sense because I was only getting half of a sentence before an emergency tone would kick in and somebody else would start talking.

Whatever was happening wasn't just on this little street on the west side. There were desperate calls being sent out all over the city. It sounded like a meltdown.

South Division was being hit hard with fires and mobs and gunfire popping up on almost every block in their service area.

The Downtown Division dispatcher couldn't get any of her officers to answer their radios.

Every available officer in the Northwest Division was being called to the hospitals at the Medical Center.

The world was collapsing all around me and it was happening too damn fast. I was absolutely mystified how destruction on that kind of scale could happen so quickly, and no matter how I tried to comprehend it, I still couldn't wrap my mind around it.

Then it hit me, so hard that I almost collapsed, and I let out a moan.

My family. My wife. My baby.

I had to get to them. Now.

I turned my radio down and crept back to the wall that separated me from the line of houses. I decided to use the wall for cover and to cross over as soon as I reached a point where there was as little activity as possible.

From there I'd grab the first available patrol car I found.

If I couldn't get out of the subdivision through the main entrance, then I would cut through the playground of the elementary school.

But I had to find a car first. And soon.

Chapter 3

I crept through one of the backyards to the east of all the commotion. Plastic toys and basketballs were scattered around the yard. A tricycle lay on its side on the porch. A rickety metal swing set off in the corner looked like some kind of giant insect in the shadows.

What little light there was came from inside the house, casting long pale streaks across the yard. My flashlight was somewhere near my car, maybe in the grass or out in the street somewhere. I doubted I'd be able to find it again, even though I needed it almost as badly as I needed a car.

I made my way over the fence and out into the front yard.

The sound of gunfire rolled away into the distance like thunder. People were still shouting and I could hear the wailing sirens of fire trucks off in the distance, but I was far enough away from the scene that I thought I could risk entering the front yards again.

But there was no way I was going to risk going back into the middle of that mob. I planned on coming back to the original scene from the east—that way I could stay out of sight of any mobs that were still there and could move in to get my car when it was all clear.

My guess was that the original mob Chris and I encountered would have moved west toward all the lights and sounds of fighting, which would make getting to my car easier.

I worked my way through the front yards, trying to stay out of the light and keeping under the cover of trees whenever I could.

The air had grown unusually cool as the night breezes picked up, and I didn't have my jacket with me. San Antonio usually has high eighty-degree weather all the way through the middle of October, and I hadn't figured I'd need it. When I left for work that afternoon, it was sunny and eighty-six degrees, but it felt more like fifty while I was standing in that yard.

There were no dogs barking. I thought that was really strange. The only thing I could hear was the noise of the crowd from the top of the hill, and then that died away too.

I stopped and listened to the quietness that had descended on the street. Strobes filled the sky, but everything had grown very still and the only noise at all was the wind washing through the leaves of the trees above me.

The further east I went down Chatterton, the heavier the tree cover got.

The houses closest to the elementary school were a little larger than the rest of the subdivision, and they had the biggest lots with the largest trees.

Those houses were still pretty close to where I had left my car, and the cover they provided made them seem like a natural place to observe the street before I made the final dash to my car.

As I walked through one of the front yards, I came across a huge Spanish oak with a canopy almost as large

as the house it stood in front of. It had never been cut
back, and its outer branches sagged to the ground,
making it look like a gigantic dome tent.

A sharp, gusty wind blew through the top branches,
tossing them back and forth. The huge oak creaked
and groaned under the sudden urgency of the wind. It
was strange and beautiful music.

I walked around its canopy and saw an opening
where one of its larger branches curved down to the
ground from the central bole.

There was enough room for a man to walk under it
and the space seemed to form a quiet sanctuary, a cave
with walls of leaves. I swung open the curtain of leaves
and entered it, thinking that if nothing else I could
catch my breath there.

But I saw immediately that it was no sanctuary. A
man was already there, on his knees, eating large pieces
of viscera from a gaping hole in a dead woman's ab-
domen. A long, lumpy rope of intestine dangled from
his fingers.

He wore a blue button-down shirt and his face was
soaked in blood. His pants looked brown and very dirty.
He wasn't wearing shoes. His mouth hung open, forming a mean, vacant hole.

But the most awful part of his expression lingered
around the eyes. They were milky white and opaque, a
perfect image of death.

Blindly, I felt for the curtain of leaves behind me and
grabbed them, steadying myself for support. I kept my
eyes on the man's eyes, not wanting to look away, and
backpeddled into the yard.

But as I moved, so did he.

A piece of dark meat fell from his teeth. He stood up
slowly, gangly and rickety on his damaged legs, and
came after me.

"What's wrong with you?" I asked, but didn't expect
an answer.

What I was looking at was simply impossible. It was wrong in every way. I wanted to yell out at the man that he was an abomination, but when I opened my mouth to speak, nothing came out.

I felt like I was headed for a meltdown. My heart was beating so fast and so hard it hurt. I could hear the blood roaring in my head. I wasn't breathing.

"No," I said. "You need to get back."

I let the branches fall from my hand and I stumbled backwards into the yard, still staring at the oak tree that no longer seemed beautiful, but mangled and unnatural.

The man appeared from the veil of leaves and came after me.

The battle I had just escaped didn't seem real. The crowds of people walking into a wall of armed policemen, fighting with their bare hands and teeth, hadn't seemed real. But that man, that gore-stained monstrosity, he was real. Looking at him, I no longer had any doubts I was looking at a zombie.

I reached for my gun.

As I backed up, I pulled it from the holster and worked it into my grip.

I saw the green glow of the night sights and centered the front dot on the man's forehead.

He never even acknowledged the weapon. The void in his eyes never changed to recognition of the danger. He walked straight at me, and his face remained blank right up to the end.

I squeezed the trigger, and he fell. The only witness to one of the worst moments of my life was the rustling murmur of the wind through the trees.

Chapter 4

After I shot that man, I stood there looking at him, fighting off the urge to touch him. I could almost feel the cold, wet sponginess of his skin against my fingertips, and the thought turned my stomach.

I still couldn't believe what was happening. When I left for work that afternoon, the world had seemed normal. Now, everything was upside down.

Were those people really zombies? I fought against the idea, but it wouldn't leave me alone. I had seen horror movies. I watched them and I laughed at how stupid they seemed, because the zombies in the Hollywood movies never looked real. Once you've seen death in all its splendid horror, a movie version just doesn't cut it. The walking disasters I had seen certainly looked worse than anything I had ever seen on film.

As I stood there thinking about it, my doubts continued to grow. The way I understood it, zombies were dead people that went around eating living people. The man I shot under the tree had been doing that. God, he had been doing that. But was he dead? That part I didn't believe. It went against everything that made up my reality. Besides, he'd bled when I shot him. Dead bodies don't bleed.

And that made the horror of what I'd seen even worse. It wasn't enough that the world was crashing down around my ears. Worse than that, I had actually shot somebody. I'd shot several people. How was I supposed to live with that? They'd been trying to kill me, sure, but that didn't make it any easier. Killing somebody ain't easy, not under any circumstances.

My head was swamped by the enormity of it. I'd seen a lot of good men and women die in the fight at the top of the hill, and I had just stumbled blindly through the worst of it. I was lucky to be alive, and I knew it.

I turned and headed west, where I hoped to find my car again.

But I didn't have far to walk before I saw just how badly my shift had been gutted.

As I got closer to the spot where Chris and I ran into trouble, I started to see wrecked cars and broken glass and every kind of debris spread out over the lawns and into the street. There were hundreds of bodies strewn across the battlefield, and many of them had faces I recognized.

An echo of the fight still covered the street like smoke.

Not far from where I was, a man with useless legs pulled himself along through the grass, trying to reach me. There was gravel in the noise that came from his throat.

I had to look away, but it took an act of sheer will to do it. He was a human train wreck.

My police car had been demolished. All four windows were smashed in, and the front windshield was a spiderweb of cracks. It looked like the front fender on the driver's side had been hit with a shotgun blast. There was a jagged, gaping hole in the metal, and the tire below it was flat.

The driver's-side door was open, and the inside was even worse than the outside. The shotgun was missing. My briefcase was in pieces and spread all over the floorboard. A bullet had pierced the steering column and the ignition wires were hanging from the hole. Somebody had knocked the computer out of its mounting bracket. My cell phone was nowhere to be found.

"Fucking perfect," I said out loud, and slammed the door closed. What little glass was left in the window frame collapsed and came tinkling down on the pavement. "That's just great."

I stood in the street beside my car with my fingers in my hair, wondering what in the hell I was supposed to do.

There were no other police cars at the scene.

I could see long skid marks leading back up the hill. I guessed the officers who came down this far did the same thing Chris and I had done and got the hell back up the hill as soon as they realized their little .40-caliber cap guns weren't doing the trick.

But they had left their dead behind. I saw six dead policemen and one firefighter amid thirty or forty dead civilians. It looked like it had been an expensive battle for everyone.

Chris's flashlight was in the grass on the other side of the car. The bodies of two men in their late twenties and an older woman were less than ten feet away, and when I reached down to pick up the flashlight, I was careful to keep my eyes on them.

A voice from somewhere in the shadows said, "Don't worry, they're dead."

I fumbled for my gun as I turned on the voice. "Who's there?"

"It's me, Eddie."

It was Carlos Williams, one of the field-training officers from my shift. He was stretched out with his back against a tree over by the corner of the house, his gun still in his hand.

"Carlos?" I said. He looked bad. "Where are you hurt?"

"They bit me," he said, and shrugged his shoulder so I could see where. He was wearing his short sleeves, like me, and his left arm was torn up pretty bad. There was a nasty wound on the side of his bicep so jagged and deep black with blood it had to be a bite mark.

I went over to him. "Can you stand?"

"I think so. Help me up."

I got my arm under his and heaved him up. "I nearly shot you," I said. "Don't scare me like that."

"Yeah, you looked pretty jumpy." He laughed to cover up the pain. "I wasn't worried. I've seen you shoot."

"You're funny. Come on. Let's clean that off."

I guided him around the side of the house and turned the water hose on his arm.

"Hold still," I said. "I know it hurts."

I turned the flashlight on the wound. It was still bleeding freely, but I got most of the dirt and grass and shredded bits of his shirt out of the wound.

"It looks deep," I said.

"I'll be all right."

"Come on. I think there's one of those blood-borne pathogen kits in the trunk."

There were dead bodies all over the yard, and it seemed like everywhere we stepped there were brass casings sticking up through the grass.

"You guys really shot the place up."

"It takes so many shots to kill them," he said. "I've never seen anything like that. They just kept coming."

I nodded without listening.

His wound was starting to scare me. The blood was still pouring down his arm, and he looked pale. I remembered how bad Chris got and how fast he started to go downhill, and I didn't want the same thing to happen to Carlos if I could help it.

He was bigger than me by about eighty pounds and holding him up was difficult. I sat him down in the backseat of the patrol car and had him turn his arm so I could see it.

I got a look at his face in the pale white bulb of the car's dome light. His eyes had turned piss yellow, with deep red pools at the edges. His chin and the front of his uniform were stained with a foul-smelling black liquid that I guessed was vomit. I forced myself not to gag, focusing on the wound.

"Keep that in the light," I said to him. "Let's see if we can stop the bleeding."

"Look at those guys over there," he said, pointing with his chin.

"Where?" I turned quickly, half expecting to see more of those zombies coming after us. "What guys? I don't—"

"I shot them. I shot them all. Look at them. Each one's got a hole in the middle of his forehead. They kept coming, but I shot them all."

It sounded like he was trying to convince himself it had really happened.

I got the blood-borne pathogen kit out of the trunk and tore it open. Fancy name, but there's not much to it. It comes with a couple of rolls of bandages, some latex gloves, a paper filter mask, a plastic squirt bottle, some hand sanitizer, and that's about it.

I put on the gloves, poured the whole bottle of hand sanitizer directly into the wound, and then unwrapped the bandages.

"This is gonna hurt, okay? Try not to move."

I worked the bandages around his arm, trying to make it snug without hurting him too badly. He growled under his breath, but he let me fix him up. The blood was already soaking through by the time I had it secured.

"Fuck," he said, pushing my hands away. His voice sounded like a growl. "That's good enough."

"We'll have to change the bandages again in a bit. They're already soaked."

"Yeah, okay. Here, get out of the way. It's too damn cramped in here."

I backed off and let him climb out. When he finally got himself out of the backseat I realized just how big a guy he really was. He wasn't over-muscled, but he wasn't fat, either. There was just a lot of him. A big square block.

He was a few years older than me, maybe 37 or 38. His hair was thin, light brown, and he wore it short and trimmed.

Even if he hadn't been in uniform, and I didn't know him from Adam, I think I would have recognized him for a cop. He just had that look about him.

"Look at her," he said, pointing at an old woman laid out in the grass. "I shot her, too."

"You had to do it," I said. "She would have come after you like the others."

"She's the one who bit me. Her name's Sylvia Perades."

"You knew her?"

He nodded. "About twelve years ago I caught her son in the backseat of a stolen car. I brought him home instead of booking him and held him down while she slapped the fuck out of him. After that, she used to make me tamales to bring home to Kathy every Christmas. She made dinner for me and brought it to the hospital the day Matthew was born."

"You needed to protect yourself," I said.

"It didn't look like she recognized me at all."

"She probably didn't."

He stared at her for a long time, saying his good-byes. He stared at her so long I thought he was fading out on me.

"I forgot you were a dad," I said, not really knowing what else to say to him but feeling like I had to say something. I remembered that he took a lot of time off a while back when his kid was born, but until he said his son's name I hadn't even remembered whether it was a boy or a girl. "What is he, about a year old now?"

"Nine months," he said, but I think he knew what was really on my mind. I'm sure my face showed it plain enough. "Have you called your wife yet?"

I shook my head. "I can't find my cell phone."

"Me either. It was here on my gun belt, but it looks like it's gone now." He felt around his belt without looking at it. "Looks like my baton's gone, too."

"We need a car. We should get you to a hospital."

"A car, yes. Hospital, no."

"You're hurt."

"And I'm sure bunches of other people are too. Imagine what the hospitals are going to be like. Everybody who's injured is gonna head to a hospital. How long do you figure before the hospitals are all overrun with those zombie things?"

"I hadn't thought of that."

"We need to get to a fire station. They have medics there. Besides, whenever the radio system goes down, we're supposed to head to the nearest fire station. The rest of the shift is probably headed there now."

While he was talking, I watched the street to the west of us. Through the flickering strobe lights I could see zombies moving down the hill. Coming our way.

"Carlos," I said. "We need to leave."

"We need a car."

"Well, we're not going that way." I pointed up the hill

where there were plenty of cars but absolutely no way of getting one.

He turned to see where I was pointing, and then hung his head. "Crap, Eddie. I don't have many bullets left."

"Save them. We're not gonna shoot if we don't have to."

Chapter 5

The crowd coming down from the top of the hill grew steadily larger. To me, they looked like streams of dark water overflowing an embankment, coming downhill without direction, following the path of least resistance. They seemed driven only by a vague impulse to keep moving.

"Got any ideas?" Carlos asked.

"You're the senior man. You tell me."

"I'm not gonna be able to make it very far. It's my head. I feel really dizzy. It hurts."

I knew he was hurting. There was pain in his voice, even though he tried to force it down.

"There's the elementary school. Can you make that?"

"Yeah," he said, but he sounded doubtful. "We ought to avoid any kind of place where a crowd might gather."

"School let out at three."

He nodded, and together we started toward the school, his arm over my shoulder.

Feeling his dead weight on my shoulders, I was stunned by how bad he looked. His bite was serious, there was no doubting that, but even so, I thought, there was no way it should be tearing him up like it was doing. The piss yellow in his eyes was starting to deepen to a dark crimson, and he was coughing, hacking up huge wads of black phlegm that stank horribly. His whole body shook each time he coughed. He was slick to the touch too. From sweat. Every step was a labor, a painful, gut-wrenching labor, and it said something about the inner strength of the man that he was able to walk as fast as he did.

Together we made it past the bodies and the trash in the street and all the way to the end of the block, where the slope of the street flattened out and a wall of trees marked the back ring of the cul-de-sac.

The edge of the school's property was protected by a seven-foot-high hurricane fence.

I climbed up first and then reached down for Carlos.

He pulled most of his own weight over, which was lucky. I doubt I could have carried him.

He did so well coming over that I let him come down the other side by himself. Bad idea. He lost his grip near the top of the fence and fell, landing on his side so hard it knocked the wind out of him.

"Are you okay?" I asked, kneeling down next to him. I offered him a hand up.

He pushed it away, but didn't move to get up. He stayed there on his hands and knees, head bent down, trying to catch his breath.

"Why do people always say that?"

"What?"

"Why do people always say, 'Are you okay?' after someone falls and busts their ass? I mean, look at me. Do I fucking look okay?"

I didn't answer him.

"Forget it," he said. "Just help me up."

I helped him to his feet and balanced him there. He

was swaying badly. Off toward the school the flood-
lights on the corners of the building lit up the playground and the parking lot beyond it.

I looked over the field separating us from the buildings and then at Carlos.

"We've still got some walking to do. Can you make
it?"

"I don't have much choice, do I?"

The closest building to us was the gym, and we
headed that way. Halfway across a field where years of
kickball had worn dirt lanes into the grass, Carlos
stopped walking and bent over. He vomited all over his
boots, and kept on vomiting. Long after I was sure he
couldn't have anything left inside him, he was still vomiting.

It stank.

But finally, it stopped, and he stood up again.

Before I could say anything he looked up at me and
said, "Don't you dare ask if I'm okay."

I shrugged.

"It feels like I've got the flu," he said. "My back is
fucking killing me."

"When we get inside maybe we ought to head to the
nurse's office first. Maybe there's something there we
can—"

I stopped myself midsentence. Carlos looked up at
me.

"What is it?" he asked.

"I thought I heard something."

"What?"

"Shhh."

It sounded like keys rattling. I turned my flashlight
on the playground and swept it with the beam. It didn't
look like there was anything there, but it was hard to be
sure because the beam didn't penetrate very far into
the dark.

I heard the noise again.

"What is that?"

And then I saw one of our SWAT officers named Anthony Moraga walking between the monkey bars and the seesaws. He wore a black tactical uniform, different from the French-blue patrol uniforms Carlos and I were wearing. He had his Glock in his hand and an AR-15 slung over his shoulder. It looked like he was walking with a bad limp.

"Tony," I said to him, and then just as quickly wished I hadn't.

He slowly turned to face us, and even before I could see the vacancy in his eyes I knew he was one of those things. A zombie.

"Why did you do that?" Carlos said.

"I don't know. Come on." I tried to pull Carlos along with me, but he wouldn't move.

"Just shoot him," he said.

I raised my gun to fire at Moraga. Every part of me rebelled against the act of shooting a fellow cop—even one who had been so horribly changed. It was almost impossible to pull the trigger.

I hesitated.

Waited too long.

Moraga raised his hands as he started to walk toward us, and with the hands came the gun. I watched in stunned silence as he swept the air with the muzzle, firing several rapid-order shots as his arm described a sloppy arc through the air.

He wasn't aiming. I don't think he was even capable of that. I don't even think he was trying to fire.

It looked more like sympathetic trigger-pull to me. The fingers of his hand clutched for us, and because they were wrapped around the trigger, the gun went off.

But none of that went through my mind at the time—at least, not in any organized way.

When I threw my arms over my head and ducked down next to Carlos, I was operating out of pure fear. I pushed and carried him in the opposite direction, yelling for him to move as we ran.

Behind us, Moraga fired again, and this time the shots were closer, kicking up little umbrellas of dirt at our feet.

He kept firing until the magazine was empty and the slide locked back in the empty position.

And then he quickened his pace.

I stared back at him in disbelief. His right leg was bent slightly outwards at an awful angle, obviously broken, giving his gait an up-and-down rolling motion.

It slowed him down, but not by much. Between carrying Carlos and my own exhaustion it was hard to keep ahead of him.

He chased us past the playground equipment and out into the parking lot and never fell more than twenty steps behind us.

"Fucking SWAT," I panted. "The bastard's a zombie and he's still in better shape than me."

"Get to those doors," Carlos said.

He meant a pair of green metal gym doors at the other side of the parking lot. I didn't see any other way to get away so I did what he said.

As we reached the doors I could hear Moraga coming up behind us. The dragging slide of his footsteps mingled with the rattling of his keys and when I reached for the handle I could have sworn he was right on top of us.

I grabbed the door and pulled. It wouldn't give. I tried the other door. It wouldn't give, either.

"Locked."

"Hurry up."

"It's locked."

"Here he comes."

I turned just in time to see Moraga drag himself up the curb and step into the grass.

"Shoot him."

I pointed my gun at him and I wanted to pull the trigger. I wanted to, but couldn't.

Moraga never flinched. He just kept hobbling toward us and I stood there, frozen by a mental block that wouldn't let me shoot a cop.

Then I heard the sudden explosion of a pistol shot next to my ear.

I flinched out of the way and fell to one knee. The ringing in my ear was fierce.

Moraga stopped just in front of me and teetered backwards on his heels. He fell, landing in a pile on the grass, his legs tucked under his body like a child sleeping in the grass.

I looked back at Carlos and saw him panting heavily, his Glock still pointed at the space where Moraga had been standing.

"What the hell is wrong with you?" he said.

"I couldn't."

"Why the hell not?"

"He's a cop."

"Not any more. Jesus. You need to stop being so fucking sentimental and start worrying about saving your own ass."

After that, he broke down into a violent coughing fit, worn out by the effort it took to yell at me.

In between his coughs he vomited hard, and when he looked up at me his crimson eyes were a watery snapshot of hell. His face was pale and wet with sweat and tears. In that moment I knew he was dying. He was fighting it bravely, but he had already admitted as much to himself. Death was coming for him, and he was looking it in the eye.

"We need to keep going," I said.

"Get bent."

"Let's get inside, Carlos. Please."

"I said leave me the fuck alone. I don't want your—"

The pained look melted from his face and changed to that of a professional policeman once again. I saw it happen almost instantly.

His eyes narrowed to a point just over my shoulder, and he said, "Behind you."

I turned and looked across the parking lot.

At first I only saw five zombies shambling toward us. Then eight. Then more than I could count. There had to be a hundred of them or more in a narrowing half circle around us.

Carlos fell back against the doors of the gym and slid down to the ground. He sat there looking around us and coughed.

"You've got to help me," I said, trying to pick him up. "Come on. We've got to go."

"There's nowhere to go. You go if you want to."

I tried to lift him again, but he wouldn't let me. "Please get up. Come on."

He wouldn't even look at me.

"You son of a bitch. I'm not gonna die here. Get up."

I pulled him up from his shoulder, but couldn't hold him. He slipped back down and fell over to one side.

"Get up."

The zombies behind me were getting closer. I could hear their feet scraping along the pavement. They all moved at different speeds, some of them closing in faster than others depending on their injuries. The ones with their legs intact were the fastest.

One of them stepped over the curb to my left and I shot her.

After that I just started firing at any of them that got too close. By the time I fired through all three of my magazines there were piles of dead bodies all around us, but there were still a lot more of them closing in on us.

"I'm out," I said over my shoulder. I holstered my gun and pulled out my baton.

I took a deep breath and waited, watching the crowd for the best place to strike. I knew the first move would be the most important. If I read the crowd wrong and let them get between Carlos and me, there'd be no way to double back and keep them off him.

It had to be right the first time.

But before I got a chance to move, I heard the crack of a rifle shot and the whistle of the bullet as it went by my head.

I moved left and spun around in a panic, and saw Carlos still seated against the door. But now he had Moraga's AR-15. Somehow he found the energy to lift Moraga's corpse and remove the rifle. He had his knees up in front of his chest, and the barrel of the AR-15 supported between them. His left arm hung uselessly by his side, but he still managed to fire with the right.

He cleared out the ten or so zombies closest to us, and then started shooting at the next wave. Even in his condition, he still managed to place kill shots at thirty yards.

When he fired his last round, he let the rifle slip from his hand.

I ran over to Moraga and searched him for more AR magazines, but all he had were two Glock magazines. I grabbed them both and went back to Carlos.

"You have to get up. Come on."

He muttered something, but I couldn't make it out.

"Come on," I said, begging him. "Get up."

He blinked at me, but after a moment he let me help him up.

We moved around the front side of the building, past long rows of neatly cut hedges, and up to the front door. It was an older school, built in the fifties, and the front steps were steep. I looked for a wheelchair ramp, but didn't see one.

"We're gonna have to climb up."

He grunted.

I pulled him up the stairs to the front doors and propped him against the doorjamb. The doors were locked.

"Goddamn it. It's locked."

I thought I heard Carlos laugh. "School lets out at three," he said.

"Come on. Maybe there's a window or something."

We went down to the lawn. I looked left and then right. More zombies were coming at us from the parking lot. Hedges blocked the windows to the left, so we went right.

The lawn sloped downward, away from the school. The first-floor windows were over our heads all the way to the end of the building, so we went around the corner of the building and followed the wall until we came to another staircase.

It was a narrow half-flight of stairs leading up to another green metal door.

I tried the door, and wasn't at all surprised when it didn't open.

"Where are we going, Eddie?"

"Through here," I said, and leaned Carlos against the railing.

There was a little window halfway up the stairs that looked big enough for us to crawl through. I peered inside, couldn't really see anything in the darkness, and decided we had to risk it.

I pulled my baton and punched out the windowpane. I swept the rest of the glass out of the frame and pulled Carlos over to me.

"We're going through here," I said. "Can you help me?"

He laughed, or muttered. I couldn't tell which. It was beginning to get difficult to read his gestures.

I crawled through the window and then reached back to get Carlos. He tried to help, but he wasn't thinking clearly, and his help slowed me down more than anything else. It was a clumsy, painful process, but I got him through eventually.

As he came through he landed heavily on his face, and stayed that way.

"Are you okay?" I asked.

He growled at me as he rolled over onto his back.

"Sorry," I said.

I reached down to him and he took my hand. Once he was on his feet he slumped back against the window frame and started coughing again.

"We ought to find the nurse's office," I said. "If nothing else, maybe they have a phone. We could call somebody."

"Who?" His voice sounded like it was coming through liquid.

"9-1-1, I guess. Maybe they can get an ambulance to us. Or tell us what to do for you."

"Maybe," he said, but it looked like he didn't really care.

I guided him through the utility room and into the hallway.

It was dark, and it was obvious that whatever was happening to the outside world had also happened here. Trash was everywhere. A few classroom doors hung open haphazardly. Disorder reigned.

I looked down the banks of lockers to the end of the hallway, where it split into three directions.

"Here, come on. I think it's this way."

We took the hallway to the right even though I didn't really remember how to get to the office. The front doors led directly into the cafeteria, I remembered that much, but I wasn't sure where the office was from there.

In most elementary schools the office is right there in the front, but I remembered this one was different. I thought it was on the other side of the gym, so I worked that way.

The hallway in front of the office was littered with loose-leaf paper and large pieces of office furniture toppled over at odd angles.

One of the overhead light panels was dangling from the ceiling by a tattered rope of electrical wires. I watched it spin in a lazy circle like it was the center of the world, and I wondered how in the hell it had fallen down like that.

Carlos groaned something.

Off to the right, coming around into the hallway from another direction, was a man in brown corduroy pants and a collared shirt. He was dragging a bleeding stump that used to be his leg across the floor, smearing the tile behind him with gore. His neck was broken, his head bent over at a disgusting angle. A huge red knot had swelled up from the other side of his neck.

Behind him were five more zombies.

I let Carlos rest against the wall while I loaded a magazine and chambered a round.

With my flashlight up, I walked toward the lead zombie in the brown corduroys and shot him. Once he was down, I stood over his body and shot the other five, single-tapping each one to the forehead.

When the last one fell, I went over to the glass doors of the office and tried to pull them open. They were locked.

"Damn it. This place is killing me."

I pointed my flashlight into the office and poked the light around. I was right about to turn around and get Carlos when I saw a flash of green pant leg and a brown boot below it.

Whoever it was had seated themselves behind a desk, but I couldn't see anything besides the leg and the boot.

I kept the beam on the leg, waiting.

Suddenly, a Hispanic man with straight black hair and very brown skin peeked around the corner of the desk. He smiled at me, and in the bright white light of the flashlight beam I saw his teeth sparkling like veiled diamonds.

Chapter 6

"Hey Carlos, there are people inside here."

He made a weak, strangled noise, and I turned the flashlight on him. He had pulled himself up against the wall and he was holding his side, muffling his coughs with his shoulder. It seemed like he was trying to hide from the light.

He was slipping, and it worried me.

I tapped on the glass doors of the office with the butt of my flashlight. The man in the green pants didn't want to stand up. I guess he thought he was safe as long as he stayed in his little hiding spot.

He probably figured if he waited there long enough, I would just go away.

"Come on," I said as patiently as I could. "Come over here and unlock the door."

He shook his head.

"Open the door," I said, like I meant it.

I brought the flashlight back and made like I was going to break the glass with it.

That made him sit up and take notice.

He raised his hands as if to say *okay, okay* and came

over to the door. Looking back at his hiding spot, he turned the key.

When I heard the bolt click, I pushed the door open.

"Thank you," I said, and moved around him into the main reception area.

The place was a mess. Office equipment was everywhere. There were books and papers and notebooks strewn across the floor.

The school's mascot must have been the cougar, because there was a large fake bronze statue of one laying on its side beneath a plaque that said, THIS IS A BLUE RIBBON SCHOOL.

I nudged a picture frame out of the way with the toe of my boot. "Where's the nurse's office?"

He didn't answer.

"Where's the nurse's office?"

The look on his face wasn't exactly a helpless one. It was more neutral than that, like he just wanted me to leave.

"No English."

"That figures," I said.

There was a hallway on either side of the wall behind the cougar. Both hallways disappeared into blackness and I knew I didn't have the time to go exploring.

"*Médico*," I said. "*¿Dónde médico?*"

He gave me an uncertain shrug. I knew I wasn't saying it right, and it frustrated me that he wouldn't at least try to meet me halfway. He was going to make me fumble through it.

I pushed past him and went to the corner where I first saw his pant leg. Four more people sat there, tucked into a narrow aisle between the desks and the wall.

One of them was an older man, dressed in the same green landscaper's uniform as the first man, and the other three were women dressed in gray housekeeping outfits.

I looked down at them and they looked back at me with completely neutral expressions on their faces.

I showed them the palms of my hands in a gesture I hoped they would take as friendly. I wanted to say something to put them at ease, but I didn't know the words to say in Spanish. About the only thing I knew how to say was to ask for their license and insurance.

"Do any of you speak English?"

All I got was the same blank look.

There was no used dragging it out. I made my way down the hallway, glancing in all the offices until I found the one labeled NURSE.

Only a few of the cabinets had anything useful in them. There were some more latex gloves, some bandages, and some antibacterial soap, but very little else.

There was a phone on the wall and I tried that, but all I got was a strange electronic squelch that sounded like I had called a fax machine by mistake.

I tried the operator.

I dialed 9-1-1.

Hoping against hope, I even tried calling home, but I got the same weird noise each time and finally gave up on it.

I stuffed some of the latex gloves in my pocket and headed back up to the front.

The four silent ones were still hiding behind the desk. The first man was standing near the door, looking up and down the hallway.

"Do not lock this door," I said to him. I pointed to the door. "Don't lock it."

He didn't look like he understood.

I walked into the hallway and found Carlos was still leaning against the wall. He was coughing, and there were wet lines of black fluid around his lips.

"Hey," I said, shaking his shoulder gently. "Carlos, can you hear me?"

His eyes were speaking volumes about how much it hurt.

"There wasn't much back there. Just some children's aspirin. I got some clean bandages, though. I'm gonna change this one because it's soaked through."

He turned his face to the wall as I unwrapped the bandage on his arm.

The wound was much worse.

The first time I cleaned it the wound looked dirty and mean, but at least it looked like a wound.

It didn't look like that anymore. It had festered and changed from the white and pale red of a fresh, deep cut, to a sickening yellow and black crust. If I hadn't known better I'd have said it had been festering for days, not just an hour or two. It actually looked like it was decaying while it bled. And it stank of rotting meat.

If he had been more aware, he would have heard me force the bile back down my throat

I changed the bandage as quickly as I could and gently put his arm back down at his side.

The hallway had been quiet while I worked on him, the only sound coming from the swinging light panel as it rotated on its wires, but now I heard something new coming from farther off.

Even before I could separate out the elements of it, I knew it was the sound of footsteps sliding across the tile somewhere off in the dark ends of the hallway. I let out a deep breath of frustration.

"They're coming again. Can you hear me, Carlos? We have to move. They're coming again."

I slid a hand under his shoulder and tried to lift him, but there was no strength in his legs.

The man in the landscaper's uniform was standing by the office door, watching me, and I called over to him to come and help me.

He didn't move.

"Help me, damn it."

He shook his head. *"El está enfermo."* He seemed horrified I had even asked him to help.

"Come here and help me."

He shook his head again and stepped back. "No."

From behind me I could hear the footsteps getting closer and I knew we only had a minute or two at the most to get going.

As I watched him back up toward the office I got so angry I stood up, drew my gun, and pointed it at him, muttering something under my breath about him being a fucking little coward.

"Get over here and help me," I said, closing the distance between us.

He stared at the gun, and for the briefest moment I'm pretty sure he was thinking about running the other way.

But he didn't run. He nodded and walked over to where Carlos sat against the wall. Together we lifted him up and carried him over to the office.

"We have to get out of here. It's not safe. Entiendes?"

He didn't understand.

"Más muertos," I said, pointing down the hallway. "We have to go."

That much he understood.

"Do you have a car? Maybe a truck?"

Again, I got that puzzled look.

"A truck, damn it. You know—" and I made a hand gesture like I was steering a car, "—a truck."

He nodded. *"Sí, una troca. La escuela tiene una troca."*

Glory hallelujah, now we're getting somewhere.

"Great. *¿Dónde?*"

He pointed toward the corridor Carlos and I had taken to get to the office.

That wasn't good.

I didn't remember seeing anything down there except classrooms, and that was the same direction the footsteps were coming from.

"Are you sure?" I asked.

"*¿Cómo?*"

I pointed down the same hallway. "*No. No troca. Muertos. Mucho muertos* that way."

"*Sí.*" He nodded at me like we were speaking the same language.

I shook my head at him. I didn't understand.

He pointed at me, and then at my gun. He pointed down the hallway again and made like he was shooting a gun.

"Oh," I said. "I get it. You're fucking insane."

There was no way in hell I was going to go down that hallway with those things while he and his friends made for the truck.

"No," I said, showing him an empty magazine from my belt. "*No más* bullets. *No más.*"

It takes a trained poker face to cover up the realization that you're completely screwed, and he didn't have it.

Seeing that empty magazine melted all the smugness from his face and I didn't need to speak Spanish to know exactly what was in his mind.

He swallowed a lump down his throat.

"What about that truck?"

"*¿La troca?*"

"Yes," I said. "*Sí.*"

His eyes went down to his feet. He looked back at the office. The others were standing up at the windows now, watching the two of us argue.

Finally, after he couldn't stall any more, he pointed down a hallway that led past the office and toward the back of the school.

It was the opposite direction he had pointed out to me the first time.

"You were going to leave me here, weren't you?" I said.

He looked at me blankly.

I was pissed, but I didn't let it show. I pointed to the hallway. "Go on," I said. "Lead on."

Just then his gaze shifted to the hallway behind me and his eyes got big.

I knew that look.

I turned just enough to see two zombies entering the main hallway in front of the office.

He almost dropped Carlos in his hurry to back away.

"Hey." I reached across Carlos's back and grabbed the man's shirt.

He tried to pull away, but I held him tight.

He looked at me pleadingly.

"No," I said. "You help me with him."

"No, señor, por favor."

The zombies behind us shuffled closer. The one in front was close enough that I could see the blood-stained floral print running up the side of her skirt. The heel of her left shoe had come off, making her clop and scrape the ground with each advancing step.

I didn't move and I didn't let up on my grip. I wanted him to know I meant business.

"Señor."

Clop and scrape, clop and scrape.

"Okay," he said at last, and put his shoulder under Carlos. To his friends he said, *"Octavio, vamos a la troca."*

The others were gone in a flash. They poured out of the office like runners at the gate and went down the hallway so fast we could barely keep up.

We followed them through the hallway to the gym, where we made a right and then a quick left again.

When we came around the corner we nearly ran into their backs. They had stopped, and were staring at a sight almost as gory as the one I had seen under the tree.

Maybe as many as twenty zombies were on their knees, eating arms and legs and other unidentifiable bits of human detritus.

The floor was awash with blood.

Beyond them was a doorway, green metal just like the gym doors, and I guessed that was the way out. It might as well have been on the other side of the ocean, though. There was no way we could reach it.

One of the women gagged.

"¿*Señor?*" the second gardener said to me. He pointed his finger like a gun, hopefully.

I shook my head. "*No más* bullets," I said.

He said something to the others, quietly, in Spanish, and I guessed he was telling them we had to leave. The others backed up, but not before several of the feeding zombies looked up.

A few of them got to their feet.

"Let's go," I said, and we all turned around and headed back the way we came.

But that was a bust, too. There were six or seven zombies coming our way, and I could see more behind them.

"*Señor,*" the gardener said, and I caught the obvious implication that this wouldn't be happening to him if I had left him well enough alone.

We were caught at the bend in the hallway, only a short few feet from our escape.

Carlos groaned and tried to make me drop him.

"Not a chance," I said, and tightened my grip on him.

He winced and stopped fighting.

Just then we heard somebody whistling. All of us stopped and looked at each other. It was a carefree, lilting sound—one high, one low, over and over.

We heard it again, and that time I placed where it was coming from. I looked beyond the feeding zombies and I saw a man in a white, short-sleeve collared shirt and brown slacks.

Our eyes met. He pushed his glasses up on his nose and nodded to me.

Then he whistled again.

A few of the zombies turned around to face him. Calm as could be, he walked over to the wall and banged on it with his fist.

That got the rest of the zombies looking at him, and while the others and I watched, dumbfounded, he yelled at them, baiting them with his own body away from the door that led to the truck.

He walked slowly backwards, making sure they followed him around another corner at his end of the hallway.

As the last zombie disappeared around the corner after him, my little party ran for the door. It had a little slit window in it, looking out on a small courtyard.

I tried to get a good look, but it was too dark to see much beyond some vague hulking shapes that looked more or less like a truck and some machinery.

"La troca," Octavio said to me.

I nodded to him and then helped Carlos take a seat along the wall.

I propped the door open and poked around a little with the flashlight.

The truck was right where they said it would be. It was an old white dualie one-ton, a big Ford F350.

The trailer wasn't hooked up, which was good, and most of the equipment was out of the way, so it would be fairly easy to get the truck out of the courtyard.

There was a dark pile of mulch near the front of the truck, and beyond that was a hurricane fence like the one Carlos and I had climbed.

A few zombies were on the other side, alerted to our presence, I guess, by the movement of the flashlight beam. They were slapping the fence with slow, incessant slaps.

I closed the door. Then, while I was trying to figure out what to do, I heard a door open from around the corner where the man with the glasses had gone.

He was yelling again, but not for help. It sounded like he was herding the zombies. I could hear desks and chairs being thrown around.

I heard a door slam.

A moment later, he came trotting around the corner and made his way through the gore strewn across the hallway like he didn't even see it.

"I locked them in the classroom," he said, and pushed his glasses back up the bridge of his nose. "Are you guys leaving in that truck?"

"Yeah," I said.

"Mind if I come?"

"Suit yourself," I said.

He was smiling, but when he saw how bad Carlos looked, his smile slid off his face.

"You still want to come?" I asked.

He studied my face, and I think he understood Carlos was something we weren't going to argue about.

He nodded.

I looked back at my little group and asked, "Do any of you speak English?"

They all shook their heads.

"Just my luck," I said.

"You're a cop on the west side of San Antonio and you don't speak Spanish?" the man with the glasses asked, incredulously.

"No," I said. "Do you?"

"Well, no."

"Well then, you're part of the problem, not the solution."

I turned back to the others and said, "Look, I have to get that truck. We're going to have to bust through that gate. *¿Entiendes?*"

Blank stares all around.

"Of course you don't."

I tried again to make them understand. "I'm going to come back and get you. Don't worry. I won't leave you." I looked around for some kind of understanding, but it wasn't happening.

"Do you have the keys?" I asked, making a sign like I was turning a key.

"*Sí,*" the first landscaper said, nodding his head vigorously. "*En la troca.*"

"In the truck?"

"*Sí.*"

I took a deep breath and tried to get a grip on my situation. This was going to have to be quick, but that was no reason it had to be sloppy. Sloppy gets people hurt, and I wasn't going to let that happen if I could help it.

Finally, I said, "Wait here. I'm going to come back for you. Wait."

"What are you going to do?" the man with the glasses asked. He looked as worried as the others.

"I'm going to get the truck. Some of these people are going to have to ride in the back. I can't bust through that gate with them in the back. They might get knocked out. Or worse."

"Oh," he said. "That's right."

As I opened the door and got ready to run to the truck, the first man grabbed me by the sleeve.

"No," he said. "We come too."

"Yes," I said, nodding. "Wait here. You come too."

He still wouldn't let me leave.

But I couldn't make him understand what I had to do. We were having a first-rate breakdown in communication.

Then I heard something from Carlos. It was a wet, barely intelligible string of words in Spanish. I couldn't understand it. I barely recognized it as his voice.

But the others understood it. The first man let go of my sleeve and said, "Okay." He nodded toward the truck.

"Okay," I said.

I sprinted out the door and over to the truck. As I opened the driver's side door I could hear the zombies beyond the gate, still slapping against the fence. I didn't even look at them. The keys were still in the ignition, just like the landscaper promised they would be, and the big diesel motor fired up with a roar.

When it settled down to a steady knocking chug I put the stick shift in reverse, stepped on the gas, and left two sets of parallel ruts through the grass all the way to the gate.

The whole truck jolted when I hit the fence. The back end on the passenger's side bounced up and lost traction for a second before it slammed back down to the ground.

I think I hit two or three of the zombies after I broke through the fence, because I felt two smaller jolts—like I was going over a big speed bump.

I didn't waste any time worrying about how many of them I'd taken out. I put it back in gear and peeled out toward the doors where the rest of the group was watching, dragging a huge section of hurricane fence behind me.

I slid the truck sideways right up to the door.

"Jump in," I said.

The first landscaper was a stronger man than I gave him credit for. He picked Carlos up from the floor and dragged him all the way up to the front seat without any help at all. I hadn't even been able to lift him.

He jumped into the back of the truck and he and

Octavio got the section of fence loose and tossed it to the ground.

The man with the glasses helped one of the women into the truck bed, while the first gardener got everybody loaded up.

He slapped his fist against the back window of the cab. *"Vete,"* he said. *"Vete pronto."*

I stepped on the gas and tore through the courtyard.

At the gate two of the zombies were already coming through and two more were trying to get their mangled bodies to stand up.

I ran over the first two and tore off towards the parking lot.

I let off the gas a little and relaxed my grip on the wheel. It was a boat compared to the Crown Victoria I was used to, but I got the hang of it pretty quick.

Soon we were flying across the playground, over the curb, and into the street.

I looked in the rearview mirror and saw everyone was still secure in the truck.

The first landscaper gave me the thumbs up sign, a huge smile on his face.

"You said it, brother."

Chapter 7

The closest fire station to the school was Independence Station at the corner of Resolution and Independence.

Getting there should have been as simple as turning left on to Elgin, another left on Fern Hill, then a right on Independence and go ten blocks up to the station. On any given day it was a five minute drive. Ten, if I caught all the red lights.

But I should have known better than to go to that fire station. I should have known better than to go right into the thick of things.

Elgin and Fern Hill weren't too much trouble because they both went through small neighborhoods that hadn't seen a lot of activity yet.

I saw a car on its side after we turned on to Fern Hill. Once I looked between some houses and saw a dark figure moving through the bushes.

But what I saw on the smaller side streets was nothing like the absolute carnage erupting on Independence.

Independence was one of the biggest and busiest streets on the west side—five-lanes-wide both ways and every inch of curb space filled with restaurants and car lots and grocery stores and strip shopping centers. There was almost always a lot of traffic, but what I saw put even five o'clock rush hour to shame.

Traffic was completely gridlocked, and there were people all over the street. That's what it would have looked like from a distance, anyway.

The truth was that the cars were all abandoned, and the people moving through the gaps in traffic were zombies, looking for a meal amongst the ruins.

They moved in knots, and the street looked like the host of a thousand separate slow-moving riots. The knots broke apart and reformed with amazing speed, especially considering how slow most of the zombies were.

At one point, I saw a woman fighting to get away from a group of the zombies. They knocked her down on her stomach as we were driving by. She turned her face toward us, and her expression was confusing. It seemed, even as they tore into her with their fingers and their teeth, not to be a look of pain, but rather of someone who just doesn't care anymore.

Zombies were everywhere. We were the only vehicle still moving, inching through traffic that was set in place like a river under a hard freeze. The outbreak had caught so many people while they were on their way home.

It disturbed me to see the images of everyday life frozen in place and then corrupted like that.

From the way cars were abandoned at the intersections, I could imagine how it must have happened.

I pictured rows upon rows of cars sitting at the red lights, waiting, waiting. And then from one side or the other, the zombies would have descended on the people in their cars and attacked them, breaking their windows with the palms of their bloody hands and pulling innocent people from their cars like chunks of meat from a can.

The people in their cars were probably so mentally blunted by years upon years of routine that they sat there shocked and let the attack happen rather than step on the gas and blow through the light.

Perhaps some of them got out of their vehicles and tried to help the ones being attacked. There were quite a few car doors left standing open. If so, those helpful few were probably among the first to die.

The man with the glasses poked his head over the driver's side of the truck and asked me what my plan was.

"I don't have one," I said.

"There's no place you guys are supposed to go in an emergency?"

"Are you kidding?" I said, and steered the truck past a group of zombies eating something next to the driver's side of a brand new Ford Mustang. "You really think the San Antonio Police Department has a procedure for something like this?"

He frowned. "No. I guess not."

"We're headed for a fire station," I said, just to mollify him. "Sit back, okay?"

He did, reluctantly.

Our little group moved up the street through the center turn lane. I kept the truck at a reasonable speed—fast enough to avoid the zombies, but not so fast that I didn't have time to react when obstacles came up in front of us.

Doing that got us most of the way to the station.

The sounds of the riot got louder the farther down Independence we went. We could hear the piercing tone of a police car's siren ahead of us. Hearing it gave me a moment of hope.

That moment faded pretty fast, though. The car making that tone was stationary, and no cop ever leaves his car's siren running unless he has to abandon it in a hurry.

We were less than a block from the station when I realized we weren't going to make it all the way there. Just before we got to the intersection, I turned off Independence and drove up the curb to a grocery store parking lot across the street from the station.

From where I parked, we could see the front and most of the west side of the station, and it was obvious that it had been the center of fighting as bad as any I had seen.

Almost all of the windows on the bottom floor were broken inwards and all three truck-bay doors were ripped open. The police car making the piercing tone was parked in front of the station near a couple of others, the driver's door open and the flickering strobes painting blue and red streaks across the red-brick façade of the station.

Dozens of dead bodies were sprawled out in a half circle around the police cars. Some of my brother officers had fought their last stand there.

A zombie in a water board uniform stumbled across the front lawn and disappeared around the corner. As he blended into the night, I knew the world was crumbling down around our ears. Our first line of defense had folded right before my eyes.

"Officer," the man in the glasses said. "What are we doing? We need to get somewhere safe."

"I know," I said.

Yet even as I watched the crowds stumbling into the street, I had to linger over my memories of that place.

Independence Station used to be a sort of community center for the people of the near west side. Most of the families living close by were extremely poor, and the place loomed over their modest homes like a medieval cathedral.

Mothers brought their children there to have EMS look them over when they were sick or hurt because the firefighters at the station would always help them, and even though they were supposed to report how they used their supplies so the city could send out a bill, the firefighters there rarely reported the stuff that didn't really need to be reported.

The César Chávez Parade kicked off from Independence Station every year.

Community-action groups held rallies in the break room.

For the past decade, the city used the station as a free clinic where they passed out flu shots.

A good number of the people who died in front of the station were probably brought there by friends and family in much the same shape as Carlos. The thought of how horribly they must have died and how hopeless they must have felt brought me back to my own problems.

I turned to Carlos and looked him over. It was uncomfortable for him to bend over at the stomach, and he had to stretch out across the seat so he didn't put pressure on it. Cold night air blew in through the open windows, but he was still sweating profusely. His eyes had started to swell and, though he tried to close them, the eyelids weren't quite able to make it over the swelling.

"Carlos," I whispered. "Carlos, we can't stay here. Can you hear me? We have to go someplace else."

He turned his head away from me and coughed some black phlegm onto the door panel.

"Hang on."

I wanted to tell him something else. I wanted to tell him we were going to get him some help. But I didn't believe that and it seemed cruel and pointless to lie when he already knew the truth.

The first gardener leaned in the driver's side window and tapped me on the shoulder. He pointed to a few zombies that were coming our way and said, *"Señor, los muertos."*

"I know," I said, and motioned for him to sit down.

I put the truck in gear and we were off again.

Chapter 8

I had no idea where we were going when I pulled out of the parking lot and headed up Resolution.

The streets I drove everyday and the businesses where I made calls and bought sodas and went to the bathroom were being gutted by the crowds. The destruction was spectacular.

Off in the distance I could see patches of orange haze and wind-whipped smoke in the treetops. I knew that San Antonio, my home for nearly thirty years, was burning.

Most of the shop windows facing the street were broken out and every few moments we'd see somebody running, trying to find someplace to hide.

We stayed on Resolution for about fifteen blocks, but turned off at Herrick because the road was jammed up with traffic.

I could actually feel the fog leaving my brain as we turned off the commercial streets and put the frenzy behind us.

Down in the neighborhoods, I saw a family cramming clothes and a few other things into their car. The wife watched us drive by, her eyes alert and skittish like the eyes of a wild deer.

I felt an overpowering need to talk to April, as I watched the woman load her two small children into the backseat. With any luck, she was already strapping Andrew into his car seat and heading someplace safe.

It struck me at that moment that I had no idea how far and to what degree the outbreak had spread. Was there such a thing as a safe place? I didn't know, and even if I had been able to talk to her I had absolutely no idea what to tell her.

I stepped on the gas and got through the neighborhood as fast as I could. I remembered there was a fire station on Thorn Street, less than a mile away, and I steered us in that direction.

Thorn Station was an old-style, single-truck barn on the edge of the municipal golf course that had been converted into an EMS supply station.

My plan was to keep Carlos and the others there until somebody from the Fire Department came by to restock their EMS wagon and we could get a real medic to look him over.

The station was quiet and dark when we pulled up. It hadn't taken any damage like Independence Station had, and there were no signs of activity in the area. The one truck door was closed up, but I expected that.

I got out of the truck and looked over the station. The others got out too and, out of the corner of my eye, I saw them looking around apprehensively.

The man with the glasses came up to me. "Why here, officer?"

I studied him for a second before I answered. He had a medium build, sturdy, but not muscular, with a narrow, delicate jaw and intelligent, questioning eyes. He seemed to be taking the situation pretty well.

"This is the safest place I can think of," I said. "It's

not close to any businesses or main streets, and with that golf course there, we can see those zombies coming from a long ways off."

His eyebrows went up when I used the word "zombies."

"Plus," I said, "all fire stations have emergency generators, bathrooms, food in the kitchens, and this one is an EMS supply barn. Maybe I can find something inside to help Officer Williams."

He had been smiling as I rattled off the advantages, nodding in agreement with each one, but when I mentioned Carlos, his smile melted away.

"What?" I asked.

"Your friend," he said, pushing his glasses back up his nose. "There's nothing you can do for him. You know that, right?"

I knew it. I knew it all too well.

"Maybe," I said, and glanced back at the truck. Carlos was still in the passenger seat, and I lowered my voice because I didn't want him to hear. "Maybe. But I can at least make him comfortable. And I can keep those zombies from getting him."

He nodded.

"By the way," I said. "I never did thank you for helping us back there at the school. I'm Eddie Hudson."

I offered him my hand and he shook it. "Ken Stoler," he said. "I used to teach science at the school."

"Used to," I said back at him, noticing the past tense.

"Used to."

"Come on, let's get inside."

I asked the two gardeners to help me carry Carlos to the door. He was trying to stay alert, but he was just too far gone. His legs were useless.

The front door was locked. There was a card-key reader next to the door, but I didn't have a card. I looked around for a window and found one big enough for the first gardener, the smaller one, to climb through. It was locked, too, so I broke it out with my baton.

"Go through and open the door," I told him.

He gave me a blank stare.

I made a series of gestures explaining what I wanted him to do, and eventually he understood.

He crawled through the window, and a moment later we were standing inside.

I looked around for the lights and turned them on. The others chattered to themselves, smiling with obvious relief to be out of the darkness.

"Every fire station's got an emergency generator in case of blackouts," I said. "I don't think they had this in mind, though."

Again I got that blank look.

"Never mind."

The first floor of the station was mostly business. There was a kitchen and a little dining room with a couch and a few cheap lawn chairs in a back corner. The rest of the first floor was dedicated to supplies and equipment.

Octavio and I guided Carlos to a cot near the truck bay and tried to make him comfortable. He refused a cup of water that I brought him, and he wouldn't let me look at the wound. He muttered something about me leaving him alone and turned his face to the wall.

I let him go. There was a serious problem, and I knew I'd have to do something about it soon. He was going to turn into one of those things, but I didn't want to confront that truth just then.

I went back to the kitchen instead.

The others had found a TV and were hunting for a picture. They flipped through all the channels, and eventually found a snowy news station. The broadcaster was talking hurriedly in Spanish.

We all gathered around it, glued to the images they were showing, even though Ken and I didn't understand most of what was being said.

Right away, I recognized pictures of downtown Houston, and I wondered why in the hell they were showing Houston when it was San Antonio that had been turned into zombie land.

Everything they were showing looked like old news to me. More flooding, more blackened corpses floating in the rivers that had once been the streets of Houston.

One of the women began to sob, and Octavio put an arm around her.

"Why are they showing Houston?" I asked Ken, not really expecting an answer. "Why aren't they talking about what's going on here?"

"I think they are," he said. "The cause of it, anyway."

"What do you mean?"

He pushed his glasses up the bridge of his nose with his thumb and said, "You've heard the same reports I have out of Houston, I'm sure. Rescuers being attacked and mutilated by the survivors."

"Sure," I said.

He turned back to the screen. "I think what we're seeing here is the same thing that's been happening down in Houston for the last few days. I think it's spreading."

"But how?" I asked. "You think the evacuees are doing this?"

"Maybe a few came here that way, but that wouldn't be enough to spread violence like we've seen so quickly. It has to be something else."

"Like what?"

"I don't know," he said, still watching the TV. "A virus would be the most logical guess. Something that spreads quickly and causes massive necrosis."

"You mean decay?"

"That's right. I heard you and that other man talking. You used the word 'zombie,' and I heard him say *'los muertos.'* I don't think that's completely accurate. Those people we've seen aren't dead. They are decaying on their feet, just like a dead body would do, but they're still alive."

I shook my head at that.

"What?" he asked.

"I'm not sure about that," I said. "I thought I was sure, but the more I think about it, the more confused I am. I've seen those things take a whole magazine of bullets in the chest and still keep walking. Hell, I've shot them myself. If they were living, they wouldn't be able to take that kind of damage."

"I know they're alive," he said.

"But how?"

He pushed his glasses back into place. The things seemed like they wanted to jump off his face. "Because I caught one back at the school. Back when this first started."

"You're kidding?"

"Nope," he said. "I tied her to a table. I studied her, and found a heartbeat. A pulse. They bleed, too."

"Yeah," I said. "I've seen that."

A moment passed. We watched footage on the TV from other cities, and they looked a lot like what was happening in San Antonio. New Orleans. Dallas. Miami. Mobile. Matamoras, Mexico. The destruction was total.

"I can't believe they're alive," I said. "How can living people act that way?"

"It's hard to believe, I know. But I do think you were pretty close to right when you called them zombies. Whatever it is that's causing them to decay is probably causing them to go mentally deaf and dumb, too. They probably don't have any idea what they're doing past satisfying an instinctive hunger."

"They would have to know what they're doing," I said. "At least on some level. Why else would they eat people? Why not just go to McDonald's?"

He closed his eyes for a moment. When he opened them again he said, "I don't have all the answers. My guess is that they have some consciousness; but if so, it's only a little. I never thought it would happen like this."

I turned and stared at him. "Like how? What do you mean?"

"I mean, I never thought the zombies would be living people. I thought they'd be dead people."

"What in the hell are you talking about?" I asked him.

"I run a website on zombies," he said, like it was the most natural thing in the world. "Livingdead.com. It's a big deal on the web, and in philosophical circles, too. There's a group of us that usually do the discussion groups and we talk about all kinds of zombies. I got into it because of the philosophical issues they raise. Zombies raise all kinds of issues about consciousness. The biggest one of course is about the existence of consciousness itself. Why do we have it? Do I have any way of knowing if other people have consciousness? That kind of thing."

I stared at him for a long moment, trying not to lose my temper. Finally, I said, "People are dying out there, Mr. Stoler. This isn't a bunch of geeks on the web talking about consciousness or whatever you people do. This is people dying. My wife and child are out there, somewhere."

"Hey, wait," he said, showing me the palms of his hands. "I'm not making light of this. I know it's not a game out there. I'm just saying, that's all. Just thinking out loud."

"Sure," I said. "If you'll excuse me, I'm going to check out the rest of this place."

I left him and made my rounds through the station.

All the doors were secure, and none of the windows were large enough for the zombies to break through.

From what I saw, they didn't seem able to climb very well, and the window we had broken out was above eye level.

The station had several phones, and I tried them all. None of them worked.

One of the phones was in the station commander's office. Evidently, even he had been forced out into the field in a hurry because his sport coat was still hanging on a peg on the wall. I brushed up against it on my way out of his office, and when I did I heard what sounded like his keys jangling in one of the pockets.

Out of curiosity I went through it and found his personal keys. One of them said Chevy on it. I had seen a maroon Chevy stepside in the parking lot behind the station and I thought there was a pretty good chance the keys went to that truck.

I put the keys in my pocket. When I searched the rest of his coat I found a cell phone in the breast pocket. It didn't seem very likely, but I flipped it open and dialed April's cell phone. I pressed SEND and put it up to my ear, not expecting anything.

When it actually started ringing I got so excited I nearly dropped the phone. The ringing took forever. One ring, two, three . . . "Come on, come on," I prayed out loud. "Come on, April. Answer."

I heard a click on the other end. "Hello? Hello. April, it's Eddie."

"Eddie?" She was talking through waves of static. "Eddie, is that you?"

"Sweetie, it's me. Are you okay?"

"Eddie, what's going on? The TV said—"

"It's real, sweetie. It's all real."

The ocean of white noise between us roared. "April. April. Are you there?"

"Where are you, Eddie? Are you okay?"

"I'm fine, April. I'm okay. I'm gonna come home as soon as I—"

"The TV said—" The rest was static.

"April? Are you there?

"—there were sick people all over the city."

"April, stop. I need you to listen to me. I need you to stay away from everybody. Don't go outside. Don't go near the windows or anything like that, okay? Don't let anybody inside, even if you know them. My other pistol is in the closet in that blue bag. Remember? Remember how I taught you to use it? I need you to get that gun and keep out of sight. Okay? Can you hear me, April?"

There was nothing on the other end. I wasn't even getting static anymore. I tried calling again and again and again—more times than I could count—but the phone wouldn't send.

In a rage, I threw it against the wall and broke it all to pieces.

Ken appeared in the doorway just in time to have the debris whistle past his ear.

"Whoa," he said, backing up. "What did you do that for?"

"Get bent."

He looked at the pieces all over the floor. "Did that work?"

"Yeah."

"And you broke it?"

I didn't answer him. Instead I sat down in the station commander's chair and simmered in my rage.

I was hoping desperately that April had heard enough to remember the Springfield Armory .45 automatic I kept in the closet. She hated guns. Always had. But I was hoping she would remember it, and use it if she needed it.

"We could have used that phone," Ken said.

"That was my wife," I said.

"Yeah, but—"

"Mr. Stoler, in all those little powwows you and your buddies have on your website, did any of you ever stop to consider the human side of it? Did it ever dawn on you that every zombie wandering around out there equals a wasted life? I'm not dealing in philosophy, Mr. Stoler. I have a wife and a six-month-old son out there. That's not philosophy. That's humanity."

He looked like he wanted to respond, but thought better of it.

"What are you going to do now?" he asked.

"I'm leaving," I said. "I have to find my family."

"You're leaving? What about the rest of us? What are we supposed to do?"

"I don't really care," I said. "Maybe you could discuss the philosophical existence of consciousness."

"Officer Hudson, please."

"What are you complaining for?" I said. I was being nasty, and I knew it. I didn't care. "This place is secure. You've got food. You've got a TV. When the phones come up, you'll have those too."

"Yeah, but we'll be stuck here."

"No you won't. I'll leave you the truck. I'm taking that Chevy parked out back."

As far as I was concerned, the conversation was over. I didn't want to hear anything else from Ken Stoler.

I walked out of the office, down the hallway, and was five steps from the door when Octavio came bounding down the stairs in a rush of knees and elbows, yelling at me in Spanish and pointing back up the stairs.

I thought I heard the word *'baño'* and I knew that meant bathroom, but there was no calming him. I tried to hold him there and get him to slow down, but he broke away from me and ran back to the kitchen, yelling the whole way.

There was a light on at the top of the stairs, but the stairs themselves were dark. I looked back at Ken and he shrugged, but I saw fear in his eyes.

I pulled my gun and started up.

As I mounted the steps I felt something sticky beneath my boots. I shined my light on the stairs and saw a long smear of blood leading up to the landing.

I took a deep breath and kept going.

Chapter 9

There was a puddle of blood at the top of the stairs and a long black smear leading down a corridor to the right. I kept my gun up, working the corners to maximize cover, and followed the blood trail into the locker room.

The locker room was at the far back corner of the second floor, and I knew there was no other way out. Whatever it was, I was about to meet it face-to-face.

The blood trail led into the bathroom. The floor was white tile, and the black blood glistened against it like a poorly made brush stroke. The smell made me want to vomit.

I passed the banks of urinals and turned the corner into the showers, my finger on the trigger, ready to fire. There, propped against the back wall in a puddle of his own blood, was Carlos. He had pulled his bandage off and tossed it aside. His eyes were cloudy white, but streaked with crimson. They were vacant and sunken into his face like pits. The barrel of his gun was resting across his chest.

I lowered my gun. "What are you doing up here?"

He didn't seem to hear me.

"Carlos?"

His hand and his gun fell from his chest and hit the tile beside him. He still held it loosely.

"What are you doing, Carlos?"

"Did you come up here to stop me?"

His voice shook me. It was coming out of lungs that even as we spoke were filling with blood.

"What can you say to stop me?"

He was right, of course. There was nothing I could say. I had no idea what kind of pain he was in, and it wasn't fair for me to judge him for wanting to put it behind him. It still horrified me, though.

"Are you . . . you gonna say . . ."

"No," I said quickly. "No. I won't stop you or say anything."

I watched him roll his eyes to the ceiling. His chest rose and fell with the pain of breathing.

"Carlos," I said softly. "I'm so sorry."

He coughed hard. "There's nothing to be sorry for," he said. "You didn't bite me."

"That's not what I meant. I'm sorry that you're hurting and I can't do anything for you. I don't know anything about how to use the stuff around here."

He coughed again, and black bits of his lungs landed in his lap. He looked down at the pieces of himself and moaned horribly.

I didn't know how to comfort him and I felt like all I was doing was making his last moments painfully public.

But at the same time, I don't think he wanted me to leave. He wanted to talk, to say anything, just to keep his hold on his humanity for a little while longer.

I lowered my eyes to the tile, feeling like an idiot. He needed to hear something from me, something that acknowledged his humanity, but I couldn't think of anything that made sense.

"Eddie?"

"What is it, Carlos?"

"I'm really scared. I don't want this to happen. I want to hold my son again."

"I know, Carlos. I'm sorry."

"I'm going to miss hearing people speak," he said. "I'm going to miss the sound of words."

"Carlos, I don't know what to say. I wish I could say something to make this all better, but I can't."

"It's fine," he said, and let his chin fall to his chest.

He was quiet for a long time after that. Finally he said, "Did you call your wife?"

"Yes."

"Is she okay?"

"Yes, I think so. She's scared."

"And Matthew?"

"What?" Matthew was his son's name.

"You have a boy, right?"

"Yes. I think he's fine, too."

"I have a son."

"I know. I've seen his picture."

"Yeah. I'd like to see him. Can you get it for me? In my wallet."

I nodded quietly and got his wallet out of his back pocket. There was a picture of his wife and his son and I took it out and put it in his hands.

He looked down at it and coughed. His chin sank into his chest and I saw his whole body deflate as the breath left his body.

For a moment, I thought he was gone. But then his eyes flew open and he screamed—or tried to, anyway. It turned to liquid in his throat.

He was panting heavily. I had my finger wrapped around my trigger, the gun tucked out of sight behind me, just in case he turned before he got what he wanted to say out.

When at last he settled into a series of shallow breaths he said, "Do you know what's so scary about dying like this?"

I shook my head. My finger fell off the trigger.

"I'm losing my mind. I mean, I'm really losing it. I can't think."

"It's the pain. I know it hurts."

"No, not the pain. It's the forgetting, the not feeling anything."

"Carlos, I—"

"I have a wife."

"I know."

"But I don't know her. I don't remember her. I can't even think of her name. I try to think of her and I don't see anything in my mind. There's nothing there. It's a blank space and nothing else. I know I'm supposed to love her, but I don't remember love or pain or any of it. My son . . . don't tell him I couldn't remember his name."

"I won't."

"I won't have a soul, will I?"

There was no use in me saying anything. Nothing I could say could reach him anymore. He was becoming a shell.

"Leave me alone," he said, suddenly sounding lucid again.

"What are you going to—"

"Leave me one bullet."

"Carlos—"

"Hurry." He coughed several times, hard. "Please."

I hurried. I took the magazine from his gun and checked to make sure there was one in the chamber.

"Okay," I said as I helped him put his fingers around the grip. I had to help him lift it to his mouth. It took two hands, it was so heavy.

"Okay," he said.

"I'll be outside."

I turned and walked away. Just around the corner I stopped, and waited, and listened.

I flinched when the gun went off. The sound of it reverberated so loudly in the shower stall I thought it would split the floor under my feet.

My head fell back against the wall and I let the tears fall freely. When I caught my breath I wiped my nose across the back of my arm and went back to his body.

He was dead. The gun was down by his side and his head rested peacefully against the wall. His mouth was slightly open in a mock expression of surprise, but there was very little blood on the wall behind him. I was surprised by that. It almost looked clean.

I kneeled down in front of him and wondered how something so awful could have happened. None of it made sense.

I heard footsteps on the tile floor coming up behind me—fast, hurried footsteps. I didn't bother to turn around.

It was the gardener, Octavio. His voice was soft, apologetic. "*¿Señor?*"

"Get out," I said in a hoarse whisper, turning my head only slightly in his direction.

"*¿Señor?*"

"God damn it," I said, spinning around and stabbing my gun at him. "Get out. Get out. Get the hell out of here!"

On his face was tenderness. There was no sign of fear in it. Only grace. He looked beyond me to Carlos and crossed himself. Then he turned and walked away and left me with my gun pointing at nothing.

Chapter 10

I closed his eyes with the palm of my hand.

There was nothing I could do for the body. It would have to stay there until the world was back on its rails, and that looked to be a long ways off from where I was standing.

Besides, my own family was out there, somewhere, and they needed me.

But I was also thinking about his wife and son not knowing whether he was alive or dead.

At least I had been able to talk to my wife. The cruel change that killed Carlos had robbed him of even that kindness.

I took the gun from Carlos's hand. The slide was still locked back in the empty position. I collected all the remaining ammunition and divided the bullets evenly between our two guns. It worked out to fourteen rounds a piece.

I took his driver's license out of his wallet, and slipped it into my gun belt. His address wasn't far from the station.

Downstairs, the others were sitting in the break room

around a cheap plywood card table. Ken was over by the sink, watching me warily.

When I walked into the room they all stopped talking and stiffened nervously. I probably looked a little crazy. I'm sure Octavio told them what he had seen upstairs in the shower.

I didn't try to change their minds. I put the gun on the table so that one of them could grab it.

"There's a gun for you. *Una pistola.* And here are the keys to your truck. *Sus llaves para la troca.* You've got fourteen bullets for the gun. I don't know how to say bullets in Spanish. I'm sorry. Lock the door behind me when I leave. Or go somewhere else. I don't care."

With that I walked away. None of them said anything to me. They just watched me walk out the door and into the night.

Ken followed me out to the parking lot. "Officer Hudson," he said. His voice sounded winded. "Officer Hudson, wait. Please."

I slowed, but kept walking.

He caught up with me. "Officer Hudson, where are you going?"

"I told you," I said. "I'm going to find my family. I'm not staying here."

"You can't leave us."

"We've already had this conversation," I said. "You're as safe here as anywhere."

"But the other officer? Did you—"

"No."

"But I heard a shot—"

"He did it himself."

"Oh."

I got to the truck and unlocked it. The inside looked like crap. There were empty soda cans and fast food wrappers and packs of cigarettes everywhere. It smelled like stale smoke and sweat. The dashboard was blistered and cracked from years of exposure to the south Texas sun.

I swept all the trash off the seat and climbed in.

"Officer," Ken said. "I don't want to stay here. I want to keep moving. That's the best way to stay alive."

"I'm not taking you anywhere," I said. "I'm going to pick up Carlos's family and then my family. Nowhere else."

"That's fine," he said. "Just as long as I don't have to get boxed in somewhere."

"Suit yourself," I said, and waited with the truck in gear for him to climb in.

He wrinkled his nose at the smell, and had to push his glasses back up.

"This is the station commander's truck?"

"Yep," I said, and peeled out of the parking lot.

He held on to the door as we turned onto the road. "You'd think a high-ranking firefighter like a station commander could afford something better than this."

He was bouncing all over the seat.

"It runs," I said. "That's all that counts."

Carlos's address was on the near west side. It was pretty close to downtown, but still on the west side of Jewett Street, which serves as the boundary line between the West and Downtown Divisions.

Most of the neighborhoods west of Jewett were rough, but the families there tried to keep their homes in good shape. They mowed their grass and planted trees and had contracts with termite companies.

But the people on the east side of Jewett had given up a long time ago.

In the old days, those streets had been the heroin capital of San Antonio.

My district was just a couple of miles north of Carlos's neighborhood, and I used to make calls on both sides of Jewett when the downtown guys were getting hammered with calls. I knew the area well enough, so I was able to stay away from the high-traffic areas and still make pretty good time.

I rolled the windows down and let the breeze cool my head. Carlos's death upset me in a way I couldn't really understand. He and I were never really anything more than passing acquaintances, yet I felt his absence like I was missing someone I had known and cared about for years.

I couldn't see any lights, and I found my thoughts mirrored by the uncertain darkness surrounding me. Almost directly overhead, the clouds were backlit with moonlight and shined like wet pewter. On the horizon, the clouds were tinged with a dull orange and streaked through with charcoal scars.

Ken saw me watching the darkened houses slip past and said, "I'm sorry about your friend."

"Thanks," I said, not really wanting to talk with him.

"I mean it," he said. "I know you don't think I understand. After what I said earlier, I mean. But I do. I do understand."

We passed two men on their knees who were eating a body they had ripped apart. They looked up as we drove by, blood and gore oozing from their lips.

"I lost somebody too," he said.

"Yeah?"

He nodded. "That zombie I told you about? That one I tied up back at the school?"

"I remember."

His glasses were hanging on the tip of his nose, but he didn't touch them. He looked down at his lap and took a breath.

"Her name was Margaret Sewell. She was a teacher at the school."

"Were you guys—"

"No," he said quickly. "Nothing like that. I would

have liked us to be, but I never got the nerve to ask her out."

"I'm sorry," I said.

"Thanks." And then it was his turn to look out the window.

We drove on for a little while, dodging crowds when we saw them, staying away from traffic jams, and we talked about the zombies.

"You basically have three kinds of zombies," he said. "At least that's how we divide them up on my website. You got the Hollywood zombies, like in the movies, though sometimes people call those Pittsburgh zombies because that's where *Night of the Living Dead* was made. They're dead people that have been re-animated somehow.

"Next you've got the Haitian voodoo zombies. Those are living people who have had their free will stolen by a witch doctor. They're used as slaves, primarily. Some argue that the Hollywood zombie is just an extension of the Haitian voodoo zombie, but I don't think so.

"The reason I got into talking about zombies, though, is because of the philosophical kind. They're mainly a thought experiment that philosophers use to talk about consciousness. It's really just a sexy version of the classic 'other minds' problem, but I think it's a really cool way of stating the problem. How do I know I'm not the only being in the universe with consciousness? That sort of thing."

I turned off the street we had been driving down because of a large crowd and said, "But I thought you said we were dealing with a virus."

"I still think we are," he said. "I'm just telling you about the website. These people walking around here don't really fit into any of the categories I mentioned."

"So, what's your take on them?"

"Well, first off, these people are all still alive. A lot of the hard questions would go away if they were dead. Some of the hard questions, anyway. You'd still have to deal with the religious implications of re-animated corpses, but as it is right now, those zombies are going to raise a lot of legal issues for people such as yourself."

"Questions like what?"

"Well, they all revolve around the issue of consciousness. How much of it do those people have left. If they have any degree of it, then we have to ask if they're culpable for attacking the living. Can you arrest a zombie, or even a near-zombie, for eating somebody? And what about the living? The people who aren't infected? Obviously it's self-defense if they shoot a zombie who's trying to eat them, but what about all the thousands of zombies that are just wandering around, unable to find somebody to eat? Do we shoot them because they *might* attack us? Do we have an obligation to contain them and try to find a cure for this virus? Do we take the utilitarian approach and kill them all before they have a chance to spread the virus to the rest of the world?"

I almost laughed at him. "Is that the kind of thing you guys discuss on your website?"

"Well, yeah. Those are all valid issues."

"Sounds like something for the courts to decide," I said. "Maybe the military. I'm just a cop. I enforce the law, I don't make it."

"But that's not really true, is it?" He turned to me and pushed his glasses back in place. It made him look like a fat little cherub. "As a cop, you're on the front lines of morality. The really important details, the freedoms we have, or had, as Americans, are decided in the blink of an eye by men and women like you on every street in the country. When you're called to act, you do it based on your training, sure, but you also act on your own personal standard of what's right and wrong. I hope you live through this, Eddie, I really do. I hope

your family lives through this. And I hope you realize
that what you do in the next few days and weeks will go
beyond mundane legal issues like search and seizure.
It's going to be about life and death. About humanity,
as you put it."

"You really like talking about this stuff, don't you?"

"Of course," he said. "And what better vehicle for it
than the zombie? Imagine it, a being caught between
life and death, deciding issues of life and death for the
rest of us. There's a sort of poetic symmetry in that,
don't you think?"

As he was talking I watched a man pull a woman's leg
off her body with his teeth and start to eat on the thigh.
I looked for the poetic symmetry.

He didn't notice though. He was on a roll.

"There's more, of course, than just the philosophical
side of it. I think a virus is causing this, like I told you,
and that means we have to ask how it's spread. Trans-
mission of bodily fluids is the most likely culprit. Blood,
for example. But, obviously, a bite will do it too. Maybe
even a scratch, if the fingernail doing the scratching
has the virus on it."

"But how do you suppose it got out of Houston?
From what it looked like on the TV, this is happening in
a lot of places."

"I don't know yet," he said. "That's something to
look into later, for sure. But there are precedents, you
know. The Black Death was spread by fleas on rats, and
Typhoid Mary showed how a single infected person
could start an epidemic. Maybe it's fleas, or ticks, or a
combination of insects. Fleas and mosquitoes, maybe."

That didn't sit well with me. I could shoot a zombie if
I had to. Hell, I could shoot a whole army of them if I
had to. But I couldn't shoot a flea.

"Any idea on why it formed? The virus, I mean."

"Well, that's the question of the day, isn't it? Could

be any number of factors. Unsanitary conditions in the wake of the Houston hurricanes probably. Who knows, though? Maybe it's not even a virus. Maybe it's a bacteria. A super bacterium brought on by doctors over-prescribing antibiotics."

"So what you're saying is, you have absolutely no clue."

"Basically, yeah. This is just me talking. One of the things that might help us though is the issue of cross-species contamination."

"Like zombie cats and dogs?"

"Exactly!" He said it triumphantly, like he'd just won a convert to his cause, whatever that was. "Although I was going to come back to the issue of consciousness. Suppose it's a virus that somehow thrives on the complex functions of the human mind. Another way of looking at it would be that it eats the mind away."

"Like Alzheimer's disease."

"Unfortunately, yes. Only this virus would work much faster. In hours instead of years. And when it's done with the mind, it eats the body."

"Can a virus do that?"

"I don't know. Maybe. We'll be able to say more if there are incidents of cross-species contamination. That would tell us how much of a mind you have to have in order to lose it. Are there zombie dolphins out in the Gulf of Mexico? Are there zombie chimps in the zoo or zombie killer whales in SeaWorld?"

"That would be something," I said. "I wonder if a zombie whale would remember to come up for air."

"Interesting," he said. "Definitely food for thought."

I saw a man moving quickly down the street. There was a good-sized group behind him, and they were obviously all zombies. I slowed down to check on the man, thinking he was running from the others.

I leaned over to Ken's side of the truck and called out to him through the open window.

"You okay?" I asked.

He stopped near the front tire on Ken's side and wheeled around to face us. The side of his face was one continuous wound, from his ear all the way down to his shoulder.

"Oh crap," Ken said. "Go, Eddie, go."

I didn't give him a chance to move any closer. I pointed the truck down the road and gunned it.

"Why did you do that?" Ken asked.

"I thought he was, you know, not a zombie."

"You couldn't tell from the way he was walking?"

"No. You mean you could?"

He just shook his head and we drove on in silence. Ken watched the destruction with pity in his eyes, and it looked like he was adding up the human toll.

"Eddie," he said, his tone suddenly very serious. "What are we doing?"

"We're going to pick up Carlos's wife and child. Then we're going to pick up my family."

"Are you sure this is the right thing to do? I mean, how do you know his family is still safe? Look at all this. The outbreak has hit this place hard."

"I didn't ask you to come along," I said. But what I didn't say was that I had been wondering the same thing. I wondered what in the hell I hoped to accomplish by going to Carlos's family and telling them he was dead. What could I possibly say to her? Yes, your husband's really dead. How do I know? Well, you see, I held the gun so he could shoot himself. No, no, it was painless. I promise. And yes, he did ask about you. Sort of, anyway.

I turned it over in my head, thinking about how to say it, but everything I could think of sounded equally cruel and inadequate.

And yet, for all that, I didn't turn the truck around. I kept going, driving and thinking about—

Gunfire.

The muzzle flash caught the corner of my eye. I recognized the high, metallic pop of a small caliber pistol and I locked up the brakes.

I slid the truck to a stop and I jumped out, looking around for the shooter and whatever he was shooting at.

Ken jumped out behind me. "What are you doing?" he said. "Get back in the truck."

"Gunfire," I said back to him. "That means somebody back there has a gun. Maybe they can help us."

"Don't be stupid, Eddie. Let's get out of here."

"This first," I said.

"Fine," he said. "But I'm not staying."

"What?"

I was already in the yard. He never left the street. Before I could stop him, he jumped in the truck, threw it in gear, and peeled out down the street, leaving me in a cloud of acrid smoke.

I screamed for him to come back, but of course he didn't.

I couldn't believe it. The bastard left me alone and exposed, just like that. No warning. No nothing.

Just then I heard another gunshot, and that snapped my attention back to the houses behind me.

There were no zombies that I could see. I pulled my gun and started slowly toward the spot where I saw the flash.

"Police," I said.

Silence.

"Police," I said again. "Can you hear me?"

I inched my way around the back corner of the house, ready to fire. There was an officer standing in the backyard with his back to me. In front of him was a patrol sergeant and two other men, and they had that zombie look in their eyes.

There were two other bodies face down in the grass.

The officer with his back to me spun around and nearly shot me.

"Stop," I said. "It's me, Eddie Hudson."

He didn't say anything, but I recognized him. His name was Arguello, from the Downtown Division. It looked like he had been through hell. His shirt was torn at the shoulder so that I could see his body armor and T-shirt, and he was covered in dust.

When I looked at his face for some indication that he recognized me, I saw his cheeks were streaked with tears.

"Step aside," I said, and dodged around him to fire at the zombies behind him.

The one in front changed direction when he saw me. I fired once at his forehead and put him down. Then I turned to the zombie in the sergeant's uniform.

But I never got the chance to fire. Before I could pull the trigger, Arguello tackled me from the side and slammed me to the ground so hard it knocked the wind out of me.

I broke contact with him when we hit the ground and rolled away. He came after me, scrambling to keep me from getting to my feet.

I slapped at him as I rolled away, but he had the jump on me, and he was stronger and faster than me, too. He was able to kick my legs out from under me and push me face down in the dust. He held me there.

"What the hell are you doing?" I said. "Let me up."

He didn't answer. I struggled to turn my head back in the direction of the house, and saw the two remaining zombies were getting closer.

"Let me up."

"I won't let you shoot him," he said, his voice choked with tears. "I won't."

"Let me up, damn it. Hurry."

My gun was a few feet from my face. He got off me, picked it up, and tucked it into his back pocket.

I rolled away as fast as I could and got to my feet. The zombies were closer to him, and they both turned on him.

Arguello moved quickly, stepping around the sergeant and firing one shot at the zombie in civilian clothes. That one folded to the ground instantly.

But he didn't shoot the zombie sergeant. He wouldn't even point his gun at him. He let his gun fall to his thigh and as the zombie got closer, he just stood there and cried, his whole chest shaking with sobs.

"What are you doing?" I said. "Shoot him."

He turned his gun on me. "You stay away from him. Stay away!"

The sergeant's face was torn to pieces. His neck was a gaping hole, and there was dried blood all down the front of his uniform.

Arguello stood there, letting the zombie inch toward him. He didn't make any attempt to move out of the way.

When the sergeant got close enough I was able to read his name tag. It said ARGUELLO, and I didn't need to ask any more questions after that. I knew there was a Sergeant Arguello, and I knew there was an Officer Arguello, but it never occurred to me that they were father and son.

"You can't do anything for him," I said, my voice softer now that I understood.

"Shut up, Hudson."

"You have to protect yourself. No one can help him now. You have to look out for yourself."

"You don't know that. You don't know shit, Hudson. I can take him somewhere. Somebody can do something. Maybe they have a cure."

"He's too close to you," I said. "Back up."

He didn't answer. He just cried.

As calmly as I could I reached up and grabbed him by the shoulder. He shook me off the first time, but then he let me pull him back.

When I got him out of the way, the zombie turned on me.

I backed up slowly, and stepped away from Arguello so the zombie would follow me instead.

When I was far enough away from Arguello I let the zombie reach for me. As his hands came up I grabbed his right wrist and twisted it upwards, sidestepping around the body and pushing the back of his head with my other hand.

It was easy to take him off balance, and I threw him face down on the ground with a standard arm-bar take-down. I've done the same move a thousand times on a thousand drunks.

I came down on top of him with my knee on his back, wrenched his arm all the way up, and cuffed him as quickly as I could.

It happened fast. As I slapped the other cuff on, I heard Arguello screaming at me, and I braced for the impact.

He laid into me with his shoulder and sent me flying off the thing that used to be his father.

The whole time he was screaming at me, but nothing I could understand. He was totally overcome with grief and rage and there was no reaching him.

As I scrambled out from under him I saw his gun pointed at me. I slapped at him and with a lucky blow managed to knock the gun from his hands.

He didn't bother to go after it. He charged me, bear-hugged me, and threw me to the ground.

We both went down, kicking and punching. He was all over me. Every time I got a grip on him, he was able to break it and turn my weight against me.

He swung his elbow up and caught me in the bottom lip. I saw purple and tasted blood. Then he tossed me to one side and I landed hard on my back.

As I hit the ground all I could see was a spot of ground lit up by my flashlight.

He got to his feet first and charged me. I grabbed the flashlight and swung it at him, catching him hard under the jaw with a good solid stroke.

He fell to his knees, bleeding, and I didn't wait for him to get up again. I swung the flashlight again and hit him right behind the ear. He fell backwards, and stayed down.

I staggered up to my feet, swaying all over the place. The yard was spinning so fast I had to double over and put my hands on my knees just to keep from falling over.

"Holy crap," I said, wheezing through the blood. A long rope of bloody spit fell onto the ground between my boots.

I picked up both guns from the ground, holstered mine and unloaded his. Arguello had six rounds in the gun and a full magazine on his belt.

I took the full magazine and put the magazine with the six bullets back in his belt. He rolled over and groaned, but was nowhere close to getting back on his feet.

"Don't you hurt him, Hudson," he said. "I swear to God I'll fucking kill you."

"I'm sorry," I said. "I really am."

I threw his empty gun in the dust in front of him and walked back to the street.

I could hear him yelling at me the whole time.

There were zombies in the street. Not many at first, but enough to make a break for it into a suicide run. And there were more coming. Some of them stayed close to a nearby car, while others entered the yards on either side of me.

I wondered briefly if Ken had seen this coming.

I knew I wouldn't be able to make it to the car. They had it surrounded. I could have dodged some, and shot some more, but there were so many of them they would have overwhelmed me long before I could get the car moving.

I ran back between the houses. Some of the zombies were close enough to grab at me, but I was moving fast, and their reaction time was slow. I never let them get a solid grip.

Arguello was on his hands and knees, trying to stand up. He had crawled part of the way across the yard, over to where his father was still trying to get back on his feet, but he hadn't gone very far from where I left him.

I ran by him and took the back fence at full speed, jumping onto it, and swinging myself over without bothering to look at what I was jumping into.

As soon as I hit the ground, I froze. There were more zombies entering the yard from the next street, pouring into the backyard on both sides of the house. I looked to my right, prepared to move that way, but the next yard over was already overrun.

I couldn't go back, and I couldn't go forward. Somehow I was surrounded and I hadn't even seen it coming.

My heart was hammering inside my chest. I backed up into the fence and looked around for I don't know what.

There was a small storage shed back in the corner of the yard. I ran to it and jumped up on the roof.

From the roof, I could see the zombies pouring into the yard and surrounding Arguello. He was back on his feet, but he was still groggy and he staggered as badly as the zombies.

A group of them closed in on him.

He picked his gun up and tried to fire, but nothing happened when he pulled the trigger.

He stared at it stupidly for a moment before his training kicked in. Arguello came up with a magazine, slapped it into place, and pulled back on the slide, ready to shoot.

The first shot wasn't even close. It hit high up on the corner of the house. The next shot hit one of the zombies in the shoulder.

After that he started firing wildly into the crowd, wasting all his ammunition.

The zombies took him down, and ripped him apart, but through it all he never made a sound.

"I'm sorry," I said.

But I had problems of my own. I was completely surrounded. There were dozens of zombies slapping their hands against the sides of the shed, reaching for me.

I pushed myself up to the highest part of the roof, looking everywhere for a way out.

They couldn't reach me—at least not yet. But there were enough of them that the weight of their bodies pressing up against the shed could topple it over. They had already torn down a section of the wooden fence and were moving back and forth between the two yards.

The yard where Arguello had just died was crowded with zombies. There were just as many around me. I couldn't go into either yard and expect to last very long. I turned around and around on the roof of that little shed, looking for a way out, but I kept seeing the same things and same shredded faces over and over again.

As I turned I slipped, and my knee hit the shingles.

Off balance, I started to slide.

I panicked, shot a hand out, and caught a corner of the roof. The suddenness of it caused my head to jerk up, and I managed to get a quick glimpse of the yard to the left of the one I was in.

It wasn't more than six or seven feet away, but I was so panicked I hadn't even seen it until just then.

I counted eight zombies. They were banging against the fence to get to me, but there weren't enough of them to break through.

It was a way out. I thought if I could jump into that yard I could hit the ground running and keep going.

The only problem would be fighting off the zombies when I landed.

But then I remembered I didn't have to fight them. All I had to do was shoot them. I had a pistol. There were almost thirty rounds in the gun. I could just pop them from where I was and jump into an empty yard.

Piece of cake.

But I hadn't figured on aiming while the zombies below me were rocking the shed.

The distance to the target was no problem. My shooting wasn't the greatest, but three yards was pretty easy, even for me. At least I thought it would be easy.

It was like trying to shoot from a surfboard on choppy seas. Getting a clean head shot was hard, and I knew from past experience that it took too many body shots with a pistol to put even one zombie down. I put a lot of rounds into their faces and glanced a few off the sides of their heads, but I only got a kill shot every six or seven shots I made.

By the time I ran out of ammo, there were still two of them left on their feet.

And the zombies below me were rocking the shed. It was getting harder and harder to keep my balance, and I knew that if I was going to make a break for it, it would have to be right then. It was the last, best chance.

I crouched down like a sprinter at the gates and tried to focus on the jump. The yard below me was a seething carpet of faces and hands. I took a breath, forcing down the nausea and the fear, and jumped.

One of the zombies grabbed me as I landed. We both tumbled to the ground and I rolled off him. Once I was on my feet I took off running and didn't stop until I was out in the street, all the zombies behind me.

I stood there huffing, looking around in utter disbelief. I had heard people talk about mental exhaustion, about getting to that point when the mind refuses to go any further, but I had always thought it was just hyperbole. I didn't realize it was actually possible to get to that point.

But even as I stood there, listening to the hordes behind me as they crashed through the fences like an approaching tidal wave, a little voice inside me pleaded for a little more. You've got to move.

Ken Stoler's act of treachery had left me without a ride, and I felt like a doomed man, waiting for the gallows door to drop.

The zombies were wandering back through the houses, and as I looked behind me, I saw more and more of them filtering into the street.

You've got to move.

Chapter 11

I ran for it.

I passed dark, beat-up clapboard houses that leaned in on themselves at unsafe-looking angles and sagged under the weight of years of neglect. Few were painted. Most were worn gray from the weather and their porches looked like there was no way they could hold a man's weight. The yards were small, the grass thin and scraggly. They were strewn with old machine parts and junked cars.

I ran down the center of the street because I didn't want to get boxed in again. With no ammunition, I had to avoid a fight. There was no way I would be able to fend off a whole crowd of zombies with just my baton. Even a small group of twenty or so would be able to overpower me.

The zombies I had just escaped were blocking the street to the west, so I headed east.

When I got to Appleton Street, I got my first good look at the highways. Appleton ran north-south across the near west side, then curved east and went straight up to the highway. Whenever I made arrests, Appleton was the street I used to get on the freeway for the drive downtown. From there it was a quick five-minute car ride to the jail.

I was used to running into traffic on Appleton because it was a major road, but I wasn't prepared at all for the mess waiting for me. The street was a bumper-to-bumper junkyard of abandoned cars.

I looked up and down Appleton and saw cars crashed out all over the road. Off to the south, I could see most of them still had their headlights on, and they looked like cats' eyes.

I used to enjoy watching the ebb and flow of traffic. It always fascinated me the way it pulsed, gathering up in knots at the stoplights and then spacing out again at the green, like the movement of blood through the body.

San Antonio had once been a living entity, with vigor in its veins driven by the pulse of its streets, but now the streets that were the city's arteries and blood vessels were frozen, the blood congealed in the veins.

The city itself had become a zombie, dying on its feet.

I kept my head low and started checking the cars that looked like they could be driven away.

Most of them were hung up in traffic and couldn't be moved, but I finally found an old beat-up Monte Carlo resting in the grass near the turnoff to a small side street. It looked like crap, but the keys were in it.

The dashboard was covered in trash. I swept it off with my hand and a little clear plastic baggie of marijuana fell onto the passenger seat. It caught my eye immediately, and it made me laugh, not because it was especially funny but because of what it represented.

Back when the world was normal, I'd search cars looking for stuff like that bag of weed. I used to find plenty of it, too. But as I looked around and saw how thoroughly the world had changed, that little bag of weed seemed a pathetic link to the way things used to be.

I turned the key, but all I got was the lame whirling noise of a bad starter. I tried it again and got the same noise.

"Come on, you piece of crap," I said. "Come on."

I hit the steering wheel. Mashed down on the gas. Nothing. The engine wouldn't turn.

I saw a group of zombies moving through the back patio of a bar across the street, and they turned towards me when they heard the noise.

There was one zombie out in front, moving faster than the others. I cranked the engine again and kept an eye on him.

The Monte Carlo still wouldn't start, and the fast-moving zombie entered the street. In the time it took me to crank the car again he was already across the street and banging at the passenger window.

When he started around the front of the car I stepped out and snapped my baton open. He came around the fender with his hands already reaching for me.

I waited for him to get within striking distance and then I dropped him with a full baseball bat–style swing to the side of his head.

He landed face down in the grass and didn't get up again.

But while I was fooling around with him, the others were getting closer. I got back in the car and kept cranking. There was nothing, nothing, and then all of a sudden the engine roared up. It was knocking and chugging, but it was running.

One of the zombies grabbed at the windshield just as I dropped it into gear and took off. I caught his arm in the side-view mirror and spun him around violently.

He landed in the grass next to the fast-moving zombie, and I was off before he could stand up again.

I headed west for two blocks, and then south again. Driving that Monte Carlo was a pain in the ass. The seat was busted. It was stuck as far back from the steering wheel as it would go, leaning into the backseat, so that I had to sit up with no back support just to keep control of the car.

I didn't want to get it going too fast either, because every time I stepped on the brake it felt like I was stepping on a wet sponge.

But I was lucky to have a car at all, I told myself. And I was lucky to have gotten away from Appleton Street with my life.

I kept telling myself how lucky I was as I drove through wreckage that seemed to be getting worse.

When I got to the intersection of Beaumont and Fletcher, I had to slow down to go around a wreck, and I just happened to look off to my right.

There was a police car down there! I could tell right away that it was one of ours because it had the parking lights on. They train us to leave them on when we're out of the car so we can see each other from a long way off in the dark.

I turned the Monte Carlo toward the cruiser. When I pulled up I saw that it was a traffic car. It had a video camera mounted on the inside of the windshield and there were radar antennas all over the place.

I walked around the police car. It was beautiful, not a scratch on it. Compared to the crap they give us on patrol, it was immaculate. There was even a brand-new shotgun in the trunk. Those bastards in traffic always get the best toys.

I got in, cranked it up, and it purred like a kitten. Everything worked. It was strange to sit in a police car that didn't smell like sweat and oil and cheap air fresh-

eners and a drunk's puke. There was even a little trash
bag tied to the inside of the passenger door.

I flipped on the PA speakers and said, "Can anyone
hear this? If you can hear me, come out in the street."

I was risking another zombie encounter by doing
that, but if the traffic officer who was assigned to this
car was anywhere around, I didn't want to leave him
stranded.

But no one came out. He was either dead or injured,
and, in either case, I couldn't help him. I took Carlos's
driver's license from my belt and placed it over the
gauges on the dashboard.

The car handled like a dream. On patrol, we have to
drive through fields and jump curbs and do all kinds of
crazy things to our cars, but obviously traffic didn't do
that kind of stuff.

In no time at all I had the windows down and I was
cruising down Fletcher Street towards Carlos's house.

Chapter 12

Carlos's neighborhood was nicer than the neighborhoods I had just come from.

As I turned into the main entrance, the streets seemed to open up. There were no cars on the curb, and no front yard fences to chop up the views.

I saw open spaces, and trees, and yards with green healthy grass reaching all the way up to the front steps. They were old houses, but they were sturdy and well-maintained.

"Well done, Carlos," I said to myself as I passed a rather impressive red-brick house with a little fountain in the front yard. This neighborhood was a good catch on a policeman's salary. Maybe his wife worked, too.

But the destruction had come to Carlos's neighborhood, too.

Just off the main entrance I saw a burnt Tudor-style house at one corner. I probably would have missed it completely if I hadn't seen one of the curtains billowing into the air like the swish of a girl's skirt. It floated on the breeze, sticking out of a charred hole where the kitchen window used to be. It seemed so sad and silent.

And there were zombies here, too. They filtered into the street behind me as I drove by. None of them were a threat, though. The front yards were so big that I was halfway down the block before they could make it to the curb.

Carlos's street wasn't all that different from any other in the neighborhood, except that there was a car crashed into the fence on the corner. The wooden slats of the fence were scattered around the yard like exploded matchsticks and the back right tire was sticking up into the air.

I turned my spotlight into the passenger area and saw a body slumped over the wheel. It wasn't moving.

I stopped in front of Carlos's house. It was done up in gray brick and brown siding, with well-trimmed hedges lining the front of the house and a black, wrought-iron light pole in the garden. The light wasn't working.

There were three large windows on the front of the house, and I turned the spotlight into each one of them, trying to see inside. There was no movement. The house was dark and the spotlight didn't penetrate very far.

I was hoping Carlos's wife would see the spotlight and come out on her own, but it didn't happen. I waited there in the car, looking around for more zombies, and wondering again if this was really such a good idea. Every minute I was away from April and Andrew was an invitation for something bad to happen to them. After all, I didn't even know Carlos's wife's name.

But I had come this far already, hadn't I? Wasn't it worth the chance that maybe I could do something good for Carlos's family, even if I hadn't been able to do anything for him?

The question seemed to me to answer itself, and so I threw the shotgun over my shoulder and started up the front walk.

My flashlight beam wasn't much use either. I lit up the windows next to the front door, but couldn't see anything. The whole house seemed strangely quiet.

Cops always talk about *that feeling*. What they mean is that sensation when the hairs stand up on the back of your neck and you just know a situation is about to get really fucked up.

Imagine wading through the ocean and suddenly feeling something big brush against your leg.

That's what *that feeling* feels like.

And that's pretty much the feeling I had as I walked around the house.

The back door was blasted open. It had been one of those sliding glass doors that I thought every cop knew better than to put on his house. Pieces of glass were everywhere, inside and out. The house was wide open, and I thought I saw blood on the carpet. It was hard to tell for sure because the carpet was a deep pile brownish-maroon.

All I knew for sure was that it was wet and sticky.

The inside was split into two parts, with the kitchen, master bedroom, and dining room off to the left of the living room, and the smaller bedrooms off to the right. I started my sweep with the kitchen and worked back from there.

As I entered the hallways leading off to the smaller bedrooms I tightened up. There was blood on the carpet, and more blood on the wall.

I turned the corner into the first room I came to and saw baby clothes and toys all over the floor. A crib and a bookshelf were off near the back and there was a changing station near the inside left corner, away from the door.

Matthew was there and there was blood on the changing pad and blood on the wall behind him. There was so much blood.

And then it became abominable.

He moved. His head lolled over and he looked at me, eyes vacant and milky white, like candle wax.

I turned away.

My head was swimming, and I staggered backwards from the changing station.

The shotgun fell from my hands.

My legs went weak and couldn't hold me. I half fell, half slid down the wall into a pile in the corner.

I couldn't hang words on shock of that magnitude. As a parent, looking at that torn little body, I felt such a deep sense of violation that I was unable to pull myself back from it. Surely this was hell, because nothing else could ever debase the human condition as much as the sight of an infant made into such a horrible thing.

A few moments passed.

I finally looked up at the changing pad again and saw his arm hanging over the side, his hand grasping at the slick wooden paneling, unable to get a grip, and I wondered why it took something that horrible to convince me the world was dying. I would have preferred just about any death to this. Instead of a war or an asteroid or global warming, something that killed us from beyond ourselves, we were dying by implosion.

I saw movement in the hallway. A woman's body fell against the door to the nursery. She was wearing a T-shirt and panties. Her legs were sliced up in a hundred different randomly crossing angles. Blood was caked to her skin. Her hands and bottom jaw and the side of her head were torn open and black with infection.

She stumbled into the room and stretched out her mangled hands to grab me.

"What have you done?" I said, though I knew she couldn't answer me. Besides, we were well beyond the point where answers mattered.

When she was close enough to put her hands on me,

I pushed her aside and stood up behind her. If there had been more range I could have used the beanbags, but we were very close together, and at less than five feet shooting someone with a beanbag is basically the same as shooting them with a really big bullet. The effect is the same, anyway.

I didn't want to risk splattering her blood all over me, not after what Ken had told me, so instead of shooting her I punched the back of her head with the butt of the shotgun. She went down, but not for good. I didn't do enough damage. When she tried to get up I swung the butt of the shotgun down and put her away once and for all.

Then I went over to Matthew's body and tried to do the same thing to him. But I couldn't do it. I stood over his small body with the shotgun raised over my head, and I kept telling myself that he was just a husk.

But I couldn't do it.

I took the coward's way out. I went to the garage and got the gas can Carlos used for the lawnmower. I poured it out on the carpet, and on Carlos's wife, and threw a lit candle into the middle of the room.

The fire caught hold, and I walked out of the house, leaving the flames to take their course.

Chapter 13

I thought maybe the house would blow up behind me as I drove away, something dramatic like that. The truth is I didn't even know if that kind of thing worked in real life.

I've handled plenty of house fires, but I've never seen a house blow up like they do in the movies. All I could do was hope the fire did take hold, and that mother and child were burned up in it.

If there is such a thing as small mercies, then that is what happened. But I don't know for sure. I took off down the street and never looked back.

As I drove away, I tried to make myself believe there was a sense of closure in their deaths. They wouldn't have to live without Carlos, and Carlos wouldn't have to live without them.

But even as I tried to convince myself that there was something good in what I'd seen, I knew I was being foolish. There was nothing good at all about it, and any attempt I could make to somehow put a good spin on it was just more moral cowardice.

I focused on the street lamps. They weren't working,

but counting them was a mind-numbing diversion. I glided past them without having to think about problems that made my head hurt.

I drove on until I got to Crane Street. Crane was another major cross street for the highway, and it was jammed up in the same horrible way Appleton had been.

The only difference was that from Crane Street I could look down on the highway, and it gave me a good view of the intersection, and the highway beyond it.

All the traffic was clogged up in the outgoing lanes, but the incoming lanes were empty. From the looks of it, all those people had tried to get out of town at the same time.

The traffic jam was predictable. As soon as someone's car broke down, or there was an accident, the flow shut down behind it like a clogged drain. Every single person stuck in the break down had been forced to foot it, and they were probably all dead, or worse. Not one person in that whole doomed parade had been able to think outside of their mental box and simply drive the wrong way up the highway.

As I drove up the exit ramp, passing all the red signs that said WRONG WAY DO NOT ENTER, I remembered what my driving instructor at the Police Academy used to tell us. "The road is not a mandate," he had said, standing on a picnic table in the middle of the Academy's driving track. "It's merely a suggestion."

It felt strange to drive the wrong way on the highway, even though mine seemed to be the only car moving. I kept expecting a huge truck to come barreling over the next hill and smear me across the pavement, but I went for miles without seeing any movement at all.

I wasn't far from my house when I saw the police car lights still flickering on the other side of the retaining wall.

When I got close enough to see that it was one of ours, I pulled alongside it and put a light on it.

I recognized the driver. His name was Martin Jackson, and he was unquestionably dead. No chance he was getting up again. His black skin and the brass captain's bars on his collar were covered in blood from a long, jagged piece of metal that was stuck through his right eye and out the back of his skull.

I didn't know him very well, but rumor around the department was that he would make chief one day. Just forty years old and already a captain with a PhD in Criminal Justice, he had the world at his feet. The department had spent millions on his training in anticipation of the great things he would do one day, and now all that potential was bleeding out across the fender of his patrol car.

I stepped over the wall and poked around his corpse with my flashlight. There were empty shell casings all around him, and it was obvious he had gone down fighting. I was glad for that. It was somehow fitting for someone with his reputation for being bigger than life.

The magazine in his gun still had four rounds in it. I thumbed off the live rounds and put them into my own gun, but he didn't have anything else I could use.

I hesitated near the body, feeling like there was something else that needed to be done, but in the end I just got back into the traffic car and drove off.

My own family was waiting.

Chapter 14

I drove up the freeway, passing miles of cars massed into gridlock, and it felt like driving through my worst nightmare. From a distance, things looked normal. But close up, with the veneer pulled down, reality seemed to blur and bend.

The freeway was flanked on both sides by strip malls and apartment buildings and gas stations and all the areas people gravitate toward in their daily routines.

I figured most of the people injured on the highway would have wandered down into those areas, looking for help, which meant everything down there was absolutely unsafe.

When I turned onto Mariner Boulevard, I saw a huge crowd of zombies milling around between the cars. There had to be hundreds of them.

The intersection was completely choked up with wrecked cars, and I ended up driving through some bushes and across a gas station's landscaping just to get around it.

Most of the zombies could only watch as I drove up the sidewalk on the other side of the street.

I almost made it through the intersection without incident, but the sidewalk I was driving on ran out in front of the Fish Shack, where a group of about ten zombies had gathered. I was stuck between them and wall-to-wall traffic. There was no way to go around them, and backing up would have put me right back where I started from.

I used the takedown lights to flood the entire area ahead of me with light. The zombie out in front never even flinched. He didn't respond at all to the lights. I've never seen anyone look into the takedown lights and not have to turn their eyes away, but that zombie wasn't fazed.

He didn't look away, but I did. His face was torn up, the whole lower half of his jaw gone. From his nose to his throat, his face was one gaping hole with clumps of dirt and shredded pieces of skin hanging on like pennants from the wound. His shirt was black with dried blood.

Behind him the other zombies were a knot of arms and faces. They were coming into the narrow gap between a low concrete wall and the traffic.

I punched it. I hit the zombie with the shredded face and heard the plastic bumper crunch under his weight. He slammed face down into the hood and tumbled across it, straight toward me. His forehead hit the base of the windshield and cracked it, and as he rolled off to my left he pulled one of the windshield wipers out of the cradle.

I hit the others at a run, and I learned the hard way that it isn't easy to run over a crowd of people.

One went under the car and, as I drove over the others, the front tires lost traction.

The car seemed to hover in the air for just a moment before it rolled to the right, like it was gradually going over on its side.

I went off the curb and hit the side of a minivan.

The car bounced back onto the sidewalk and I kept on the gas, pushing it through the bodies as fast as it would go.

I could hear the car groaning with the impact.

"Sorry, traffic," I said. "I fucked up your pretty toy."

The back tires hit the ground with a thud as I rolled over their bodies, and the next thing I knew I was looking at an empty sidewalk.

I didn't let off the gas until I was past all the fast food places and into the residential part of Mariner.

Once the road opened up, my mind cleared and the only thing I could think of was holding April and Andrew again. It never even crossed my mind that what had happened to Carlos's wife and son could happen to my family.

I was in denial, I guess.

I entered my subdivision at the Alfoxden gate, and then went north on Swinburne to my street.

But as I turned onto Lighthouse, all my confidence dissolved. The air in my street was heavy with smoke, and somebody's trash had been scattered all over the pavement. Little pieces of paper were blowing down the street and across the yards like empty promises. There was a car smashed up on a brick mailbox about six doors down and a fat man in a white T-shirt and khaki pants was lying motionless, face down in the street.

I drove around the body and stopped near my house. My front door was wide open, and I jumped out of the car in a panic. I didn't even bother to grab the shotgun.

I drew my gun and hit the front door running.

My neighbor was standing in the doorway to my kitchen. Most of his right arm was missing and the side of his head had been torn away by somebody else's teeth.

He never even got a chance to turn around. I put my pistol up to the side of his head and fired.

A man and a woman I didn't recognize were on opposite ends of the couch in the living room and I shot them both.

"April. April!"

I shouted it over and over again as I ran from one room to the next, getting more and more desperate with every empty room I searched.

They were gone. I stood in our bedroom, my chest heaving and my mind uncertain, unable to focus on anything. I must have retraced the same paths through the house five or six times before it began to sink in that they weren't there.

There were clothes on the floor and Andrew's toys were all over the place. I looked at the mess, and for some reason thought, *Garage!* I hadn't checked the garage.

I ran through the kitchen, over the body of my dead neighbor, and into the garage.

It was empty.

April's car was gone. I had bought her a brand-new black Nissan Xterra about three months after she got pregnant because I didn't want her driving around in that crappy Ford Taurus she drove all through college. But it was gone.

I stood in the doorway, and felt totally lost.

I would have still been standing there, looking at my empty garage, if I hadn't heard the crunch of broken glass behind me.

When I turned around, I saw three zombies walking toward me through the kitchen. The girl in front was wearing jeans and a torn blue bra and no shoes. Smeared tracks of blood spread across the floor from her feet.

Behind her were two older men, and behind them I saw dim shapes moving into the house through the front door.

I fired at the girl and she went face down into the stove. The slide of my Glock locked back in the empty position and I was forced to toss it aside. The others kept coming.

I backed up into the garage. The two older men were just entering the laundry room between the kitchen and the garage when suddenly a third zombie broke in between them, moving fast.

I recognized him from around the neighborhood, though I didn't know his name. He was just somebody I saw jogging all the time.

When he entered into the garage he was practically at a run. He came up on me so fast that I didn't even have time to throw a punch.

He grabbed me, and his momentum knocked us both to the ground.

I kicked at him. I slapped and punched him. I rolled one way and then the other, but he was incredibly strong and he pinned me down so that I couldn't break his hold.

He tried to bite me, but I forced the palm of my hand into his neck, pushing as hard as I could to keep his face away from me. His breath smelled like blood and the skin around his neck felt wet.

I tried flipping him, but no matter how hard I tried to move him, he wouldn't go over.

We stayed locked up like that until some more zombies grabbed at my shoulder. The strong one on top of me shifted a little under the weight of the others and that gave me the leverage that I needed to knock him off balance.

After that, he went over easily, and when I threw him off me he landed hard near the garage door.

Before the others could grab me I jumped up to my feet and ran for the rack of shovels on the far wall.

I grabbed one and swung it at the zombie closest to me.

It knocked him back, but he didn't go down. The shovel was too long and I couldn't swing it with enough force to make it an effective weapon. Instead of swinging it again, I used it to jab at them, hooking them with the blade and pulling them away from the door.

The fast-mover came at me again just as I pushed the last one away from the door, but he couldn't force his way through the ambling crowd in time to reach me.

I jumped through the doorway and pulled it closed behind me, then steadied myself on the washing machine while the zombies banged at the door behind me.

From where I stood in the laundry room I could see through the kitchen to the dining room and through the front windows to the street where the car was parked. I had left the headlights on, and I could see at least three zombies walking through the glare. They were cutting through the grass toward the house.

The front door, I thought. Oh crap, it's open.

I ran through the kitchen and into the entry way just in time to push one of the zombies back onto the front steps and shut the door in his face.

Through the window I saw a small crowd gathering in the front yard. They formed around the headlights like moths.

I could hear the ones in the garage banging on the door and I stood there, breathing hard, feeling trapped. The front door was solid, but the door leading out to the garage was paper thin. I doubted it would hold very long.

I looked down on the floor and saw the night sights of my Glock glowing against the white tile of the kitchen floor and I prayed that April and Andrew had managed to get out of here before things got out of control.

Wait a second, I told myself. Eddie, you're an idiot. There's a whole case of bullets in the closet. Shotgun shells, too. Not those stupid beanbag rounds either. Real ones.

I picked up my gun and ran to the closet in the master bedroom. It was a mess. All my gun stuff that I usually keep on the top shelf was on the floor, and the blue box that I kept my .45 in was missing.

I pushed some stuff out of the way, looking for it, but it wasn't there. That was good, I told myself. That meant April had it. At least she had heard enough of our conversation to get the gun, and that meant she had some protection with her.

I had three magazines with me, and I topped each one off with fifteen rounds apiece. I looked for my shotgun, but couldn't find it. Maybe April had that too, I thought.

I did find my extra flashlight, though.

With my Glock reloaded, I went back to the kitchen so I could clear the zombies out of the garage. I wasn't going to chance April and Andrew coming home to a house full of zombies if I could help it.

I paused just outside the garage door to catch my breath. There wasn't any room to screw up on this, and I had to make every shot count. They weren't banging on the door anymore, but I knew all I had to do was open it and they would come pouring out.

The fast-moving zombie was my biggest concern. He was stronger than the others, and I had already seen how he could force his way through the others. If he was anywhere near the door he would have to be the first to get it.

I kicked the door open, stepped back, and leveled my gun.

There was a man on the other side of the door in blue jeans and a dark blue mock turtleneck. I shot him in the forehead and then turned my light past him, looking for the fast-mover. He was towards the back. He had been facing the wrong way when I opened the door, but when he saw the light he turned around and headed towards me at full speed.

I shot three more zombies before he got all the way to the door, and I had another one in my sights when he broke through. He forced the one I was going to shoot to one side just as I pulled the trigger and my shot ended up hitting a different zombie in the shoulder.

He knocked the others out of the way in his rush to get me, and he was inside and had me backing up before I could fire off another shot.

I had to back-pedal to keep my distance, and it was impossible to do that and fire with any accuracy.

My first shot hit him just below the nose. That shot would have stopped anybody else, but not him. It snapped his head back, but the rest of him kept coming forward.

I fired at him again and hit at the corner of his left eye. That put him down on the ground, but it didn't put him out completely. He was still twitching, jerking his shoulders like he was in a seizure and trying to get back on his feet.

I fired three more shots at point-blank range, turning his head into a puddle of soup.

By that time the others had filtered into the kitchen. It was exactly the situation I had hoped to avoid, because now they were spread out, coming around both sides of the island, with plenty of room to move. I had to keep moving and shooting at the same time, keeping my eyes on targets coming from two directions.

By the time I put the last one down I had a trail of bodies spread out across three rooms and brass casings all over the place.

The magazine in my gun was empty. It had taken me

sixteen rounds to put down ten zombies, which was a pretty bad ratio. Shaking my head, I swapped out magazines and went back to the closet to load up on more ammunition.

I took one last look around the bedroom and then walked into the hall. As I was walking by Andrew's room, I accidentally kicked one of his toys, a phone shaped like a puppy that bobbed its head up and down as you dragged it by its leash. It started singing "London Bridge Is Falling Down" and the song grabbed me by the heart.

It's funny how the smallest things can cause such massive storms in the mind. Andrew hardly ever played with that damn toy, but the sound of it was enough to awake half-a-year's worth of memories in me.

I found myself turning the corner into his room, looking at the diaper bin and the sock puppets and the little blue turkey baster-looking thing that we used to clean out his nose and I really started to hurt.

It made me wonder how anyone could live through losing a child. My Adam's apple pumped up and down in my throat like a piston, and I tried to push down the grief. I had no idea where April and Andrew were, and the stress of not knowing was breaking me.

They were still alive, waiting for me somewhere out there in the night. I believed that sincerely. But the thought of them ending up like Carlos's wife and son kept nagging at me until I was ready to take one bullet out of my gun and put in my pocket to keep for myself, because there wasn't going to be anymore me if there wasn't going to be anymore them.

I closed my eyes and thought of my wife and son while the sound of "London Bridge Is Falling Down" faded to silence in the hallway behind me.

Chapter 15

I stood in Andrew's room for a long time.

There were still zombies in the front yard, and I still had to get the extra ammunition from my closet to the car out in the street, but moving took so much effort, and I was so tired.

Finally, I don't know how much later, I straightened my uniform and went to the living room window so I could look out into the front yard.

The three zombies I had seen earlier were still there. They stayed close to the car, attracted to the light, I guess. Luckily, none of them were fast-movers.

I went outside and put the three of them down in quick order. Then I moved all the ammunition from the closet to the car.

It wasn't until I was out on the road, looking for empty lanes to work through, that I realized I had no idea where I wanted to go or what I was supposed to do.

When I worked dogwatch in the Northwest Division I used to go to the Exxon at the corner of Cereno and Budd. They gave cops free sodas there, and they had an office in the back where I sometimes went to catch up on my reports.

Miles and miles of roadway disappeared beneath my wheels, and I drifted aimlessly, like a cloud of dust in a desert wind storm, until somehow I found myself in the parking lot of that Exxon. When I put the car in park, I realized that I had driven fifteen miles, at least, and yet had absolutely no memory of it. Where the memory should have been was a hole, swirling with grief and uncertainty.

I stopped so that I was facing the building and stared at it for a second before I realized there was something wrong with it. The power was on. The lights inside the store were still on. And there were people inside. Three of them.

I got out of the car and ran to the front door, but as I got closer I saw that they were zombies. They had that recognizable half-dead walk.

The door was locked.

When I tried to pull it open, one of the zombies came up to it, and slapped on the other side of the glass.

Behind him on the floor was a puddle of blood, and beyond that, coming toward the door, was an older man with red, sunken cheeks and no hair, dressed in a clerk's uniform. The third zombie was near the beer and ice cream freezers.

I walked down to the far side of the window for a better look at the rest of the store. When I did finally make entry, I didn't want to be surprised by an unseen zombie.

The two at the door followed me. I watched them approach, and then moved down to the other side of the store once they blocked my view.

I stared at the man near the beer. There was a transparent reflection of my face in the glass, and just beyond that were the grotesque, vacuous remains of a man so thoroughly numbed by what his life had been like that he couldn't take his eyes off of the beer, even as a zombie.

Wondering what Ken Stoler would have thought of that man's consciousness, I tapped on the glass, but he didn't respond. I banged my fist against the glass, and that did it.

He turned, and in an instant I saw that almost all of his face was missing. The skin had been completely torn away, and though he was wearing a flannel shirt, there was so much blood that it was difficult to tell where his body ended and the cloth began.

I looked away, suppressing a gag. Out of the corner of my eye I saw him approach the glass, but it was obvious that he couldn't see me.

He walked in my direction, but not quite at me. He didn't stop walking until he ran into the glass about two feet to the right of me.

By the time the other two zombies had made it to my end of the store I had a plan. I picked up the trash can near the front door and threw it into the window on the opposite side of the store. The glass window exploded all over the store's floor and I was able to waltz right in.

I was completely inside, gun drawn, and waiting for them by the time the zombies were halfway across the salesfloor.

I shot the first two and then walked over to the zombie without a face. He was reaching for me, or at least where his addled senses told him I was, but he was really nowhere close.

I put a bullet in his head and left him on the floor next to the candy aisle.

Then I walked over to the soda section and grabbed a Diet Coke. I went to the windows and leaned against the glass, watching my reflection and thinking about everything that had happened. Off in the distance I could see an orange haze hugging the horizon and grayish-black smoke clouds piling up to the sky. The city was really burning.

Beside me was the overstock bin where they kept the cartons of cigarettes. I glanced at it and then did a fast double take.

Usually, they lock the cigarettes up so people can't steal them, but the doors weren't padlocked like normal. They were wide open. Anyone could just reach in and—

It had been over a year since my last smoke. I had been cigarette-free ever since that morning when I came home from a late call and saw April sitting at the kitchen table with a glass of water in front of her and the most thoroughly puzzled expression I have ever seen on her face. That very minute I knew something special was happening to our lives and, when she told me she was pregnant, I went out to my car and crumpled up my pack of cigarettes. That was the last pack I thought I would ever smoke.

But now, as I looked at carton upon carton of Marlboro Lights, I figured there was no better time than the end of the world to start smoking again. I opened the bin, took out a pack, and walked over to the registers for a lighter. My hands were shaking when I lit it up.

But, oh, that old familiar taste. I breathed it in slowly, letting the flavors fill up my lungs slowly so I wouldn't choke. It was like heaven to feel that nicotine rush again. I felt light-headed and giddy, and kind of dizzy all at the same time. I blew out the smoke above my head and watched it grow into wreaths.

Then, from behind me, I heard an amused voice say, "I thought you gave that junk up."

Chapter 16

"Marcus!"

I knew that voice the moment I heard it. It was Marcus Acosta, my old district partner before I transferred to West.

"Eddie," he said. God, he was so calm about it.

He wasn't in uniform. He was wearing blue jeans and a heavy black jacket, his pistol tucked into an off-duty holster and his police radio in his back pocket. He stood there with his arms crossed, a twisted, devilish smile on his face.

It had been three months at least since I'd seen him last. Police work is like that. The shifts are so screwed up that if you don't work with someone every day, you never see them. And yet there he was, standing in the middle of all that broken glass and smiling like he had just done something naughty, and I couldn't help but smile myself.

One look at him was enough to wipe out an awful lot of pain.

He kicked some of the glass around with his toe as he looked at the bodies on the floor and said, "So, zombies."

"Yep," I said.

"I have to confess, I didn't see that one coming." Then he smiled again. "It looks like you've had a rough night."

"Yep. You?"

He shrugged. "Are you in that traffic car?"

"Yeah."

"Looks like you wrecked it."

"Yeah." I looked out to the parking lot and didn't see any other cars besides mine. "You have a car around here?"

"It's about four blocks west of here."

"Your pickup?"

"No, that's back at the station. I was in a marked unit."

"What happened?"

"I wrecked it."

He walked around the store, looking at the bodies, making sure they were all down for good.

When he came to the old bald guy in the clerk's uniform he said, "Hey, you shot Gummers."

"Who?"

"Gummers." He kicked the dead man's foot.

"Friend of yours?"

"No. He was the new guy here. Started about two months ago. Man, that guy talked and talked and talked. Drove me nuts."

"Gummers?"

"Ain't got a tooth in his head." And he curled his lips over his teeth and smacked his lips together. "You know, Gummers."

"Got it," I said. "Say, how come you're not in uniform?"

"Uniform's back in the truck. I heard about all this on the TV when I woke up, so I came in early. By the time I got to the station everything had already gone to hell. And by the way, I don't recommend going to the Northwest Division station."

"That bad?"

"Most of B-shift is dead."

I nodded.

"How about out west?"

"About the same. What did the news have to say?"

"Nothing, really. At first it was riots and looting, that kind of thing. Nobody on TV said anything about zombies, though. First time I heard zombies was when I got to work."

"What else did they say?"

"Sounds like it's happening all along the Gulf Coast. They're saying it's because of that stuff down in Houston. The news didn't really say anything else. Besides, all the local channels were off the air by the time I got to the station."

"How does that happen? How does everything crap out like that so fast?"

He shook his head at Gummer's corpse and said, "I'm surprised you're not at home."

"Already been there."

"And?"

"They weren't there. The car's gone. I don't know where they went to. I don't even know if they're okay."

"You haven't talked to her at all?"

"Just for a second or two. Earlier. I don't know how long ago. A lot's happened."

"But you did talk to her?"

"She sounded scared."

"Well, that makes two of us." He watched me closely for a moment. "Eddie," he said, "she's a smart girl."

I nodded. "I hope she'll know what to do. I'm scared for her. And for Andrew."

"They'll be okay, Eddie."

"I hope so," I said, and a long, uncomfortably empty

silence followed. I changed the subject. "We ought to find a new car, Marcus. That one out there has about had it."

"Where did you get that one?"

"Found it."

"You haven't been downtown yet?"

"No. I heard all the emergency tones going off on the Downtown channel though. Sounds like they got it bad."

"I think everybody has it bad," he said. "Still, we probably ought to head that way."

"What on earth for?"

"Headquarters. If there's some sort of plan in the works, they'll know about it."

"What makes you think headquarters is still operational? All the radios went down."

"Yeah, but they may have only lost the mainframe. The Emergency Operations Command Center is probably still secure. They're supposed to have dedicated lines to Homeland Security and FEMA."

"Maybe," I said doubtfully. "But I don't plan on cruising halfway around the city just to find out. If there's any chance at all that I can find April, that's what I'm gonna do."

"But do you have any idea where to start looking? You said yourself that you don't know where they went. They could be anywhere."

"Yeah, and wherever they are, that's where I want to be too."

"Fair enough," he said. "We'll look for them together. What about your car?"

"It'll run, but the right front tire's about to shred away to nothing. It's rubbing bad."

"Then the first thing we do is find another car."

"What about yours?"

"Eddie, I put it halfway up an oak tree."

"Oh."

"And there weren't any left at Northwest, either."

"That figures," I said. "You think we'll have a better chance downtown?"

"Yeah, I was thinking we could go to Fleet and get one of the cars out of the ready lot. They've got hundreds of Crown Vics out there just waiting to get the decals put on them."

That made sense, I admitted.

"And while we're down there, we ought to go over to headquarters. It's only a couple of blocks away. It couldn't hurt. From there we can go wherever you want us to go."

"You really want to check out headquarters?"

"I think we need to. Look, if they do have a plan, it's bound to include a safe area for civilians. Let's say you find April and Andrew. What then? You need a place to put them where you know they'll be safe. You can't do that if you don't have a plan."

"That's true." It did sound like a good idea. It was better than the plan I had, anyway, which was no plan at all. "Can we get to the freeway from here?"

He smiled. "This is still my district, remember?"

"Okay," I said, and stepped aside. "After you."

"Thank you."

Chapter 17

We stepped through the shattered store windows and into the parking lot. It was starting to get really cold. I shivered against it, wishing I had a thick jacket like the one Marcus was wearing.

The front of my car looked like the face of a boxer who has just lost a fight. The passenger-side headlight was busted out, and the remaining one looked like a swollen, open eye. Part of the plastic bumper was rubbing against the ground on the passenger's side, and the hood was smashed in. A little more driving time and the whole car would be history.

"Oh, man," Marcus said, laughing.

"I know," I said, still trying to figure out if we could pull the front bumper off so that it wouldn't fall off while we drove. "I really smacked it up."

"Not that, stupid," he said. He slapped my arm and pointed across the parking lot. "I'm talking about her."

He was pointing at a really fat, dark-haired girl at the other end of the lot. Zombie. I could tell by the way she walked.

At first I thought she was completely naked, but

when she moved I could see a flash of white underwear appearing and then disappearing into the folds of her thighs.

She pivoted around on one foot and then the other in an uncertain, tottering kind of way, so that we saw her in profile with every step. There was a large, nasty gash across the top of her leg that went from the top of her knee all the way up to her hip that looked like rotten, blackened flesh.

"Is she wearing a thong?" Marcus said, still laughing. "God, that is the most obscene thing I have seen all night."

"Shut up, Marcus."

The woman kept walking toward us at the same laborious pace, but she was still far enough away that we could have just climbed into the car and left.

"God, she's really fat."

"Forget about her, Marcus. Let's get going."

"Hold on, would you? I mean, look at that. I didn't know they made thongs that big. That thing must be holding on for dear life. 'Help. Help me. I'm breaking!'"

"For God's sake, Marcus. Drop it, would you?"

Marcus was a clown. That was just his way. He could turn a trip to Internal Affairs into a stand-up routine and still write a report good enough to get us out of just about any kind of trouble. But this time I wasn't amused. I found it more annoying than anything else.

"Let's just go, Marcus."

"You're seeing this, right? Look at that. It's like trying to cover up a watermelon with a rubber band. You mean to tell me you don't think that's funny?"

"She's a zombie, Marcus. Zombies aren't funny."

"You have to get your humor wherever you find it, Eddie."

"I'd like to go now, please."

"Hey, what do you suppose she's at right now? About twenty yards?"

I gauged the distance. "Yeah, about that."

"I'll bet you a pack of smokes you can't land a head shot in less than three shots. What do you say? Come on. I'll make it a whole carton. I know you want some. I'd do it myself, but I'm out of ammo."

"There's a whole case in the car," I said, and walked over to the driver's-side door. "You can have all you want if you shut up and get in."

"Just a second. Come on, give it just one shot."

"No."

"About fifteen yards now, I bet. Piece of cake. Even you could hit her from here. Come on, you're not scared, are you?"

"No."

I know he thought he was being funny, but he sounded cruel to me. Marcus could fight like a son of a bitch, and I'd seen him rip up plenty of bad guys, but I had never known him to be unnecessarily cruel, and that's the way he sounded to me just then. It disturbed me.

He snorted. "I bet you couldn't have hit her any—"

I glanced over at him. "What is it?"

"Eddie," he said, "there's something I forgot to tell you."

"What?" I followed his gaze.

Four zombies were coming around the corner of the store. He watched them as they came around the dumpster and then looked back at me.

"You said you've got some bullets in the car, right?"

"Yeah."

"Fat chick," he said, pointing over my shoulder with his chin.

I turned. The fat woman was way too close to ignore anymore. I fired one shot into her forehead and then turned back to Marcus.

"You're killing me, Marcus. What did you forget to tell me?"

He looked at the fat woman on the pavement and then back at the zombies near the corner.

"Remember how I told you I hit an oak tree about four blocks back?"

"Just tell me, Marcus."

"We're about to have company," he said. "A lot of it, actually."

"Great," I said. "Now will you get in the car?"

"Yeah," he said. "Okay."

I started the car and Marcus climbed in. The four zombies stepped onto the pavement. Beyond them, I could see more zombies coming our way.

I backed the car up and took off in the opposite direction. At the exit from the parking lot we hit a dip and the front end crunched against the pavement. We ended up driving over the bumper.

"Ouch," Marcus said. "Next car we get, I'm driving."

Chapter 18

As we drove away, Marcus reloaded his pistol and his two extra magazines. He was fast with it, too. Shooting came naturally for him.

While we drove, he told me about his first encounters with the zombies. "I shot the couple that used to live downstairs from me," he said. "Remember them? The woman had that nasty thing on her nose?"

"I remember."

"Yeah, well, I heard her screaming. I was sitting there, watching all that crazy shit on the news, and I hear her screaming bloody murder. So I go down there, and there's the husband, eating her. I shot him. I shot her too, just in case. After that I dragged them out to the dumpster. And you're not going to believe this. I was headed back to my truck after dumping the bodies and I hear all this screaming coming from the pool. It was like everybody in the whole damn complex didn't know what else to do besides scream. I went down there and saw this old woman standing next to the pool and a zombie floating facedown in the water with a cloud of blood all around him. She wanted me to jump him and pull him out, and I was like, 'Lady, after what I've just seen, there's no way in hell I'm gonna give that guy mouth-to-mouth. He'd probably try to bite my tongue off.'"

"I don't think you're supposed to use your tongue when you do mouth-to-mouth," I said.

"Then you ain't doing it right, brother. But, seriously, somebody ought to burn up all those bodies. Just you watch. In two days, this whole city's gonna smell like I don't know what. It'll be bad, though."

I hadn't thought of that—but then, I had other things on my mind last time I was home.

"You know, you and April were probably one of the last people to have a cell phone conversation tonight. Right before I turned off the TV, I heard the news saying they'd lost all communication with their people in the field. No cell phone, no radios, no nothing."

"Really?"

"That's what I heard." He suddenly got very excited and waved his hand at some zombies walking across a nearby yard. "Hey. Slow up. Over there. That's the asshole who complained on me last month. Slow up and let me see if I can pop him."

"Have you lost your mind, Marcus?"

"I don't think so," he said, aping my seriousness. "Come on, pull over. It'll only take me a second. I'll fucking teach that guy about complaining on me."

I kept on driving.

"Hey, wait a minute." Marcus watched the guy fall behind, his damaged legs unable to keep up with the car. "Damn it, Eddie. When will I ever get a chance like this again. Come on, he's getting away."

"No."

"Goddamn it, Eddie. Doesn't April let you take your sense of humor to work any more?"

I didn't answer him. That was the second time he

had mentioned April so casually, like there was absolutely nothing wrong, and it was pissing me off.

He noticed he'd upset me. "Hey, I'm sorry, Eddie. I know you're worried sick about her. We're gonna find her."

"I hope so."

I pretended like I was having trouble reading the street signs, but he knew it was just an act.

"She's a smart girl," he said. "She'll know what to do when she has to."

"How do you know that, Marcus? Do you know what to do? I sure as hell don't. I haven't got a fucking clue. This whole night's been one messed up cluster fuck."

Marcus folded the lid back over the case of bullets and set it on the floorboard next to his feet. Then he turned and watched the houses go by. It was his way of telling me he understood, and I appreciated it.

"These traffic cars are pretty nice," he said after we had driven a few minutes in silence. He played with the trash bag that was draped from the passenger door and laughed to himself. "Where did you say you found it?"

"On Fletcher."

"Fletcher? Isn't that in the 23 side?"

"Right on the boundary line between the Downtown and West Divisions."

"What do you suppose a traffic guy was doing there? I thought they usually stuck to the freeways."

"I don't know," I said.

"Well, he's got a video camera."

Marcus looked over the little index card–size monitor mounted between the sun visors and played with the controls. He was like that with electronic stuff. Any gadget at all, if it was in front of him he couldn't leave it alone until he had it figured out.

"Did you watch this already?"

I saw the picture come up. "No," I said. And then,

after a pause, "I didn't have time. As soon as I found the car I went straight to Carlos Williams's house."

He gave me a look out of the corner of his eye and I told him how Carlos had died, and what he had said about his son right before he shot himself.

"You didn't?"

I nodded.

"You went to see his family?"

"Yes."

"Eddie," he said, shaking his head slowly, sadly, "why do you do that to yourself? I swear, sometimes you can be a real idiot, you know that?"

He was right, of course. But it didn't feel like he was right.

"You're too damn sentimental. That's your problem."

"Probably," I said.

"There's no probably about it. I know I'm right."

We drove on in silence for the next few blocks while he tried to figure out how to replay the tape. All the easy ways to get to the freeway were blocked up, and I was forced to use some of the smaller streets and alleyways.

"What's wrong with taking Maldon?" he asked, glancing at the street we had just passed. "That's a straight shot."

"Too many businesses down Maldon," I said. "I want to avoid any large crowds if we can help it."

"Oh." He looked disappointed.

He kept working on the video until he got it. "Oh yeah, here we go."

I couldn't really watch it and drive at the same time, but with Marcus narrating the whole thing I didn't really need to.

"Okay," he said, "there he is. Who is that? Do you recognize him? Looks like Wainscot to me."

I glanced over, but the monitor was so small I couldn't see anything. The figures on the screen looked far away and dark.

"There goes his gun. He sees something. Damn it. Can't do much with the focus. What's he looking at? There he goes. Wait. No. Now he's off camera."

Marcus kept watching, pushing the fast-forward button and watching some more, but that appeared to be the end of it.

"That didn't tell us a damn thing," he said.

"He wasn't anywhere around when I found the car."

"Yeah, he probably got eaten."

"Nice."

"What? Oh, I'm sorry, Miss Prissy. I'm sure it was all hugs and kisses when he met the zombies."

"Go to hell, Marcus."

"Find a parking spot, brother," he said with a dismissive wave of his hand at the world outside our car. "We're already there."

Chapter 19

Marcus was admiring the brand-new shotgun. Traffic really did get the best toys.

On patrol, officers use the barrel of the shotgun as a trash can. You find everything from gum wrappers to chicken bones stuffed down inside them.

And when quail season opens, you're lucky if there's a gun in your car at all.

He worked the action and ejected one of the green beanbag shells from the gun. "Useless," he said, and tossed the bean bag out the window.

"Oh!" I said. "I've got real shells for that thing. Check that green box over there."

"Where?"

"It's over there. I don't know. Under the seat, maybe."

"Got it," he said, and started loading up the magazine tube. "Where did you get these from anyway?"

"From home."

"Your house?"

"Yeah."

"I didn't know you had a shotgun."

"It's just an old skeet gun. Nothing special. A Ruger Red Label Over-and-Under. I haven't shot it since before April and I got married."

"That's too bad. Ruger makes a good gun." He racked the shotgun's action and a huge smile lit up his face. "God, I just love the way that sounds. Don't you?"

"You can use it if you want."

"You don't mind?"

"No. Of course not. You're the one riding shotgun."

"Cool. Thanks." He looked up from the shotgun and I could tell he was checking his mental map of the area. "You're not going to go through the Medical Center, are you?"

"No. I figured it'd be best if we went around."

"Probably so. The news was saying that the hospitals are all totally overrun. They got it early, from what it sounded like."

We kept to the edge of the Medical Center, but even from there, it was obvious the destruction was total.

Most of the major roads were so overrun with traffic that there was no hope of getting into the hospitals anymore. The entire area was choked off.

As we hopped a curb and drove through the grass to get around a clogged section of Fielding Street, I looked to my left and let my eyes follow the direction all those cars were facing.

Fielding was flanked on both sides by massive earthen embankments that stretched up from the street level to the businesses at the top of the ridge. People had actually tried to drive up those embankments, and it looked like a lot of them had rolled their vehicles before they got anywhere. The street reminded me of a wild African river after a flood, the kind they show on nature documentaries, with the carcasses of thousands of animals floating on the surface and crowding the banks.

I put us back on the road. Even though I was trying to avoid the more commercial areas, it was impossible to stay completely away and still get to where we were going.

And we couldn't avoid the zombies, either. They were all over the street, and as we drove past groups of them that turned and stumbled after us, I began to understand just how far and fast the outbreak had spread.

We drove past so much destruction that I stopped trying to add it all up. Marcus didn't seem to care, though. He hummed to himself happily, like he did this everyday.

"I think you're going to have a hard time getting through at Middleton," Marcus said.

"Why at Middleton?"

"They put up a lot of stuff through there since you left. A lot of businesses. See?" He pointed ahead of us where the traffic suddenly became too thick to pass. "That's what I was talking about."

I stopped the car and looked out over a sea of frozen traffic. Zombies staggered between the cars. There didn't seem to be a gap large enough to drive through, and there were hundreds of zombies entering the street on both sides of us.

In the time it took to figure out where they were coming from we were surrounded.

"Looks like we'll have to back up and try to go around," I said.

"Not yet," Marcus said. Then all of a sudden he pushed the door open and jumped out, leaving me staring after him with my mouth gaping open.

"What the— Hey, wait."

I watched him run straight into that crowd of zombies and I thought, "He has gone insane."

Even worse was that he expected me to follow him, just like it was another Friday night bar fight.

"You idiot," I said to him, and the next thing I knew, I was standing outside the car, gun in hand. I was looking at a sea of zombies in every direction. There had to be a thousand or more.

But Marcus never hesitated. He fired all six rounds from the shotgun and then started swinging the shotgun around like a club, tearing a path right into the middle of the crowd and whooping it up like he was the whole damn rebel army rolled into one man.

He actually taunted them as they closed up behind him.

And then his rebel yell was drowned out by the bark of his pistol. I caught glimpses of muzzle fire as he moved through the crowd. He looked like a cowboy out of some old-time movie, strutting through the crowd with his gun blazing.

But the zombies weren't just closing in on him. They were all around me, too. Just before I jumped back inside the car I saw Marcus about fifty yards away. He jumped into the open bed of an abandoned pickup truck and started shooting.

I put the car in gear and drove straight into the crowd, mowing down bodies as I went. I kept my eyes on him as I plowed through the sea of bodies, ignoring their faces as they rolled off the hood.

I locked up the brakes and spun the car around so that the passenger door was as close to him as I could get it.

The car slid sideways into the crowd, and a few of the zombies were thrown with such force that when they slammed into the side of the truck that Marcus was firing from, the impact nearly knocked him off his feet. He almost went over the side.

I shot a zombie that was trying to climb through the passenger window and cleared the way for Marcus to jump back in the car.

He was hollering the whole time, still firing out the passenger window as I put the car into reverse and mashed down on the accelerator.

The back tires broke loose. Smoke was everywhere. It was like driving too fast through a bumpy field. Bodies were being thrown out of the way or pushed under and run over and there were so many of them that the car nearly high-centered on top of a still-moving pile of bodies before our momentum put us back on the asphalt.

"Go! Go! Go!" he yelled, laughing like he had never seen anything so funny in his whole life. "That's it. You're tearing them up."

I kept on the gas until we cleared the last of the crowd and then a little farther after that. We ended up going over a curb and crashing into the drive-through order box at the Burger Barn before I got the car to stop.

Marcus was laughing his head off. I wanted to punch his lights out, but before I got the chance he put his hands up and said, "No. No way, Eddie. You do not get to say a damn word. You know why? Because that was awesome. That was absolutely fucking awesome."

I looked at him and wondered who put this idiot in the car with me. The whole time, I was gripping the wheel so tight my fingers were turning white.

"Well?"

I didn't say anything.

"Come on, Eddie. Say something. You were amazing. And I know those zombies back there were impressed."

"Impressed?"

"Yeah, well, they're zombies, of course, so they can't be that impressed. But damn, Eddie. You may not be able to shoot your way out of a wet paper bag, but brother, do you know how to drive. That was by far the coolest thing I have ever seen you do."

And then he started laughing again.

I made a fist and got ready to use it.

"No," he said, still laughing.

"What in the hell is—"

"No," he said.

My frustration came out as one long, slow hiss. Instead of punching him, or choking him, I gripped the steering wheel.

"Say it," he said. "Come on, say it."

"Screw you, Marcus." But the moment to hit him passed, and my anger settled to a simmer.

We were still stuck in the parking lot and we had to figure a way out that put us on the other side of all those zombies. The lot was edged all the way around by a two-foot-high cement wall, and the only way out was starting to fill up with zombies.

"Just plow through them again," Marcus offered.

I punched it, heading for the center of the crowd. We hit the exit going way too fast and swung a hard right onto Nightingale.

The car was swaying all over the place from all the damage I had done to the suspension, and when we made the turn the back end came around on me and whipped through the crowd.

They didn't slow us down though, and as I straightened out the back end, Marcus leaned out the window and started firing at them like he actually stood a prayer of landing a kill shot.

"Awesome." he said, ducking back into the car. "Absolutely awesome."

"You're a moron."

"You know," he said, and his voice had that annoying edge to it that told me he was about to tease me. "I refuse to let a bunch of zombies ruin the end of the world for me. And you either, for that matter."

Three blocks over we turned south again and tried to finish our course around the Medical Center. We got as far as Cotton Street before another traffic jam caused us to turn into a strip center parking lot.

"Any ideas?" I asked, looking over the wreckage.

"There's a service drive around back for the loading docks. I bet we can cut through there."

"Are you sure?"

"Honest," he said. "I've been through there before."

"Okay," I said, and turned the car toward the back of the building. The drive went around the side of the building, then turned to the left, and went straight along the back wall.

We were only able to make it about halfway down the alley. There was a high concrete wall on the right, and a large brown truck parked along the left wall. Between the two of them was a space about half as wide as the car.

"Looks like we go—"

But he didn't get to finish his sentence. A fast-moving zombie broke his window and tried to pull him out of the car by his collar.

The zombie clawed at him, but Marcus was faster, and his movements, once he got over the initial shock, were deliberate.

He pushed the zombie's arm back into his face and grabbed him by the neck.

Once he had his grip, he didn't let go. He yanked the zombie's head down into the door again and again until the thing grew slack in his grip and collapsed to the ground.

"They're behind us," I said, looking back at a small group of them coming our way.

"Go!" he said. "Mow them down."

I put the car in reverse and punched it. We were twenty, maybe thirty miles an hour when we hit the closest zombie.

The car lurched up and then it seemed like the back of the car just exploded. There was a rush of color and broken glass as the zombie came through the back windshield and crashed face-first into the Plexiglas prisoner cage separating the front and back seats. Everything inside the car rolled forward with the impact.

In the rush, I lost control and scraped up against the concrete wall, killing our momentum.

By the time I regained control and rolled the car to a stop, the zombie in the backseat was moving, fumbling at the Plexiglas.

With exaggerated calm, Marcus turned to me and said, "Eddie, get us out of here, please."

The zombie in the backseat was a huge man, and he completely filled up the backseat. He slapped his broken hands against the Plexiglas and pressed his red face against it, biting at it and gouging it with his teeth. If he could have eaten his way through, I know he would have.

He was so big that I couldn't see around him. I was trying to back us out of the alley and then out to the parking lot, but there was so much going on that there was no way for me to do it without hitting just about everything.

By the time we made it out to the parking lot, Marcus had had enough. He turned around in his seat, his back against the dashboard, and pointed his pistol at the zombie.

"No," I said, and shielded my face with my hand.

"What?" he said.

"Not in the car, you dumbass. What are you, fucking nuts?"

"You keep asking me that," he said. "Pretty soon I'm going to think you mean it."

I hit one of those concrete pillars they mount light poles on and it knocked Marcus off the dashboard.

"That's it," he said, as he righted himself. He opened the car door and got out.

"What are you doing?"

He stepped to the passenger-side back window and pointed his gun at the zombie in our backseat.

"No," I said, trying to get my door open. But I was still in the car when he started firing. The window blew apart, and as I tumbled out onto the pavement, I saw the body in the backseat convulsing with the impacts.

"Goddamn it, Marcus."

"What?"

"What in the hell is wrong with you?"

"What?"

We were starting to draw a crowd, and two of them were fast-movers. I could see them pushing the other zombies out of the way.

"Behind you," I said.

He turned, aimed, and shot two fast-movers like it was target practice. They hit the ground and were still twitching when he turned back to me.

"What did I do?"

The crowd around us was starting to get thicker and I didn't feel like arguing with him. "Just get in the car, Marcus."

"No way. First you tell me why you're being such an old woman about this. What the hell did I do?"

"Are you nuts?"

He pointed over my shoulder with his gun. "There's a couple behind you," he said. "Over there."

I turned around and saw two zombies in medical scrubs stepping off the grass about ten yards away. They were slow ones though, and one had been horribly mauled. He was missing an eye, and where it had once been there were only streaks of blackened blood. I took aim and shot each one in the forehead.

"Time to go," I said.

"No. You wanted to talk, so let's talk. I want you to tell me what it is that I'm doing that's pissing you off so much."

"Marcus, please."

"Not yet. Tell me."

"We're surrounded."

"I can see that. Come on, talk to me. I want to hear what's on your mind."

"Marcus, please. Get back in the car and let's go."

The zombies were moving in from every side now, but Marcus just stood there waiting for me to crack. He was actually smiling. The crazy bastard was actually smiling.

"Behind you," he said.

I turned and fired at a woman in a blue dress. My first shot hit her in the cheek, but I was more careful with my second shot and put her down for good.

"Nice," Marcus said.

"Shut up."

"I'm waiting on you," he said. "You tell me why you're acting so fucking pissed about everything and I'll get in the car and we can go. I'll even let you drive."

I pointed behind him and he turned and dropped a zombie with a one-handed shot. He made it look so easy.

"Well?"

"Don't try to turn this around on me, Marcus. You're the one who thinks he's some kind of fucking cowboy out here. I just want to get home to my family."

"Cowboy? You think I'm some kind of cowboy? What does that mean, exactly?"

"Behind you," I said.

"You, too."

"Left or right?"

"Your left."

We both put our zombies down. Marcus was having the time of his life, which pissed me off more than anything else. To him, this was some kind of carnival shooting gallery and he was just plunking away like there were no consequences to any of it.

And he had no idea why what he did bothered me so much.

I looked around and realized there was no way we

could keep up a safe position where we were. There were just too many of them, and more were gathering at the edges of the parking lot.

"Marcus, I am scared shitless. Okay? Are you happy? You made me say it. Call me names if you want to, but I am scared out of my mind. I'm scared for what's going to happen to me and I'm scared for what's going to happen to my family. I have no idea what to do and I'm stuck in the middle of a bunch of zombies and it's all just a fucking game to you. That's why I'm acting this way."

"I do not think this is a game," he said.

"Whatever. Behind you."

He turned and fired a couple of times. Then he said, "You're going to make it, Eddie. Don't worry."

"Yeah, well, I am worried, Marcus. I don't want to be out here any longer than I have to be. I want to know that my wife and my son are safe, and I want to be with them. Just because you don't have anybody waiting at home doesn't mean the rest of us aren't scared to death for our families."

The amusement went out of his face when I said that last part, and I realized that I had hurt him. Marcus had been married twice before and both times it ended hard. He took to women like a house on fire. It was fun to watch, but the damage was usually spectacular.

He pursed his lips together into a scowl. After a long pause he said, "Behind you."

I shot two zombies, reloaded, and shot a third before I faced Marcus again. He wouldn't look at me.

"I'm sorry, Marcus. That was stupid of me."

"No, it's the truth. You said it. I ain't got nothing to go home to. Hell, I'm actually kind of glad my ex-wives got turned into zombies. Serves the bitches right. And no more alimony for me."

"Marcus, I'm sorry."

"Stop saying that."

"Behind you," I said.

He shot the zombie and watched the body after it fell. I thought maybe he was going to take off on me again, but he stood his ground.

A badly messed-up woman in a white shirt and no pants shambled up to him, and he waited so long to shoot her I almost did it for him.

When she hit the ground, he turned around and faced me again.

"Is there anything else you wanted to say to me?"

"Marcus, please. Let's just go."

"What's the point?"

"The point is my family is waiting out there some-where. I know they are, and I have to get home to them. I want to be with them. Please, Marcus, can't you see that? Help me get home. I need you to help me."

He nodded. The sadness faded from his face, and in its place the old shit-eating grin returned. "Hey, Eddie, you know I'm always there for you."

I nodded and waited for him to move, but he just stood there.

"Car," I said. "Now."

"Anything you say."

We climbed into the car and tore out of the parking lot, neither one of us saying anything until we cleared the zombie crowd.

I was quiet because I was still pissed at him and em-barrassed for the cruel things I'd said. We had been friends for so long, and relied on each other to know in-stinctively what the other was thinking and going to do in just about every situation, that it completely floored me when he did the opposite of what I expected.

I got the feeling Marcus was quiet because he was waiting for me to come out of my stupor and see all this as some sort of cosmic joke.

For him, there were no further implications to all these zombies than the end of alimony payments, and while I guess he understood my urgency on some level, he could never share it.

His laughter caught me off guard. When he saw me shaking my head at him, he said, "What? You don't honestly expect me to sit here and mope with you until all this just goes away, do you?"

"You realize there's a dead body in the backseat, don't you?"

"Who? Him? Well, it's not like he wasn't a zombie already. And besides, I'm not the one who put him there, remember?"

"Yeah."

"Oh, for Christ's sake, will you stop it? I can't ride in the same car with you if you're just gonna cry about how bad all this is."

He paused for me to say something, but when I didn't, he said, "Look, if it'll make you feel any better, we can pull over and get him out of here."

"Yeah," I said. "Let's do that."

"Okay." He looked back at the body and whistled. "Damn! He's a big boy. What do you think he weighs? About 260, 280?"

"Probably."

"Yeah, well, you're gonna have to help me with him. There's no way I'm gonna be able to lift him out of here by myself."

I looked at what I could see of the body in the rearview mirror. It was covered in blood.

"Okay. There should be some gloves in the trunk."

"Good. Pull over someplace where we can dump him."

But we had to go all the way up Dickinson Avenue before I could find a safe place to pull over. There were no businesses down Dickinson, and no zombies.

"This looks okay," Marcus said. "Stop here and we'll toss him out."

I got the gloves from the trunk and Marcus opened the back door.

"Oh man," he said, turning his face away from the sight. "You really fucked this guy up."

"Me? What the hell are you talking about? Those are your bullet holes in him."

"Relax, relax. Just come here and help me with him."

I handed Marcus a pair of gloves. The man was on his back, one of his heavy slab-o-meat arms bent under his bulk and his head down in the foot well behind the driver's seat. From where I stood, I could see his mouth was hanging open.

"What foot do you want?" I asked him as I pulled on my gloves.

"It's always the same with you, isn't it, Eddie? Can't we ever get together without having to pull somebody's stinking dead body out of the back of a police car?"

He was only half kidding. "That junkie on Queene's Court wasn't my fault," I said. "How was I supposed to know he swallowed all that dope?"

"Whatever. Just grab a foot, would you?"

He grabbed the right and I grabbed the left. It was a tight fit because the door wouldn't open far enough to let us stand side by side. We pulled on the guy until something gave way and he started to slide along the seat. On the way out, the back of his head smacked the metal part of the frame next to the seat and made a loud crack.

"Ouch," I said. It sounded very loud along that quiet stretch of Dickinson Avenue.

"He didn't feel a thing," Marcus said. "Come on and help me get him over here."

I went to move the door out of the way, but as soon as I moved, the guy suddenly sat up.

"What the—"

The zombie was on Marcus so fast that neither of us had time to react. They both went over backward. Marcus landed underneath him and the zombie's bulk pinned him to the ground.

I tried to push him off but I couldn't get the leverage. I was stuck between the two of them wrestling on the ground and the open door of the police car, and all I could do to help Marcus was to pound on the back of the zombie's head with my fist.

He moved, but he wouldn't break his hold on Marcus. I hit him some more and finally pushed him far enough from my legs for me to move. It took two hard kicks to his gut before he turned away from Marcus and focused on me.

Marcus moved fast.

As soon as the zombie got off him, Marcus was on his feet, his pistol in his hand.

I pushed the zombie back toward the car with another hard kick. He straightened up just in time to take a bullet in the forehead from Marcus's gun.

His head exploded all over the car. The impact knocked him backward and then he fell forward, right on top of Marcus. I dragged the mostly headless corpse off of Marcus and reached out a hand to help him up.

"Thanks," Marcus said, wiping the gore from his face.

I went to the trunk, got the blood-borne pathogen kit, and helped him get cleaned up a little.

"I'm surprised you couldn't lift that guy," I said. "Guess you need to work on your dead lift, huh?"

He looked at me with a stare almost as blank as that of the zombie he had just put down. "You have never told a good joke in your life, you know that? I mean it. You are tragically not funny. It's pathetic."

"What? That was a good one."

He shook his head like he pitied me. "Just get in the car and drive."

Chapter 20

Less than half a mile down the road from where we dumped the body, we saw a Channel 9 news van stopped at the corner of Dickinson and Stewart. Just around the corner, in front of the Lexington Baptist Church, was the news crew that belonged to it—two cameramen and a pretty, dark-haired reporter I didn't recognize.

It looked like they were interviewing somebody—an older white guy in a blue shirt, yellow tie, and expensive-looking charcoal-gray slacks.

"Don't slow down," Marcus said. Then he groaned. They had already seen us, and they were flagging us down.

The cameramen turned their cameras on us.

"Too late now," Marcus said. "Might as well go check it out."

"They might know something," I said hopefully.

"Yeah, right," he said. "Those clowns from Channel 9. They know how to crucify us, that's about it."

I pulled the car into the church's gravel parking lot and coasted over to the news crew. The cameramen followed us with their cameras, one of them taking extra care to record the damage to our car. He got a close up of the blood on the fender.

The reporter was stunningly beautiful. She looked about 25. Tight brown jacket. Shear white blouse. Super short brown skirt. Fantastic legs.

"Maybe it won't be so bad," I said.

Marcus snorted.

But before we could get out of the car, the reporter and one of her cameramen crowded up to my window. Behind her I could see a small group of wide-eyed, nervous-looking people coming out of the church to see what was going on.

"Sandy Navarro, Channel 9 News," the reporter said. She turned slightly for the camera, making sure the cameraman got her legs in the shot. That's what it looked like to me, anyway. "Have you come to get these people out of here?"

She stuck the microphone in my face.

The cameraman turned the camera on me, the glare from its spotlight blinding me.

"Who, me?" I asked.

She tossed the hair out of her face with an easy shake of her head, a move that made her look like a model in a shampoo commercial, and said, "There are sixty-three people inside this church, officer. They've been without power for hours. Without food or water. Some of them have medical needs. What are you going to do to get them out of here?"

Marcus chuckled. I glanced over to him, but he just held up his hands. "Don't look at me, man. There's a reason I always let you talk to these people."

"Thanks," I said.

"No problem."

Sandy Navarro stuck the microphone in my face again. "Officer?"

A light breeze carried the faint vanilla hint of her perfume into the car. "Do you mind backing up?" I said.

"These people need an answer, officer."

"Well they'll get one as soon as you back up."

She didn't move.

"Please," I said. "I'd like to get out of the car."

She huffed indignantly, but finally backed up.

I opened the car door and stepped out. So did Marcus. But I hardly had a chance to close the car door before Sandy Navarro moved in for the kill again.

"What are you going to do for these people, officer?"

She was grandstanding for the camera. Channel 9 News had a reputation for sticking it to the police any time the opportunity came around, and I knew to expect it, but I still felt like I'd been put on the spot.

Maybe that's why I let myself get angry.

"What exactly is it that you expect me to do?" I asked.

"You're the police," she said. "Isn't it your job to serve and protect?"

"I'm not the police," I snapped. "I'm one cop. Just one. I don't know what in the hell you expect me to do. My whole shift is dead. We haven't seen another living policeman or a firefighter in hours. I don't have radio contact with anybody. I don't have backup. We don't even have enough firepower to face down a small crowd of those things out there. So I ask you, what exactly do you expect me to do for these people?"

We stared at each other for a brief moment, and I think maybe she saw how bad things were in my eyes.

She blinked.

The microphone lowered a little.

When she spoke again, her hard edge had softened a little, and the words didn't come as easily.

"About an hour ago, Chief Roles held a press conference in which he said the police department was moving to Stage III of the emergency mobilization plan. Can you tell me what that means?"

I glanced at Marcus in time to see the smile evaporate from his face.

"What does that mean, officer?"

"It means things are as bad as they can possibly get," I said, which was basically understating the problem. In order for our brass to go to Stage III of the emergency mobilization plan, they would have had to admit the total defeat of the combined resources of the San Antonio Police Department, the Bexar County Sheriff's Office, and all the little unincorporated police departments throughout south Texas.

I thought of April and Andrew, and they never seemed as far away as at that moment.

"You wanted to know if help was coming for these folks." I said to Sandy. "You can tell them we're waiting on the military. They're about the only ones that can pull our irons out of the fire at this point."

Marcus came around the front of the car. "What else did the chief say, Sandy?"

Sandy turned on him, and almost immediately I saw a spark in her eye. Marcus had that effect on women. They couldn't spread their legs fast enough.

"He said that all personnel were being recalled to duty, regardless of their actual duty status. Are you a police officer, too?"

"Marcus Acosta," he said, and held out his hand to shake hers. Marcus hated reporters, but he loved women, and he had an almost predatory look in his eyes as he took in her sumptuous curves.

Sandy, for her part, suddenly seemed a lot less aggressive than she had just a moment before, when she was the no-nonsense investigative journalist ready to stick it to the police. At that moment she reminded me more of a little lamb that didn't have enough experience to realize that if she didn't cut and run right that minute, the wolf in Marcus was going to devour her.

"Sandy Navarro," she said, eyes turned down a little,

blush spreading like a field of poppies in bloom across her cheeks.

They shook hands, and lingered that way a little longer than they should have for just a polite nice-to-meet-you handshake.

"I've seen your spots on the news," he said. "You're good."

"Thank you," she said, and the blush widened.

I groaned and turned away.

"Give me a second," she said to him. "I want to finish interviewing Dr. Stiles and then maybe we can talk some more. I'd love to hear about the adventures you two have had tonight."

"I'd like that, too," he said. "I'll be here."

Sandy walked back to the older guy she'd been interviewing when we pulled up, and waited for the cameramen to get back into position.

Marcus smiled at her, then caught me sneering at him.

"What?"

"You know what," I said. "What the hell was that?"

"Give me a break," he whispered. "This may be the end of the world, but it's not everyday a man gets to have something that good. You saw those legs. Do you have any idea how good they'd look wrapped around me?"

"You're a man whore, Marcus."

He smiled.

The two of us walked closer to the entrance and stood behind the cameramen so we could hear the interview.

Sandy straightened her skirt and jacket, brushed her hair back out of her face, and then turned on the charm for the camera.

"Good evening," she said to the camera, her eyes twinkling. "I'm Sandy Navarro, Channel 9 News. I'm here at the Lexington Baptist Church in northwest San

Antonio with Dr. William Stiles of the University Hospital District, who less than five hours ago managed to lead nearly seventy people to safety here at this church. Good evening, Doctor."

"Good evening, Sandy," the man said. He was a lean-faced man with a military officer's haircut and a self-assured posture. I also got the feeling from him that he was used to people fawning over him.

"Dr. Stiles, tell me a little about your situation here."

Stiles steepled his hands together in front of his chest and frowned in concentration. "A little while ago, University Hospital was overrun by people infected with the necrosis filovirus. Most of the hospital's security staff was either killed or infected themselves. Luckily, I was able to get these people out of the hospital. We managed to make it out to the front lawn of the hospital, where we requisitioned two city buses that had been abandoned there, and drove them to this church, where we've been ever since, waiting on the authorities to get us out."

"And how many people were you able to save, Dr. Stiles?"

"Sixty-three."

"You worked on some of the first reported cases of infection here in the city, is that right?"

"That's right. We saw the first cases last night. They came in from Houston on one of the flights bound for the shelters. We had no idea at the time what we were dealing with. It was only in the early hours of this morning that we realized we were dealing with something completely new. Unofficially, we began calling it the necrosis filovirus."

"Can you tell us about that please? What exactly is the necrosis filovirus?"

Stiles exhaled deeply, his frown spreading further across his golf-tanned face. "The necrosis filovirus is closely related to the family of viral hemorrhagic fevers that include Ebola, Marburg, and the Crimean-Congo viruses. It's a biosafety level-4 agent, which makes it about as dangerous as any virus you're ever likely to deal with. Laboratory protocols call for a pressurized, heavy-duty biosafety suit to handle a level-4 agent. AIDS is a level-2 agent, if that gives you some measure of comparison. The thing about the necrosis filovirus that makes it different from the other hemorrhagic fevers is the incubation time. A person who contracts Ebola or Marburg is likely to exhibit a headache, backache, and other flu-like symptoms within five to ten days. The necrosis filovirus, on the other hand, seems to amplify within the host in just a few hours. After that, well, you've seen the infected walking the streets. They experience depersonalization to such a degree that they essentially become a zombie. The illusion is all the more complete when you see the clouded pupils, the smell, the rotting skin, and the almost complete lack of sensitivity to pain."

"What about the unbelievable acts of aggression we've seen, Dr. Stiles?"

"That, unfortunately, is a recorded symptom of the hemorrhagic fevers. Though truthfully, I've never heard of any disease that turns people into cannibals. The thing is, in Ebola and Marburg, the disease devastates the host's ability to move around. Those diseases are so deadly, so incapacitating, that the host usually does not get a chance to spread the disease very far geographically before quarantine measures can be put in place. Up to this point, every recorded outbreak of a viral hemorrhagic fever has been restricted to a relatively small number of victims. The necrosis filovirus, though, incubates faster, allows its hosts to move around with comparative ease, and, as you just said, makes them very violent.

"There's one thing I want to point out though,

Sandy. None of the hemorrhagic fevers have a one hundred percent mortality rate, and I have no reason to believe that the necrosis filovirus does either. We may not be able to save every person infected with the virus, or even most of them, but we can save some, and that puts us in a delicate situation ethically. These are not criminals we're dealing with, after all. The infected are normal people, and they can't be held responsible for their actions. That's just not fair. The problem demands a more delicate solution than just sending in the military to shoot all the infected. After all, if this were an outbreak of another kind of disease, such as the bird flu, or something comparable, we wouldn't go around shooting the victims. We can't do that here, either."

Stiles went on talking, but Marcus and I both had had enough. Marcus turned to me and said, "This guy is nuts if he thinks he can cure those people."

"I know," I said.

"We need to get out of here."

"I know."

While the others were listening to Stiles, Marcus and I headed back for the car. We didn't make it very far though. I had my hand on the door when Sandy and one of her cameramen came up behind me.

"Are you leaving, officer?"

I dropped my chin to my chest and sighed. Then I turned around and braced for another round with Sandy Navarro, Channel 9 News bulldog.

"Yes," I said.

"Just like that? You don't plan to do anything for these people?"

"I thought we'd settled that," I said. "I can't do anything for them. And I have a family of my own out there. I intend to find them."

Before she could say anything else, Marcus stepped back around the car. "Sandy," he said, taking her by the arm and leading her away from me a little. "Why don't we go inside? Officer Hudson and I will talk to the people. Let them know help is on the way. It'd be a good shot for you guys, and maybe you could tell me a little more about what you know about what's going on. After all, if I'm going to be out in the middle of all this, it sure would be helpful to know a little more than I do now."

She brushed the long black hair from her face and smiled warmly. It was amazing to watch, the way she changed. That same flip of her hair turned her into a serious professional journalist in front of the camera, but around Marcus, it made her look like a schoolgirl who's just been introduced to her favorite rock star.

Unbelievable, I thought. How does he do it?

Marcus nodded to me. I knew the look. Go in and put on a good show for the public, it said. I'm right behind you.

I sighed, turned, and went inside the church, Sandy, Marcus, Stiles, and the cameramen trailing behind me.

The door led into the gymnasium, which was large and barnlike, decorated with banners from the church's youth group, announcing them as the Baptist Youth Basketball League Champions of 2002 and 2004. The whole place danced with yellow candlelight, and people were everywhere. They had taken the tumbling mats down from their brackets on the wall and laid them out in one corner of the gym so a few of the older folks would have a place to sit down. That handful of older folks watched tiredly from their corner as the others bustled around them with a sort of aimless agitation. Nobody looked to have a plan.

I caught bits and pieces of conversations as I walked through the crowd. People were complaining about the cold, about how hungry they were, about how scared and worried they were.

I didn't blame them. Most of them were echoing the same feelings I had, and again I thought of April and Andrew, wondering if maybe they had left our home for someplace like this. Thinking of them made it hard for me to say anything reassuring to the folks who asked me when they could expect to be rescued.

I lied as best I could. I told them not to worry, that they were safe, that there was no way the military would take one minute longer than they had to before coming to our rescue.

If they knew I had doubts of my own, they didn't let on. Most just walked away, wide eyed and still very frightened, mumbling to themselves.

From somewhere behind me I could hear Marcus laying it on thick with Sandy, and she couldn't get enough of it. Once, I even heard her giggle, a bubbly, nasally sound that seemed totally out of place amid the stunned survivors around us.

I separated myself from the crowd and walked down a hallway that led back into the church, looking for a bathroom. I had mud and blood and bits of other stuff all over me, and after listening to Stiles talk about level 4 killer viruses, I had a renewed desire to get cleaned up.

The hallway went about fifty feet into darkness, past a number of offices and classrooms with locked doors, then opened into a high-ceilinged vestibule.

It was even darker there, and I turned on my flashlight.

Two other hallways went off to my right, and there was a flight of stairs on my left. A sign next to one of the hallways said RESTROOMS, and there was an arrow beneath it.

I followed the arrow.

The bathroom was a few doors down on the right, and I almost made it. I had my hand on the door when I heard somebody coughing, a mean, wet hacking sound that reminded me of the noises Carlos had made before his end had come.

I clicked off my flashlight and stood perfectly still, listening in the dark.

The coughing came again, and so did other noises. Worried voices. Calming voices. More coughing. A woman making a noise somewhere between a groan and a scream.

I drew my gun and inched along the wall, following the sound. Around the next corner I saw flickering yellow candlelight. The voices were clearer now, and so were the sounds of people in pain.

Slowly, I walked around the corner, into the candlelit main entrance to the church, and I gasped.

The entranceway was rectangular in shape, long and narrow, with a high, three-story ceiling. A massive wooden chandelier hung in the middle of the room. A narrow balcony ran the length of the room on both sides, and looked to go off to the upstairs levels of the main sanctuary, which was off to my right.

About thirty people were stretched out on makeshift cots, and all of them looked in really bad shape.

A couple of people who looked to be nurses were busy tending to the sick, trying to make them as comfortable as possible.

None of the injured seemed to have turned—yet.

Three things went through my mind all at once.

First was that Dr. Stiles must be using this place as some sort of hospital for the infected among his group. I remembered what he had told Sandy about a less than 100 percent mortality rate, and how he hoped at least some of the infected might recover, and a shudder ran through me. These people, I gathered, were relatives of those farther back, in the gymnasium.

My second thought was that Dr. Stiles had conveniently not mentioned his little hospital to Sandy or to Marcus and me. I shuddered again. What possible reason could he have for not mentioning it, I wondered. And then I answered my own question. He probably figured it would hurt his chances of being rescued if the rescuers knew this little virus bomb of a menagerie existed. Why would they risk spreading the infection, or catching it themselves?

My third thought had nothing to do with the sick people groaning on the floor, or even with the unscrupulous Dr. Stiles. It was all about the four men with rifles that had stepped out of the shadows on either side of me as soon as I entered the room. All four of them shifted their guns to their shoulders and, before I knew it, I was looking down the barrels of each of them.

I hadn't noticed them at first. I was too busy watching a pair of nurses who were tending to the sick, and trying not to look into the red, swollen eyes of the few people on the cots who had strength enough to look at me.

The gunman closest to me looked about thirty years old. He had a golden complexion and deep black, unruly collar-length hair. He had a narrow build, and between that and the hair, he reminded me of some sort of Colombian soccer star.

But he was an amateur with the gun. He held the stock too high up, so that he had to point the barrel down at me in an uncomfortable-looking angle.

Untrained, no question. And twitchy, jumpy. A bad combination.

Behind him was a short, gray-haired man with a considerable paunch. He looked like he had fired a rifle before, but he was nervous, like pointing a gun at a cop was something he never imagined himself doing as long as he lived.

The other two guys, who were standing off to my left, were nondescript. Just regular-looking guys of average height and average build. They held their guns loosely, uncomfortably.

I focused on Twitchy.

"What's going on?" I said.

"We don't want you here," he shot back quickly, angrily.

"Fair enough," I said. I kept my voice calm, my moves slow and minimal. The last thing I wanted to do was get Twitchy twitchier.

"Leave us alone."

"I'd like nothing better," I said. "Let's just put those guns down, okay? I don't want to be here any more than you guys want me here. Just put your guns down and I'll turn around and leave you to your business."

There was an awkward pause.

Paunchy lowered his gun, almost dropped it. The two on my left did the same thing. It was like I thought with them. They didn't want any part in this.

Twitchy didn't drop his, though. He saw the others lose a little of their conviction, and it scared him.

Suddenly he was animated, his voice quivering with nerves. He stabbed the air with his rifle and spoke frantically, so frantically I could barely understand him.

"No, you put your gun away. Not me, no. Yours. Yours. Put it down first. You go first. Kevin, Robbie, watch him. Don't let him talk you down. He puts his gun down first. Burns, get up here."

He nodded at Paunchy behind him without ever taking his eyes off me.

"Burns, get up and take that gun from him."

"Malin," said Paunchy. "I don't—"

"Nobody's taking anybody's gun away," I said. "Everybody just stay cool. I'm backing up now. Just relax and everybody's gonna be just fine."

"No," shouted Twitchy.

He said something to Paunchy that I didn't catch. I was too busy watching the room behind him. Out of the corner of my eye I had seen movement under a sheet covering a cot, and as I watched, I saw a woman with a blood-stained face, blackened gore in her hair, and milk-white pupils, sit up in bed.

Her head turned slowly in our direction, the eyes dead.

Twitchy and Paunchy were still arguing about taking my gun. Without looking at them, I said, "Behind you."

"Shut up," Twitchy said.

"Right there," I said, nodding at the woman getting out of the cot. "Shoot her."

That was the wrong thing to say in front of Twitchy. I had meant to say something diplomatic, something calm, but even as I was thinking what to say, the words "Shoot her" just came out.

Twitchy exploded in anger. He took a couple of steps forward and shook his fist at me.

I saw a well-worn band of gold around the third finger of his left hand.

"You leave her alone," he yelled. "God help me, I'll kill you if you touch her.

Tears were streaming down his face, fat and round.

"That's fine," I said. The zombie that had been his wife was now lumbering at him. Paunchy had seen her in time and was backing away. "That's fine," I said again. "Take my handcuffs. Secure her to the cot if you need to. She can stay there till someone can help her."

The zombie was five feet from him. Three feet. Too close.

"Malin," Paunchy said. He was pleading with the man.

The zombie grabbed Twitchy by the shoulder and dug into the bare flesh of his arm with her teeth.

He let out a girlish squeal and yanked his arm away. The next minute he was pushing the zombie away, trying to speak to it like it was still his wife, trying to coax it back to the cot.

The zombie fought for another bite, and when Twitchy finally realized he couldn't talk her back to the cot, he called for Paunchy to help him.

Paunchy dropped his gun and ran to help. Together

they dragged the zombie back to the cot and forced her onto her back.

I took out my cuffs and walked toward them.

"Here," I said, holding them out to them. "Take these."

Twitchy wheeled on me, gun in the air. He fired a shot that whistled somewhere over my shoulder and hit the wall behind me.

"Stay away from her, you son of a bitch. Get back!"

I was frozen for a second, the shot still ringing in my ears. The cuffs fell to the floor.

Everybody in the room was looking at us. The two men with rifles off to my left were fidgeting nervously, still uncertain what to do. Both nurses were standing in the middle of the room, their feet rooted to the floor. A few pairs of miserable, blood-red eyes peered up from nearby cots.

Only Paunchy seemed to be focused on something other than the two of us. He was still struggling to keep Twitchy's wife from getting off the cot.

Two more zombies sat up in their cots. A moment later, another one.

They lumbered to their feet, their bloody blankets falling down to the floor. One of them was closing in on the nurses. I yelled for them to move, but not in time. A zombie fell on one of the nurses, grabbed her by the hair, and pulled her to the floor.

She went down screaming.

Instinctively, I made a move to help her, and that set Twitchy into hysterics.

He fired at me.

The first shot missed me, went past me, and grazed one of the men on my left, striking him in the arm. The second shot thudded into the wall.

Twitchy didn't stop firing. Each time he pulled the trigger, he stabbed the rifle at me like there was a bayonet attached to it, which was lucky for me. It kept him from aiming. All he was doing was spraying and praying, which sounds like a good way to manage a gunfight, but isn't.

I ran to my left, clamoring over the injured in their cots, knocking them to the floor while I hit my belly and crawled behind a pillar for cover.

Twitchy was yelling and shooting wildly. I peered around the edge of the pillar and Twitchy fired again, forcing me back behind cover.

All I could see of the direction I'd come from were the three cots I'd knocked over, and the people who were now on the floor, holding their stomachs and vomiting a black, tarry goo onto the wooden floor.

The man closest to me was staring me right in the face when he slipped under and became a zombie. It occurred to me then that he must have been using all his strength to stave off the change, and I had pushed him over the edge, or distracted him, which amounted to the same thing. Either way, by upsetting his cot, I had broken his concentration, and now a zombie was staring me in the face.

The other two behind him changed in the same way. It was like watching a row of lightbulbs flicker out. One minute they were human, suffering. The who of what they were, or had been, was gone, leaving only an angry blank slate.

The three zombies stood up, and then the whole room erupted in screams and the clanging of beds being overturned and bodies colliding.

Over the din of it all, I could still hear Twitchy yelling at me. Despite everything going on around us, he seemed to have focused on me, treating me like the root of all his troubles.

He fired two more shots. One of them hit the floor next to my left hand and kicked up little pieces of wood that peppered my arm, burning like wasp bites.

I ran for the next pillar, not giving him the chance to

close in on me. As I landed on the ground behind the next pillar, I turned, raised my gun, and almost fired.

I didn't pull the trigger, though, because just then Marcus broke into the room right behind Twitchy. Dozens of people ran into the room behind him, Sandy and Stiles and the two cameramen among them.

Sandy gasped. Stiles's face was lit with rage. There was a mad rush of people as Stiles and a few others tried to take the cameras away and pull Sandy from the room. At the same time, people continued to rush into the room, running to the cots in the room to check on their injured friends and family.

Twitchy wheeled around and pointed his rifle at Marcus.

Wrong thing to do.

Marcus grabbed the barrel in his left hand and pushed it away. He dug the heel of his right hand under Twitchy's chin and forced his face to the ceiling. Then he kicked him in the balls so hard that Twitchy's feet actually left the floor.

Twitchy collapsed, gurgling in pain.

Marcus turned on Stiles and snarled something at him. I couldn't hear what he said, but I gathered it was something similar to what I had said to myself when I first saw the room.

People were screaming, fighting, dying. We were packed in so close together that it was hard to tell the healthy from the sick.

I couldn't shoot my way out. The room was too crowded for that. Instead, I kicked and punched my way to the front door. I thought if I could only make it out the doors, and put some distance between myself and this crowd, I'd stand a chance of making it back to the car.

I fought my way to the doors and pushed on them, but they were locked. When I turned back to the room,

I could see people getting knocked down and de-
voured. Arms were waving, faces bent into horrible
masks of rage and pain, and in the middle of it all was
Marcus, swinging the butt of the rifle around like a
club, tearing a path through the crowd.

From off to my left I saw Sandy Navarro. She had
been pushed into a corner by two zombies.

I fired a single shot and dropped one of them.

Sandy turned toward the shot, saw me, screamed for
me to help her. The other zombie put his hands on her,
and she pushed it away. I couldn't fire at that one,
though. He was too close to her for me to risk it.

I ran that way, fighting my way through the crowd,
and came up behind the zombie she was wrestling with.

The zombie was a skinny man in a white shirt and
brown slacks. His shirt was stained with rust-colored
gore under one arm. I kicked him in the back of the
knees, knocked him off balance, and threw him to one
side.

He landed faceup, and I didn't give him a chance to
regain his feet. I fired once, catching him in the left
eye.

"Are you hurt?" I asked Sandy.

She was staring at the zombie I'd just killed, very
near to throwing up.

"Are you hurt?" I said again.

She shook her head no.

"Good. Stay close. I'm gonna get you out of here."

I grabbed her hand and pulled her towards the hallway at the far end of the room, but she was scared, and
she resisted.

"Come on," I said, snarling it at her. "Come on."

"Eddie!"

It was Marcus, directly above me. I looked up and
saw him leaning over the balcony, looking down at me.

"Marcus—"

Under different circumstances I would have asked him how the hell he'd gotten up there, but as it was I grabbed Sandy by the arm and pulled her out so he could see her.

"Grab her," I told him, and hoisted Sandy up. It took some doing, but I managed to get her into position so she could stand on my shoulders.

Marcus reached down, caught her by the hand, and pulled her over the railing.

When she disappeared behind him, he was staring down at me, an inexplicable grin on his face.

A zombie put a hand on my arm. I pulled away and shot it twice, once in the chest, once in the ear.

Marcus was still smiling. "Did you get a peek?" he said.

"What?"

"Up her skirt?"

"Marcus!" The zombie I had just shot got pushed back on me by the frantic crowd, and I was forced to kick it away.

"Marcus!"

He rolled his eyes at me, but lowered the barrel of the rifle down for me to grab.

I caught it, and he pulled me up. Once I was even with the balcony I was able to swing myself over.

I landed next to him. Sandy was huddled up in a ball on the floor next to the wall, sobbing.

We picked her up and carried her out to the car, the sounds of the battle dying away behind us.

Chapter 21

Sandy was a mess. We had to prop her against the trunk while we cleaned up the broken glass and spilled blood from the backseat, but by the time we had it clean enough for her to sit down, she was a little more in control.

Not much, but a little.

"What about my cameramen?" she asked, looking up at Marcus with large, uncertain eyes. She had wiped her face with a baby wipe from the vehicle's blood-borne pathogen kit, but there were still little black rivulets of mascara on her cheeks that made her face look like a desert of dried-up creek beds.

Marcus put an arm around her shoulder and guided her to the backseat.

"Sandy, we have to worry about you, okay?" he said, and I was shocked at the delicacy in his voice, the naked humanity. "I'm sorry about your friends, but we have to go."

She looked into his eyes and brushed the hair away from her face. Another change. This time, the gesture made her look vulnerable, and yet very sensual at the same time.

Nothing is as protean as a woman.

"Okay, Marcus," she said, and climbed in.

I turned the car onto the upper level of the freeway. The bottom level was only two lanes wide, with no shoulder, and there was no way we were going to make it through there. The upper was a little more open.

Once we got on the freeway, we were in darkness. All the overhead street lamps were out. None of the Trans-Guide traffic displays were working. The freeway was a black ribbon against the night skyline, and off in the distance we saw towering pillars of black smoke and the orange glow of structure fires.

Looking around at all the destruction, I realized how lucky I had been the last time I was on the freeway. Had I run into this mess earlier, without Marcus, I would probably still be looking for a way home.

Or worse, not looking for anything at all.

I turned on the takedown lights and the car's high beams, flooding the road ahead with as much light as the car could put out.

Wrecked cars were everywhere. Clouds of dust floated sluggishly on the breeze, and the cold night air seemed to glow with a greenish sheen. The car's lights caught the dust, and as I snaked us through the gaps in the snarled traffic, I had the feeling we were drifting through an underwater landscape of sunken ships and warplanes, the graveyard of some long-ago and distant naval battle.

In places the freeway was so thick with wrecks that we had to use the push bumpers to ram our way through. Whenever possible, Marcus would get out and drive the wrecks out of the way, but we still ended up beating the crap out of the car. It started making a mechanical whining noise, a sickening groan, every time I hit the gas. I could feel it straining, slipping out of gear.

We saw a car that had run up onto the bed of an

older model Ford pickup. Inside the car I saw a woman slapping her bloody hands against the passenger window in a slow, pointless gesture, and when we got up close enough to see her face, there was no doubt that she had been changed. Death spoke through her eyes.

Sandy gasped in the backseat.

"You okay?" Marcus asked her. He had to raise his voice to be heard through the shattered Plexiglas divider. There was still blood on it, despite our best efforts to clean it up for her.

She nodded, wiped a tear from her face. I actually pitied her then, despite the attitude she had given me back at the church. Seeing her like that, softened, made me realize that she was genuinely hurting. It also made her seem even more beautiful than she had been before the situation at the church got so out of hand.

"What's that smell?" Marcus asked.

He was right. Something smelled bad. I wrinkled my nose at it as I looked around.

It wasn't death. I know what death smells like. This was something else, something just as earthy and foul, but not as ominous. Like manure.

We saw the source of it just ahead. An eighteen wheeler had flipped over on its side and was blocking two of the three lanes. There were a few cars in the remaining third lane that looked like they had run into the retaining wall when the big rig flipped over.

Marcus drove one out of the way, and I rammed two more with the car to get us clear.

Once we cleared the gap and got around the truck, we saw that the rig was a cattle hauler, and the smell that we thought was manure really was manure.

The scene was gut-wrenching, easily the worst display of blood and bone and brown, puddled viscera I had seen all night.

The side panels of the truck had been ripped away

when it rolled over, but there were parts of the paneling that looked like they had been pulled apart by human hands. Zombies had gone after some of the cattle and torn them to pieces. Dripping, shredded cattle carcasses, a shoulder here, a leg or rump section there, were festooned from broken wooden slats, and there were large, steaming piles of cow shit and wet hay melting together in pools of blood on the ground.

Some of the cattle must have stampeded in fright during the attack because there were crushed human bodies on the ground next to the cattle carcasses.

About fifty feet away I saw a cow with its stomach ripped open. The wound looked like some kind of grotesque jungle orchid in bloom. Its head was resting on the retaining wall, where it had crawled away to die.

"What do you know," I said, pointing the cow out to Marcus. "There's no cross-species contamination."

"No what?"

"No zombie cows."

"What are you talking about?"

"Cross-species contamination," I said again. "There are no zombie cows. Haven't you wondered if anything else besides people gets turned into zombies? Apparently, it's a big question in zombie studies."

"Zombie studies?" He put his back to the passenger door and crossed his arms over his chest. His way of pronouncing something as bullshit when he heard it. "I took women's studies back when I was working on my Associate's degree. Is zombie studies anything like that?"

"This is a little different, I think."

"So what are zombie studies?"

"It's nothing," I said. "Just something this guy told me about earlier tonight. I think it amounts to a bunch of freaks in a chat room, talking about what they think zombies would be like if they actually existed."

"If they actually existed?"

"Well," I said, "I think they're gonna have a lot to talk about after tonight."

He nodded. "I didn't know you were into that kind of thing."

"I'm not. It was just a random thought going through my brain. No big deal."

"Oh."

We continued on in silence for a little while longer, and things were quiet enough that I could hear Sandy's sniffles in the backseat. Poor girl, I thought. She's trying hard to be tough.

"You really took women's studies in school?" I asked Marcus.

He glanced out the window at the fires burning up the west side of San Antonio's skyline. "It wasn't quite what I thought it was going to be," he said.

The wreckage blocking the roadway never seemed to end, and I began to wonder if we would have been better off taking the surface streets. The car was really starting to groan.

A short distance later we came to another wreck that was blocking the whole road. The main culprit on this one was an overturned maroon Isuzu Trooper. Evidently, it had hit two other cars, gotten airborne after hitting the retaining wall, and knocked down a light pole.

The pole was lying across two lanes and the left shoulder, and there were at least ten cars turned the wrong way. Some were crumpled together in a metal embrace.

I stopped the car and studied the wreckage.

"This is going to take some doing," I said.

"Yeah," Marcus said. "Think you can push that Isuzu out of the way? Looks clear past him on that side."

"I think so."

There wasn't really much to push against. Because it was upside down, the bumper was too high for me to catch it with the push bumper, and I had to ease up to the aluminum case for the spare tire and part of the rear window.

I made contact gently, then dipped into the throttle and started to push. The car strained, and then the aluminum spare-tire case buckled. The next moment I heard creaking metal and the pop and shatter of glass breaking. I knew we weren't going to get it moved that way.

I backed up, carrying part of the spare-tire case with me. "What do you want to do now?"

Marcus squinted at the wrecked cars. "Let's see if some of these other cars are drivable. Maybe we can use them to ram that light pole out of the way."

"Okay."

I glanced at Sandy in the rearview mirror. She wasn't sobbing anymore, but she had a fixed, road-worn look in her eyes.

"You going to be okay for a minute?" I asked her.

She nodded.

"Okay," I said. "We'll be right back."

Marcus went up to a blue Volvo, opened the door, and shot the zombie behind the wheel as casually as if he were ordering a beer at a bar. I jumped when I heard the shot. Marcus reached in, grabbed the body, and pulled it out onto the pavement. It made a dull thud as it hit the ground.

He pointed at a green Kia, meaning for me to drive it.

I nodded. There were no zombies in mine. I got in, and Marcus got in his Volvo. We backed the cars into position, then gave them some gas, and rammed the light pole out of the way.

It made a fierce grinding noise, but eventually we got

it moving, and after moving a few more cars, we had one lane open.

"That ought to work," Marcus said.

"Yeah, I can get through here no problem."

We were congratulating each other on a job well done, heading back for the car, when we heard Sandy screaming.

We ran for her at a dead sprint, but when we rounded a row of cars between us and her, we saw a thick knot of zombies beating on our police car, trying to get at the meat inside.

A few of the zombies were on top of the trunk, pulling at Sandy through the busted-out rear window.

Others had opened the driver's side rear door and were already inside the car. I thought I saw Sandy, her back against the opposite rear door, kicking at the hands and teeth clutching for her, but it was dark and I couldn't really see her that well to be sure.

I jumped onto the hood of the car, ran over the roof, and kicked a zombie that had yet to get inside square in the jaw. He flew backwards and landed on his head behind the car.

Next I grabbed a pair of legs belonging to a zombie who was headfirst in the backseat and pulled as hard as I could, extracting him from the backseat. I heard Sandy howling in pain, and I could barely see her, thrashing at the hands and faces pressing down on top of her.

Her screams filled up the night. I fired into the backseat, hitting at least two of the zombies in the head, maybe three.

Meanwhile, Marcus had gone around the passenger side of the car and got Sandy's door open. He managed to grab her beneath the shoulders and pulled her from the car. As he moved her I heard a nasty sound, like a large piece of fabric being ripped in half, only it was the sound of her flesh ripping.

Several zombies tumbled out of the car after her.

Through a gap in the mass of bodies I caught a glimpse of Sandy, and nearly gagged. She was covered in blood, and her left leg was missing below the hip. Most of her stomach was shredded.

She started to gasp, gulping for air like a fish out of water.

"Get them!" Marcus shouted.

I jumped down next to him and started firing at the faces inside and on top of the car. I did it quickly. In thirty seconds they were all dead.

When I turned around, so was Sandy. She had bled out.

Marcus pushed her body off him and then the two of us pulled the other bodies out of the backseat. It was grim work, and we did it without talking.

When it was done, we got back in the car and drove away.

After we got rolling again, Marcus happened to glance in the backseat and made a disgusted noise.

"What?" I asked.

"We left her leg back there."

"I'll pull over so we can get rid of it," I said.

"No," he said, and sat back down. "Don't worry about it. We're not going to have this car very much longer. Downtown's only two exits away."

"Okay," I said. "If you're sure."

"I'm sure," he said. "A pity, though. She really did have great legs."

Chapter 22

By the time we drove into the police vehicle ready lot to get a new car, the one we were in had almost died. Three of the tires were in good shape, but the rest of it looked like warmed-over crap. It was making a grinding noise on Marcus's side that sounded like part of the undercarriage was dragging on the ground and a thin wisp of steam or smoke was coming from underneath the hood.

We had to bust the fence at the entrance to the yard and, when we did, the car slipped out of gear and wouldn't go back in.

We left it by the guard shack, shot a zombie there that used to be a city mechanic, and stepped into the ready lot.

There were rows upon rows of white Crown Victorias, all of them exactly the same, and all of them ready to go.

I could tell Marcus was in heaven.

He clapped his hands together and said, "You ready, Eddie? Let's go shopping."

"After you."

"Thank you, sir. I hear they're not much on selection here, but the prices can't be beat."

What we wanted was on the west end of the lot. The cars there were already outfitted with push bumpers, which we figured we would probably need again. The only thing they were missing compared to a regular patrol vehicle was the decal package.

Marcus pointed to a dealer's sticker still stuck to one of the windows. I watched him run his finger down the columns with a sparkle in his eye that made it seem like he was fingering fine jewels.

"Look at this," he said. "Can you believe it? Look at how much these things cost. The city's getting their eyes poked out on this deal."

"That's a lot," I said, without even looking at the sticker. I was looking around for more zombies. We were out in the open, and it was making me nervous.

I saw one stumbling past the yard on the other side of the fence. A little farther beyond him was a homeless shelter, and dark, slow-moving figures moved through the maze of filthy mattresses and trash piles that surrounded the building.

So far, they hadn't noticed us, but I'd always hated dealing with the homeless, and I sure as hell didn't want to mess with them now that they were zombies.

"What do you think?" I asked. "You ready to go?"

"Yeah, yeah. Which one do you want?"

"The white one."

"That's cute," he said. "Get in. I'm driving."

Getting through downtown wasn't as difficult as I thought it would be. There were zombies everywhere, and most of the roads were choked up with abandoned cars, but it wasn't anything close to as bad as it had been in the Medical Center.

We got almost all the way to headquarters before we ran into our first real gridlock.

"I'm gonna turn right here," Marcus said. "We can park up front. The back gates will probably be locked anyway."

"Okay."

Marcus turned down Watson Street and we rode up the sidewalk all the way to the front steps of head-quarters.

It looked like there had been a fierce battle near the front of the building. On the other side of the street was an old Spanish-style limestone wall, and in front of that, a little strip of grass ran parallel to the sidewalk.

Three enormous live oaks draped their dew-soaked branches over the street, sheltering the bodies of a dozen or so people.

They were collapsed on the pavement and in the grass in poses that made them look like they were sleep-ing in the sun on a lazy, sunny afternoon. But there was something uneasy and unwilling about the way they laid there.

Most were on their backs, with an arm stretched out above their head or a knee cocked up into the air.

One man was facedown in the grass, and a dried puddle of his own blood had stained the grass below his cheek. Most of his right leg had been eaten and his pants were in tatters, clinging to the gore. It reminded me of a half-eaten cob of corn.

I even saw a few uniforms among the bodies.

"Come on," Marcus said from the front doors. "Don't look at it."

"Yeah, okay." I turned away and followed him up the steps, but even as I did I got the feeling that we weren't going to find our answers inside.

We walked through the open front doors and into the lobby. Debris was everywhere, and in the bluish-white glow of the building's emergency lights it looked like the seat of desolation.

The whole building was running off the generators, and they were making a monotonous, mechanical droning noise that seemed to be coming from everywhere at once.

In the middle of the floor was a dead woman in an expensive-looking dark gray skirt and a white blouse. I could see the receiver of her Glock poking out from underneath her leg. Marcus said he recognized her, but I had never seen her before.

"She's a robbery detective," he said. "Was a robbery detective, I mean."

"She's got a cell phone on her belt," I said.

"You want it?" Marcus asked, his eyebrows arched, asking why in the hell I would.

"Maybe it still works."

He shrugged. "Get it if you want it."

I walked over to her corpse and turned her over with the toe of my boot.

I reached for the phone and then backed up in a hurry, just to be on the safe side.

"Well," he said. "Does it work?"

I flipped it open, dialed April's cell number, and got two rings before it cut to static.

"It rang," I said.

"Anything?"

"No. It cut out."

"Might as well keep it," he said. "We'll try again later."

I put the phone on my belt.

Beyond the detective's body was a vestibule where the security people sat. The rest of the building was behind that and closed off behind bulletproof glass doors.

I couldn't believe the damage I saw. To the left were the cashiers' windows and the door that led to Records and Accounting. Two middle-aged, heavy-set women and a tiny little man in a brown suit were crumpled up in a pile next to one of the doors.

Through the cashiers' windows I saw a woman in her early twenties staggering between the rows of filing cabinets, unable to figure out how to get through the maze to where we were standing.

To our right was a hallway that led off to Personnel, and beside that was what used to be a glass trophy case. Now all that was left of it was crunching beneath our boots.

The stain of death was all around us. It seemed to hang from the walls and permeate the air like a fog. I almost didn't want to breathe, afraid that somehow I might become corrupted by it.

"You done looking?" Marcus asked me.

"What?"

"I don't feel like wasting time standing here, okay? First place I want to check out is Communications. I want to see if there's some sort of regrouping site."

"Okay," I said, but I was watching the zombie in the Records office. She had managed to get out of the maze of filing cabinets and was trying to climb through the glass windows.

"Right," he said, but didn't sound convinced. "Eddie?"

He shook my shoulder. "Eddie? Hey."

"What?"

"You with me? Come on. I need you sharp."

"I'm with you," I said. "I'm just tired."

"Me too," he said. "Come on. Through here."

We jumped over the security desk and started back. Most of the doors were controlled by electronic key cards, and neither of us had one. Only people with regular business at headquarters get those.

The first floor was mainly support services and meeting rooms.

What Marcus really wanted was on the third floor. That was where we'd find the 9-1-1 emergency dispatch system, and it was there, according to Marcus, that we would learn whatever there was to learn about what was happening and what those in charge were doing about it.

Marcus shot a zombie at the entrance to the south stairwell who used to be a Sex Crimes detective. Then we started up the stairs.

The generators were humming, which meant the elevators were probably working too, but neither of us wanted to risk getting stuck inside of one.

Our plan was to get in, learn what we could from anybody we could find, and get out.

But as we stepped out of the stairwell and onto the third floor, I realized we were in trouble.

The whole floor was quiet.

Usually, the third floor of headquarters was a zoo. Even in the middle of the night you could usually count on there being fifty or more people running around, stomping out fires of one sort or another, and generally filling the place with noise. It was never this quiet.

"Come on," Marcus said. "Let's be quick about this."

We headed for the Communications entrance on the northeast wing of the building and stopped around the corner from the glass doors that led into the dispatcher's pit.

Marcus motioned for me to loop around him and move to the other side of the doors. I got into position and then peered around the corner.

"Holy crap," I said, whispering to him. Inside there were more than fifty zombies who had once been our dispatchers. "We're not going to go in there."

He nodded and then lowered his head like he was thinking what to do next.

There was a sudden crash, and then the doors flew open.

A slender female in blue jeans and a bloody green shirt erupted into the hallway. I had my shoulders turned away from her when she broke out, but I spun around just in time to catch her by the neck as her face came down next to mine, mouth open and teeth wet with blood.

She was one of the fast-movers. She fought like mad, clawing and kicking and sticking her dirty mouth in for the bite that would kill me. The force of her attack knocked me backwards and my gun slipped from my hand.

I yelled out for Marcus to help, but he was already on top of her. He grabbed her by the hair and pulled her head backward, twisting and guiding her face away from me.

She went sprawling into the wall, and before she could get up, he peppered her with bullets.

I rolled toward my gun.

Marcus stepped into the doorway and start firing. He said something to me that I couldn't understand, and the rest of it was drowned out by the sound of his gun.

He fired again and again, trying to pick off the zombies before they made it through the doors, but there were just too many of them, and they swelled into the hallway like an ocean wave.

It only took a few seconds before Marcus and I were separated by a widening gulf of bodies. They were so thick all I could see was a mass of moving arms, and in flashes of pistol fire, moving farther and farther away, was Marcus as he fought to hold his ground.

I could still hear him shouting, but I couldn't see him anymore. The zombies were piling into the hallway and I had nowhere left to go. They were painting me into a corner. I fired I don't know how many rounds, but it was like trying to dig a hole in the surface of the ocean. One would fall and three more would step into the gap he left behind.

There were just too many of them. I glanced right and saw a middle-aged woman with a flattened and bloody face standing in front of a gray metal door. The others had pushed her to the wall as they poured into the hallway.

I put a hole in her forehead. She fell back against the door, but I didn't let her fall to the ground. I caught the back of her shoulders and used her as a shield against the crowd.

The others reached around her body, clutching at me.

The split second that I bought using her as a shield was enough to reach the door and pull it open. I let the woman's body fall to the floor and ran through the door, only dimly aware that I was stepping into another stairwell.

Behind me, the door was still wide open and the zombies started coming through.

I turned and fired until I was out of bullets. By then there were so many bodies stacked up in the doorway that the rest of the infected were having to climb over them to get to me.

I kicked at the bodies and somehow managed to get the door closed.

As I shut it, the sound of the crowd died to a muffled roar, and I was left alone on the top landing of the stairwell, surrounded by blue cement walls and a gray cement floor that was covered with puddles of black blood.

They were banging on the door, but they sounded miles away. Everything sounded hollow and distant except the blood pounding in my ears.

"You gotta move," I said, trying to make myself do it.

I saw the door open just a crack, and that lit a fire

under my ass. I went down the stairs as fast as I could go, but it was narrow, and the steps were steeper than a normal stairwell. I had to make each step deliberate just to keep from tumbling down.

The door to the second floor was locked. I pulled it hard, but it wouldn't budge. Only when I stepped back to kick it did I see the black electronic key card pad to the right of the door jamb.

The first floor had the same set up, and it was locked too.

I ran back to the second floor and pulled on the door again, frantic with claustrophobia and rage.

I kicked the door, then backed away and kicked it again in desperation.

"Motherfucker!"

Above me, I heard zombies entering the stairwell. I switched out magazines and ran up to get them before they could get me.

I made it to the third-floor landing just in time to see a dozen or so zombies come tumbling through the door and land right in front of me.

I slowly backtracked down the first few steps, never taking my eyes off of them as they advanced.

The lead zombie took the first step, stumbled, and came tumbling down to my feet. I raised my gun and was just about to fire when I heard a door down below me open up.

"Marcus?" I said, hoping that it was really him and not more trouble.

"Eddie."

I turned and flew down the stairs, yelling as I took the steps two at a time, "Don't close that door. Keep it open."

But he was already running up the stairs toward me.

"Catch the door. Don't let it close."

We met on the second-floor landing, him coming up

as fast as I was running down. "Can't go that way," he said, panting hard.

I jumped down next to him. "Can't go up either," I said, just as winded.

He reached for the door and pulled on it. Still locked.

"How many?" I asked, looking over the railing at the zombies that were gathering below us on the first floor. Some of them were taking their first steps up the stairs.

"A whole crap load," he said. "I don't know. I went down the south stairwell. They're all over the place."

"Great." The zombies from the third floor were turning the corner above us. "Any ideas?"

He shook his head. "How many bullets do you have left?"

"I don't know. Maybe ten."

"Me too."

The first few zombies were coming into sight above us. The ones from the first floor were having more trouble coming up than the others were coming down, but it was just a matter of time. They would make it up eventually.

"I guess we make them count," I said.

"Yep. But save your last round for me, okay?"

"With pleasure."

A couple of zombies rounded the corner above me and I shot them. Every shot sounded like an explosion in the tight confines of the stairwell.

"There's too many of them," I said.

"Keep shooting."

I turned my attention back to the zombies coming down the stairs. Marcus was pulling on the second-floor door with everything he had. He put one foot on the doorjamb and grabbed the handle with both hands. He yanked on it with his whole body weight, and the door flew open.

Marcus fell backwards and landed on his butt. Two older male zombies in very expensive suits came through the door, and in the split second before Marcus put holes in their heads, I recognized one of them as Captain Ibsen from the Media Relations office.

Marcus stepped in front of the door and kept it from closing with his foot. "Come on," he said. "It's now or never."

But he didn't have to tell me twice. I was out the door and onto the second-floor reception area before he finished his sentence.

The second floor was the home of the department's Interagency and Media Relations offices, and the ten or so zombies I saw there were all dressed in the finest style.

At least they had been.

Now all those expensive clothes were soaked through with blood and bile.

Marcus did the shooting for both of us, clearing a path through the zombies and across to the west side of the building.

"Where are we going?" I asked.

"Can't take the south stairwell again. There's too many of them that way."

"But where are we—"

"Over here," he said, and pushed open a gray metal door on the back wall. "This way."

I followed him through the door and into the night air. The sign on the door said OBSERVATION DECK, but that was a little optimistic for the scrap of cement and metal railing that we were standing on. It was maybe four feet wide and fifteen feet long, with a canopy overhead that didn't even cover the whole deck. There were a few ratty chairs next to the door and about a million cigarette butts on the cement, and the only view the observation deck provided was of the fenced-in portion of the employee parking lot and the back side of a long-since-vacated bakery.

"Where to now?" I asked.

"I don't know," he said. "I'm making this up as I go."

"That's cute. Seriously, Marcus, where to?"

"I am serious. I don't know. You got any ideas?"

He tilted back one of the chairs so that it kept the door from opening, and then looked over the railing to the parking lot below. "I guess we jump for it."

I looked over the railing and then back at him. "Are you insane? We're like thirty feet up."

"Gosh, princess, I'm sorry. Did you want to go back inside and fight zombies?"

"Fuck you."

"Where else do you suggest we go?"

He was right, of course. There wasn't any other way out of the building. I looked over the edge again and whistled. "After you," I said.

"Gee, thanks."

"Don't mention it."

Marcus climbed over the side and lowered himself down until he was hanging from the ledge by his fingertips.

Then he let go.

I heard him land, and a second later he called up to me to jump down. "It's all right," he said. "It only looks like a long ways."

"Asshole," I said, and then climbed over the railing just like I had seen him do. I held on for a second, then let go.

I knew even before I landed that I was going to mess myself up, and sure enough, when I hit, I felt a stabbing pain go through my right ankle, up my leg, and into my back.

I folded, and stayed that way.

"You okay?" he asked me.

I looked up at him and thought of Carlos Williams. "It's my ankle," I said.

"Shit." He looked around, searching the parking lot for movement. "Do you think it's broken?"

"No," I said hopefully. "I don't think so."

"Try to move it. Turn it in little circles."

I tried moving it, and it hurt like hell. Marcus helped me stand up and I put some weight on it a little at a time.

"How does it feel?"

"It hurts."

"Do you think you can walk it off?"

"Yeah," I said, taking a few tentative steps. "I think so."

"Good."

We turned toward the building just in time to see the back door bust open and a crowd of zombies come pouring out. We both stood there slack jawed at the sudden commotion. Another moment later and they were through the back door and flooding out into the parking lot, coming right for us.

Chapter 23

We stood there in the parking lot and watched as the crowd of zombies got bigger.

"There are so many of them," I said. "Why are there so many of them? The first floor was empty when we came in."

Marcus checked his magazine and then slapped it back into his gun. "I've only got four rounds left."

"We need to get out of here."

"I know. How's your ankle?"

"I can make it."

He nodded and looked out over the parking lot. I could see his wheels turning. The lot was maybe a third full and surrounded on three sides by a fifteen-foot-high green wrought-iron fence. There was a guard shack and a gate on the south end of the lot, but it wouldn't open without a key card.

"Looks like we're gonna have to climb over," he said.

Of course that was easier said than done. Every April, during the Fiesta celebrations, some drunken idiot gets stuck at the top of the fence while trying to climb over so he can piss on a cop car, and some cop has to risk his fat ass going up there to get him down. The fence did really well keeping people out, but now it was doing just as well keeping us in.

I looked around for something we could climb up on to help us get over, but there was nothing close to the fence.

"Looks like that's going to be kind of hard to do, Marcus."

"Again," he said, "would you rather we go back inside and fight zombies? I don't think the zombies would mind much."

"One of these days I just might take you up on that."

"Just follow me," he said.

We started toward the west side of the parking lot. If we could get over the fence there, it was only about twenty yards to our car.

But we hadn't made it more than half way to the fence when we heard a woman screaming to the south of us. She sounded really close.

We both stopped, and listened.

She screamed again. She was close. Marcus took off running across the lot and I hobbled after him as fast as I could go.

The zombies coming out of headquarters were spreading out, and as I looked behind me I saw a line of them backlit by the building's emergency lights. It was hypnotic in a way, watching them. They moved so slowly, so painfully, and yet with such a relentless need to put their hands on us that I found it hard to look away.

The girl's screaming brought my attention away from the zombies. I watched Marcus disappear at the edge of the lot, and I was still maybe thirty yards away from him when I heard him fire the first shot.

I got to him as fast as I could. He was standing at the fence, facing a young girl of about sixteen who was on the other side. She was screaming for help and reaching between the bars to grab hold of Marcus's clothes.

Behind her was the body of the man Marcus had just shot.

More zombies were lumbering toward us from the bakery behind the girl.

"Open the gate," she said. "Please. Let me in. Please!"

Her face was wet with tears and sweat. When I looked into her eyes I immediately recognized that look—that look that said there was nothing anybody could do to reach her. She was only seeing fear.

Marcus fired again, but even in the low light of the alley way I could tell there were more of them than we had bullets. They were thick in the darkness behind her, and there were more entering the alley farther off.

She turned her hunted gaze on me. "Open the gate. Please. You've got to let me in."

I opened my mouth to speak, but all that came out was a pantomime of the words, "I can't."

"Run," Marcus said to her. "Run. We can't open the gates."

But she was so scared she couldn't take that in. The words weren't breaking through her wall. She pounded the wrought-iron bars so hard they rocked inside their concrete mounts. She cried to be saved.

Marcus fired again, and out of the corner of my eye I saw his slide lock back.

"I'm empty," he said.

"I got it," I said, and came up next to him, firing what I had left. I fired three times, and each time I put one of them on the ground, but all I did was make room for other hands to reach for her. We had nothing left to protect her with.

"Help me. Jesus, why won't you help me?"

"Run," Marcus said to her. "Come on. Run."

"Please." She said it over and over again until she just

gave up and slid down the bars to the ground. She wasn't listening to anything anymore.

"Run."

The girl turned her huge doe eyes up at Marcus. He knelt down next to her and showed her his gun.

"Do you see that? Do you? When it does that it means I'm out of bullets. We can't open the gate. We don't have the key. If you want to live you have to stand up and run. Run. That way."

Marcus tried to grab the sides of her face through the bars.

"You have to run," he said, lowering his voice and speaking as calmly as he could. "Run."

He tried to pull her up, but she slipped out of his hands and collapsed to the ground.

"Run, you stupid bitch. Get your ass up and run. Right now."

But the zombies closed in around her. We were less than a yard away from her, and we were powerless to do anything to help her. As I watched, the color bled out of her face and she stopped struggling. Her screams were muffled into silence.

When the zombies had finished with her, some of them stood up and clutched at me through the fence with their bloody hands.

"Fuck this," I heard Marcus say from behind me. But I didn't turn to look at him until I heard the roar of an engine.

It was Marcus, behind the wheel of one of the Gang Unit cars. I saw the headlights come up, and then the back tires began to spin as Marcus backed it up.

"What the hell are you doing, Marcus?"

He skidded the car to a stop halfway across the lot, paused there for just a moment, and then the car lurched forward. He was barreling down on the spot where I was standing.

"Marcus," I said, "you are one insane son of a bitch."

I jumped to one side just before he reached me. He never hit the brakes or slowed down at all. The car blasted through the gate in a splash of sparks and broken metal.

Some of the zombies at the gate were thrown clear by the impact; others were mowed down under the car.

The Crown Victoria went all the way across the alley and smashed to a stop in a crumpled mess against the wall of the bakery.

Chapter 24

Marcus was stuck in the car, jammed up beneath the steering wheel and the air bag. I held the air bag off him like a drape. He turned towards me. There was a little bit of blood on his face and a musty-smelling white cloud inside the car that made me feel like I was inhaling ash.

"Hey, Marcus, can you hear me?"

He let out a shallow, tired sigh and opened his eyes very slowly. "Oh, man," he said, and a thin grin crossed his face, "that sucked."

I smiled too. I couldn't help it. "You're a fucking idiot, you know that?"

"You'd think I'd have that figured out by now, wouldn't you?"

"Can you move?"

"No."

"You can't? What's wrong?"

"You're in the way."

"You're killing me, Marcus. You know that?"

"Not yet," he said, chuckling as he pushed his way out of the car. "But I'm working on it."

The smile didn't last long, though. After I helped him out of the car he looked at the scene, at the bodies, at the girl whose torso had been ripped open and mostly eaten.

"What was she thinking? Why didn't she run like I told her to?"

The force of the impact had thrown her body several yards to the right of us. She had been wearing a pair of blue jeans and a soft baby-blue camisole, but the camisole was shredded now and the jeans soaked with her blood. From the neck up she looked human. From the waist down, too. The part in between looked like the floor of a butcher's shop. Even Marcus had a hard time looking at it.

"I don't know," I said. "Just scared, I guess."

He shook his head. "That's the stupidest thing I've ever seen anybody do. Why would anybody just lie down and die like that? She just gave up."

"It's a waste, that's for sure."

Marcus and I hobbled away.

Neither of us were able to make a very good pace. My ankle was still hurting, though not nearly as badly as it had been just before Marcus nearly ran me over, and Marcus was banged up something fierce. He said his whole right side felt like it had been hit by a wrecking ball.

A lot of the zombies from the alley were still moving, but they couldn't catch up with us. The ones from headquarters were still inside the parking lot, stuck behind the fence and not much of a threat. We dodged a small group that was outside the fence at the northwest corner, and then had a clear shot all the way to the car.

Both of us went for the driver's seat. "I'm driving," he said.

"Yeah, right, not after what you just did."

"I called it back at the gas station, remember?"

"What does this look like? Third grade? Plus, I let you drive from the ready lot to here. It's my turn now."

"I'm driving."

"No way. You're hurt."

"So are you."

"We're going to my house," I said.

"I know the way."

"Fine," I said, and threw up my hands. "But we're going to my house. Straight there. Nowhere else."

"I know. Get in."

Marcus pulled the car off the sidewalk and we turned north on Vespers. We were going to take Vespers northbound all the way through downtown, because it joined up with the access road for the freeway and we should have been able to take that all the way out to my house.

Provided we drove outbound on the inbound lanes to avoid all the traffic, it was less than twenty minutes from headquarters to my house.

But we didn't even make it three blocks before we were stopped by massive traffic congestion at the emergency entrance to Children's Hospital. Everything was shut down to the north and to the west of that by debris and abandoned cars.

Marcus turned the car onto the sidewalk again and drove us east.

"Maybe we can cut through Washington Square and double back."

"Yeah," I said, as I watched a group of zombies walking across the street from the hospital. "Let's try that."

While he drove up the sidewalk I went to work on the remaining ammunition, splitting it up between his gun and mine.

"Twenty for each of us," I said, and handed him back his pistol and his extra magazine.

"Is that it?"

"That's it."

"Really? I thought we had a whole—" He slammed on the brakes, hard. "Holy shit!"

"Oh my God."

My jaw went slack and I sat there gaping at a crowd so big I couldn't see the end of it. To the north of us, and again to the west, the streets were filled with zombies. Cars in the middle of the street looked like rocks in the middle of a fast-moving stream.

The bus station on the northeast corner was on fire, and the windows of the glass buildings above us were painted with fire. Large pieces of rubble filled the streets, and through the charred frame of an exploded bus we could see where the gas pumps had once been. The fire was still at a healthy rage, and in the orange and yellow glow I watched the infected coming for us.

"Where are they all coming from? Look at that, Marcus. They're everywhere."

Marcus spun the car around under full acceleration and left a pair of black looping streaks down the sidewalk as we headed south.

He took us down two blocks, and then turned east again where we hit more abandoned cars and more crowds.

It was maddening, like trying to find our way out of a maze, only the game was rigged so that every direction was a dead end. We couldn't stay on any one road longer than a block or two before having to change direction and start all over again.

By the time we cleared downtown we were on the near east side and caught between traffic and another crowd of zombies. I looked from one obstacle to the other, my mind racing for an idea of what to do next.

Marcus chose a third option. He turned the car onto a pedestrian walkway that led over the freeway and came down in the park-and-ride terminal for the Convention Center.

"Hold on," he told me as we started down two flights of steps.

I saw the ground ahead of us drop away into empty space, and then all of a sudden we were pointed straight down and the ground was rushing up to meet us.

We hit so hard I could actually hear the car's frame bending. Marcus struggled with the wheel, caught the car before it could drift all the way sideways, and then landed it in the middle of Mount Olive Street.

He let the car drift to a stop and waited for me to say something.

"What?"

"Well?" he asked.

"Well what?"

"Go on, say the words. That was some of the best driving you've ever seen, wasn't it?"

"Are you kidding me?" There were pieces of broken windshield glass in my hair and my door wouldn't close anymore. "Marcus, that was the most fucked-up thing I have seen you do all night. I never did anything like that when I was driving."

"Oh, come on."

I was still brushing glass out of my hair. I held one up so he could see it. "What did I do that was worse than this?"

"You're kidding, right? Eddie, look in the backseat. Do you see a dead fat guy back there? No, you don't. And you know why there's not a dead fat guy back there? Because what I just did was some incredible fucking driving. Tell me it wasn't. Go on, tell me and then call yourself a liar."

"No."

"Admit it."

I laughed at him. "No. No way."

"Fine."

He put the car in gear and started off down Mount

Olive, pouting the whole way. He amazed me like that. It cracked me up that someone capable of kicking as much ass as he did could still be capable of pouting like a four year old when he didn't get his way. But there it was.

The car was so messed up the best he could get out of it was about thirty miles per hour, but he still threw in a parting shot before he gave up the argument.

"I don't care what you say. That was some incredible driving, and you know it."

Mount Olive curved around the east side of the Convention Center, then went north until it turned into the on-ramp for the highway.

We weren't able to make it that far, though. There was a massive amount of traffic congestion before the ramp, and it was completely impassable. We didn't even have room to drive up the grass embankment because there were so many cars wedged into the gaps between the guardrails.

We had to back up and cross over at Dove Street into the East Division service area.

Neither one of us had ever worked the east side, so everything east of Mount Olive was uncharted territory for us.

I had heard the neighborhoods east of the Convention Center were tough, but I was shocked to see how different they were from the perfectly manicured gardens and clean streets of the Convention Center's grounds. We were just one block over, separated from the center by a long line of enormous live oaks, yet it seemed like we had stepped into another world. Even the pavement was different. Where the Convention Center's streets were smooth and accented with russet- and ochre-colored bricks, we were on raw asphalt that had buckled from the railroad tracks that crisscrossed all the streets in the area. The lingering, filthy stench of backed-up sewage and rotting garbage hung in the air.

After turning onto Dove, we were lost. Streets that seemed like they should have gone north-south seemed to fade away into vacant lots or curve back on themselves, and we suddenly found ourselves in the warehouse district with absolutely no idea how we got there or how we would get out.

The buildings we passed were dying. Graffiti covered the faces of the buildings in unbelievable profusion. In places the long, unintelligible scrawls were covered up by weeds growing at the base of the foundation.

It didn't really make sense to call what we were looking at the warehouse district, because there was really nothing more to it than one decaying hulk after another stretching on into the darkness. What I was looking at was the dead city, the cancerous growth in the bowels of a dying culture.

I was thinking that way, about the death of things, and staring out the window at the gaping black holes in the sides of the buildings we passed when Marcus slapped me on the arm.

"What's that?" he asked, pointing a good ways down the road at what looked to me to be smoke.

But it wasn't smoke. Even from a distance I knew it wasn't smoke. It was moving faster than smoke, but thicker and blacker.

"It looks like a flock of birds."

"You may be right," he said. "Probably grackles."

They were grackles. It was the biggest flock of birds I've ever seen. As we pulled up on another dead end we saw hundreds of thousands of fat black birds sitting on every available perch. They lined the edge of the roof of the building straight ahead of us, and they were all over the power lines and the parking lot and the gutted carcass of a Country Fields Bread Company eighteen wheeler. Red-and-white plastic bread bags fluttered into the air all around us. The grackles were tearing the loaves of bread apart, feeding like sharks in an ocean of blood.

The noise they made was tremendous.

We saw movement again. From off to our left, a small section of the flock fluttered into the air, flew a short distance, and then settled down to the ground again.

"Look at that," Marcus said. His voice had a strange, exhausted breathiness to it that I hadn't heard before.

Then I saw why the birds were taking off. There were zombies moving through the parking lot. At first I saw just a few, but as I watched, more zombies streamed out from between the buildings. Soon we were facing a crowd of maybe sixty or more.

A few of the grackles started screaming, and soon the whole flock was agitated and squawking like they were being murdered, though the birds didn't have any trouble avoiding the infected. Small sections of the flock took to the wing in violent fits and then settled down again a short distance away.

"We should go."

"Yeah," said Marcus. "I think so, too."

He put the car in reverse and turned his head to look behind us. He frowned, and then dropped his head and cursed under his breath.

"What is it?" I looked back in my rearview mirror and saw what he was looking at. There was a huge crowd of zombies behind us. "Crap! Where do they keep coming from?"

"I don't know," he said. "They're everywhere."

He put the car in drive again and peeled off to the left. He cut between two long white buildings and sped down a broken, puddle-filled alley. We broke out of the alley at Shiloh and he stopped the car.

Shiloh was blocked off to the west of us by a gutted fire truck. All of its hoses were laid out next to the smoldering black corner of a vacant warehouse. Either something had exploded or a section of the building had come crashing down because there was debris all over the road and there was no way we could get around it. More crowds were gathering to the right of us. Big crowds stretched out deep into the darkness.

Marcus turned the car into the crowd and punched it. I leaned back in my seat, bracing myself against the dashboard, but before I could yell at him not to do it, we were diving headfirst into the crowd.

We hit the first bodies while we were still accelerating, and then everything started happening too fast. There was a hideous rush of wet thuds as bodies hit metal and glass and rolled off the hood. I saw faces, but no features. Everything was a blur, and roaring above it all was the straining engine of the Crown Victoria, fighting a losing battle as it pushed through the crowd.

We started to drift to my side of the street. The car was rolling sideways by the combined weight of all the human bodies it was striking, like a boat caught in a strong crosscurrent. I could feel the car start to lose acceleration, almost as if it had been knocked out of gear. Marcus had it floored, but we were slowing down, and we were still caught up in the thick of the crowd.

We were an island in a sea of bodies when the car gave out altogether.

"Run for it," Marcus said as he opened his door and took off toward a three-story gray and white building to his left.

But I couldn't get out.

Already there were dozens of zombies pushing up against my side of the car, and it was all I could do to hold the door closed. If there hadn't been so many of them pressing against the ones closest to me, they would have been able to rip the door out of my hands.

Frantically, I climbed over the computer between the two bucket seats and squeezed out of the driver's side door. Even as I was climbing out of the car, more bodies were pressing down on me. I felt a hand clutching at my shoulder and my neck, and then they were all over me.

I started swinging my fists at everything. As they swarmed around me I felt their weight pushing me back into the car. I put one arm across the top of the door and the other on the broken windshield. Before they could come down on top of me I jumped straight up and got on top of the car.

From the roof I could see Marcus fighting his own way toward the building. I also saw a way to get to him. I pulled my gun and shot at four zombies standing in front of the car, and then jumped to the ground and ran after Marcus, dodging zombies as I ate up the distance between us.

He was fighting them back from the doorway, yelling at me to hurry it up. I saw him break a man's neck and then throw himself into a thick wooden door, ramming it with his shoulder. I came up right behind him and never slowed down.

We hit the door at the same time, and sent it flying off its hinges. We both crashed to the ground on the other side in a wave of dust and shattered wood.

I popped up and turned my gun back on the doorway. Zombies were already coming through. Marcus was running toward a large staircase off to the right. I fired at the first zombie through the door and was about to fire again when I heard Marcus shout, "Come on. Up here."

I ran after him. He went up the staircase and around a corner at the top of the stairs with me on his heels the whole way. There we slipped in to a deserted office and I slammed the door behind us.

"Help me move this," he said, pushing a cabinet in front of the door.

Together we pushed it flush to the door and then listened. We could hear heavy, plodding steps making their way up the stairs.

Chapter 25

I turned away from the door and the sound of the infected beyond it, breathing hard and shivering against the cold.

The building we had taken shelter in had started to rot after years of neglect. There were holes in the wall and most of the windows were broken out. A harsh, cold breeze bit through its dark cavities. It was like being in a cave.

I instinctively reached down to my gun belt for my flashlight, but it was long gone. We were stuck in the viewless dark.

Gradually my eyes became accustomed to it, and bulking shapes around us turned into the less obscure outlines of very old and very musty office furniture. The ravages of neglect were everywhere, and the place stank of wet, rotten wood. A wet, gritty sort of sawdust covered everything.

Marcus wiped some of it from his hands and asked, "Where's the shotgun?"

Oh crap.

"I think it's still in the car," I said

"Why is it in the car?" His sense of humor never failed him.

"I don't know. I guess we forgot it."

"We? You were supposed to get it."

"Me? Why me?"

"You were riding shotgun. That's what that phrase means. You ride shotgun, you're the one who's supposed to hold on to the shotgun."

"You don't really want to argue about this, do you? Because you know, I'm not the one who just took off running and left his partner's ass hanging out in the wind. I'm real sorry if I forgot it, but I was kind of busy—you know, with those zombies trying to eat me and all."

"You don't do sarcasm very well at all."

"Was I being sarcastic? Because I didn't mean to be. I'm being dead fucking serious. What the hell is wrong with you? You just left me out there."

"You're a big boy," he said. "You didn't need my help. You may not be able to shoot worth a damn, but you can fight when you need to. I've seen you do it, and I wouldn't let you watch my back if I didn't know you were up for doing it again. It would have been nice if you'd have remembered the shotgun, though."

Something crashed against the door. Both of us jumped back, ready for those things to come busting into the room.

The door shook, but it held. That first loud crash gave way to a slow, steady beating against the door, and even in the faint light I could see little streams of white dust sparkling down from the seams of the door.

At first it sounded like there was just one or maybe two of them on the other side, but gradually the noise grew louder and less rhythmic.

Soon there were dozens of hands beating against the door, and the door was moving, creaking back and forth in the hinges.

"I guess we argue about it another time," Marcus said.

"Where do they keep coming from?"

"I don't know, but we should probably get going."

"I mean it, Marcus. Where do they keep coming from? First the street's deserted, and then the next thing you know, the whole damn place is covered in them. They don't move that fast. How does this keep happening? What are we doing to attract them?"

"What do I look like?" he said. "Do I look like I have the first fucking idea about what is going on?"

"It's weird."

"No shit. Tell me it didn't take you all night long to figure that out."

"No," I said.

"Okay then. We can't stay here."

"Where to?"

"Anywhere but here." He walked to the back of the room and disappeared around a corner. "Come on," he said. "There's a hallway back here. Let's see where it goes."

For Marcus, there was no stopping and questioning what he was doing or what he was about to step into. He was tough, and he knew it. It never occurred to him that he couldn't stand toe to toe with anything or anyone he encountered.

But I wasn't that way. For me, rushing headlong in to a fight was just plain stupid. I only fought when I had to, and even then I tried to have a plan about it. They say opposites attract, though. Maybe that was why Marcus and I worked so well together. We counteracted the worst in each other.

As I followed him into the hallway I was still troubled by the way so many zombies always seemed to descend on us so quickly everywhere we went. It seemed impossible that death could have overtaken so many, so quickly. I thought about the crowds we had encountered, and I wondered if it was just our stupid luck or if there was something more to it than that. I wondered what Ken would have said about it.

For Marcus, it wasn't even an issue. He seemed to think it just happened, that it was completely random, and that we just happened to fall into the thick of it because we were unlucky.

"More of the fuckers to shoot," was all he said about it.

Behind us, I heard the sound of the door giving way, and the filing cabinet being thrown to the ground. It was a sudden, hollow sound that reverberated through the building.

"Sounds like we're going to have some company," Marcus said.

"Yeah. Better keep going."

The hallway we were in connected to a whole series of small offices. They were more or less interconnected, and the walls between them were little more than particle board partitions that didn't completely separate one cubicle from another.

Once we were past the offices we stepped into another hallway that was much narrower. There were doorways on each side that were more substantial and I guessed that they had belonged to the people who ran this place.

But there must have been another way in besides the one we took because as soon as we stepped into the hallway, two zombies came out from around a corner to our left. I stepped over and pushed the one in front into the arms of the other one, and they both fell to the ground. I took out my pistol, but before I could fire Marcus stopped me.

"Don't waste your bullets," he said. "Let's keep moving."

We took off at a trot, winding around a couple of corners before we slowed to a walk again. The floorboards creaked under our feet, which wasn't good. We were bringing unwanted attention to ourselves with every step.

Suddenly Marcus stopped, held his hand up, and listened to the darkness ahead of us.

I stopped too, and listened.

Footsteps. They were coming closer, too. Marcus looked back at me and I nodded back.

"Can you tell how many?" I asked.

He shook his head. "More than one," he said.

"Okay, I'm ready when you are."

He rose from his crouch and moved out around the corner. Then he stopped and let out a frustrated sigh. I stepped around the corner to see what he was looking at, and when I saw it, I gasped.

The hallway opened up to a landing, and beyond that was a wide staircase that led out to a row of truck bays. One of the overhead doors had collapsed, and a huge crowd of zombies was pouring in through the hole. A narrow stripe of blue moonlight ran crossways through the room below, and a small group was crossing it and mounting the stairs.

They had already seen us. I could only see a short distance beyond the door where they were coming in, but the little bit of the alley that I could see was packed in tight with bodies. From the rate they were pouring into the building, I guessed that the first floor was already overrun.

"There are so many of them," I said.

"This is getting old real quick," Marcus answered. "We can't stay here. Let's double back and see if we can get around them."

"Right behind you."

We both backed away from the landing. I could hear more of them coming up the stairs, and while they didn't seem to climb very well, it was only a matter of time before there'd be enough of them to cause us problems.

We ran into a dark hallway off to our right because it looked like it went all the way back to the far side of the building.

We made it maybe fifty or sixty feet when we heard the floorboards creaking in front of us. Marcus stopped and knelt down, listening, trying to figure their direction from the sound.

"We're surrounded," I said.

"Start trying doors," Marcus suggested, his voice a barely audible whisper in the darkness.

When I found a door I told Marcus to stop so I could check it. I found the knob, cold and gritty with dust, and tried it.

It was frail, but the lock held.

"See if you can force it," Marcus whispered.

I tried putting pressure on it, and the door felt loose on its hinges, but it wouldn't open.

"It'll make too much noise," I whispered back.

"Okay," he said. "Keep moving. Maybe one of these doors will—"

I couldn't see what made him stop talking, but I felt him move violently away from the wall, and I heard him struggling with one of those things.

"Get that door open," he said, and even as he said it he ran at me and pushed me forward against the door.

I lost my balance. Marcus didn't wait for me, though. He hit the door with his shoulder, knocking it down.

Both of us went sprawling through the doorway and landed on a pile of broken wooden slats.

There was just enough light to see the shape of the room. The whole left side wall had been knocked out, and gave us a view of the first floor. The smallest hint of moonlight made it through the windows along the west wall of the warehouse, but it was enough for us to see that the first floor was a seething mass of zombies.

Straight ahead of us, the wall only went part of the way up to the ceiling. The top half was broken away, exposing a wide, flat crawlspace that stretched all the way across to the other side of the building.

"Through there," Marcus said, pointing at the crawl-space.

The crawlspace had just enough room for us to go through on our hands and knees, and it looked pretty unstable. But even as I stood there thinking about it, Marcus was shooting at zombies in the hallway.

"Go," he said. "Hurry it up."

He fired again and that got me moving. I climbed into the crawlspace and started moving across the boards.

The floor was uneven, and it felt weak. I could feel it give a little as I put all my weight on it. Raised wooden slats crisscrossed the floor and made going forward difficult. Each time I came to one, I had to steady myself on it and swing my legs over one at a time so that I could put my weight down slowly on the other side.

"Here they come," Marcus said, and when I turned to look back at him I saw zombies climbing into the crawlspace.

"Be careful," I said. "The floor feels weak here."

I was just over halfway across when I heard Marcus fire a shot. The hollow space made it sound like an explosion. I turned back and saw him on his back, firing his gun through his knees.

"Marcus."

He rolled his head over so he could face me. "What?"

"Cut it out. Just get across."

"There are only three of them. We get them and we don't have to rush."

"Don't be an idiot. Just come on."

I couldn't see his face clearly, but I know what kind of look he was giving me. He rolled over onto his stomach and propped himself up—and then we both heard the floor crack.

"Marcus," I said, but before I could say anything else

there was a loud popping noise, like an ice skin cracking. I felt the floor move.

I saw him look down at the floor beneath him, and then the whole thing gave way. He disappeared through the floor in a rush of snapping wood and flailing arms.

"Marcus," I said, and rushed towards the spot where he had just been.

There was a gaping hole in the floor, and I crawled right up to the edge and looked down. Marcus had landed on his back on top of a huge mound of rotten wood, and all around him was a narrowing ring of zombies, moving in to claim him.

"Marcus." Even as I yelled it I was firing down onto the heads of the zombies nearest him.

"Get up," I said. "Move, damn it. Move!"

And I fired and fired and fired until the slide locked back, but Marcus never moved. I saw him roll his head to one side and try to sit up, but in a moment they were on him. He kicked at them and tried to push them away, but they weighed down on top of him and tore into his body with their hands and teeth.

"Get out of here," he said to me, his voice breaking with the pain. "Go. Get out of here. Don't waste your bullets."

I screamed for him to move, but it was wasted breath. All I could do was watch as he died in that gurgling, violent mass of bodies. A little stream of white dust sifted down from my fingertips onto the scene like the barest hint of snow.

I closed my eyes.

The floor creaked again, and my eyes shot open. The zombies Marcus had shot at were still crawling towards me. I pointed my gun at them and pulled the trigger.

Nothing happened. The slide was still locked back and the chamber was empty. The trigger wouldn't fall.

I screamed at them to stop, but of course they wouldn't.

And then I heard the floor pop again. There was another pop, and another, and the floor shifted under me. It took my breath away.

"Oh shit. Oh shit. Oh shit."

I looked up at the zombies in pure, unadulterated panic, like I expected to see some sort of echo of my own fear in theirs. But they were oblivious. They kept coming.

"No," I said, pleading with them. "Stop. Stop."

But there was no use saying anything at all. It was like talking to a wall. They crawled on and nothing would have turned them back. They didn't notice the floor beneath them. I was the only thing they saw.

I inched my way backward on my elbows, crawling away on my belly at first, and then on my hands and knees as I got farther away from the hole. Every time the floor popped and cracked I felt another wave of panic wash over me.

There was a wooden slat on either side of me, and I held on to them, using them to pull myself along. Putting one hand over the next kept me focused on movement, and helped me think about not falling through the floor.

And then I did fall through.

The wood beneath me didn't even pop. It was there and then it wasn't. The next thing I knew my feet were dangling in the air, swinging back and forth, kicking for a foothold that wasn't there. I grabbed the beams on either side of me and squeezed my fingernails deep into the rotten wood. My grip was so tight that a sharp pain shot through my knuckles and into my wrists and arms. But I would not let go. I held on with all I had, willing myself to pull up. I heaved myself up, but couldn't get over the beams.

I couldn't move. All I could do was turn my head part of the way around, just enough to see two of the zombies crawling towards me. I yelled at them to stop, but of course they didn't. They kept coming, and all I could do was shout.

The floor lurched backwards. I felt it move, and caught myself with a start. I heard the floor pop behind me, and when I turned my head, I saw one of the zombies fall through the floor. I couldn't see the others. I turned my head the other way, and didn't see them there, either.

"Come on," I said, "pull up. Pull up."

Very slowly, and very painfully, I managed to haul myself over the edge of the hole. When at last I landed on the moldy floorboards of the crawlspace, I collapsed, shaking. My friend was dead, and I had almost died.

The realization hit me hard.

Thinking of Marcus, I started the process of pulling myself along the boards again. I was so caught up in my grief I didn't even realize I'd reached the other side. I rolled over the edge and landed on the floor of another office, never so relieved to feel solid ground beneath me.

I took in the darkness. There was a door on the opposite wall, and I figured there was another hallway beyond that. There would be more of those things waiting for me, too.

I checked the door. It was locked, but from my side. I turned the thumb catch and was about to turn the knob when I heard noises on the other side.

I put my head against the door and listened.

I could hear the muffled shuffle of feet on plank wood beyond the door.

Chapter 26

The first thing most cops do after they graduate from the Police Academy is go out and buy a fancy cop wallet so they can show off their badge.

My department makes us carry our badge and police ID on us at all times, and the local cop stores sell special wallets to hold it all. The one I bought has a cutout on the front part for the badge, and two see-through panels on the inside for both halves of the ID.

When Andrew was born, the hospital staff took a picture of him. In the picture, April has him across her chest and he's holding the smallest pair of red hands up against the light. His eyes are shut tight.

April hates the way she looks in it, but she had a special copy of it made for my birthday because she saw how much it meant to me.

As I sat there in that decayed hole of an office, my back against the wall, I took the picture out of my wallet and stared at Andrew's red, exhausted face. His mother was so flushed with relief and love for the baby in her arms that I could see the emotion shining through her skin. Seeing the two of them together like that made me smile in spite of everything else I was feeling.

Outside in the hallway I could hear more of those things shuffling around, and I wondered how many of them there were, and if they could sense me somehow. It still bothered me how they always seemed to find me. I told myself that if I ever saw Ken Stoler again I would ask him that very question. That is, right after I kicked his ass for stealing that truck.

One look around the room was enough to tell me that if they could sense me—and managed to get through the door—I'd be screwed. I only had six rounds left, and nowhere to hide.

I know it sounds strange, but even with the very real threat of ending up a shredded, bleeding piece of meat on the floor of some abandoned warehouse hanging over my head, the only thing I could wrap my mind around at that moment was Andrew's picture. And of all the memories I had accumulated from the six short months that he had been a part of my life, the one that came to mind was me feeding him a bottle at two in the morning, rocking him back and forth in an old glider chair until he cried himself back to sleep.

I thought about all the times he'd fallen asleep on my shoulder, and I wanted more than anything else in the world to be back there, holding him, patting his back to make him burp, and feeling the warm, soft wind of his breath against my neck.

In the darkness of that office, I was able to imagine myself back in that glider chair. I turned my head just slightly. I could almost see the bedroom where April and I slept. The image was part memory, part self-induced hallucination, and the moment I recognized it for what it was, it was gone. The spell was broken.

I knew right then that to stay in that room would get me killed, and there was no way in hell I was going to let that happen. More than anything, I wanted to live.

I stood up and leaned my head against the door, putting my mind in order for what I was about to do.

I turned the doorknob slowly until it clicked over. I took a deep breath and got ready to move.

And that's when the cell phone on my belt started ringing.

Chapter 27

I nearly jumped out of my boots. Fumbling at my belt, I grabbed the phone and flipped it open. So many things had happened in the last two hours, so many horrible things, that I had completely forgotten about it.

The caller ID screen showed April's cell phone number, and I realized that those two rings I heard at headquarters must have gotten through to her after all.

"Hello," I said. "April?"

"Eddie. Oh, my God. Eddie?"

"I'm here, April. Where are you?"

Static filled my ears. Through the white noise I could hear her voice, scared, yet still rational and in control. She said something about an apartment building and then I heard her say Andrew's name.

"April," I said. "April, I'm losing you."

More static. It roared in my ears.

I heard her voice again, and then all hell broke loose. A zombie slammed into the door from the other side, and the whole wall shook.

There was a pause, long enough for me to mouth the words, "Oh shit," and then the door burst open.

A burly, thick-armed zombie lumbered through the door, his mouth greasy with blood and caked with little pieces of cloth.

I backed up towards the crawlspace as I wrestled my gun out of the holster. He was almost on top of me before I got a shot off.

There were four more in the hallway moving towards me. A soft orange light was coming into the building through three windows along the left-hand wall, and in the muted light they looked like gray ghosts. They shambled toward me and I ran at them, twisting one way and then the other, dodging around each one in turn, and kept running all the way to the corner.

There were more hidden in the shadows, blocking me from a very narrow staircase. The one closest to me was looking the other way, and I grabbed his already-shredded shirt and used him as a shield as I pushed my way through the others.

I hit the top of the stairs and had to stop. There was a zombie about two thirds of the way up the stairs and it was too narrow to go around him.

I fired once and sent him sliding down the steps on his back.

It wasn't a clean head shot, but it was enough to buy me some time to jump over him and make it to the foot of the stairs. I landed hard and turned the corner, right into the open arms of a huge zombie.

He was a wall of meat.

He grabbed me with one arm and pushed me against the wall. I tried to squeeze by him but he bit down hard on my shoulder.

Luckily, all he got was a mouthful of the shoulder strap of my bulletproof vest.

We wrestled in a clumsy dance. I managed to get a hand under his chin and forced his head back. I brought my gun up with my other hand and shot him just above the ear. Gore went all over the wall behind him.

The zombie I had knocked down the stairs was getting up and there were others about to come down the stairs behind him.

I took off running through an open doorway, through another small and very narrow room with a time clock on the wall, and then through a door that led outside.

Breathing in the night air, I took stock of where I was. From what I could tell, I was on the opposite side of the building from the loading docks where Marcus and I had seen that huge crowd.

But the side I was on didn't look much better. There was a large crowd at both corners of the building.

I turned to my right and tried to flank most of them with the best sprint I could muster.

They grabbed at me, and tried to latch on. I could feel their hands on me, but I pushed and dodged and just plowed through until I broke out of the alleyway and onto a dark and broken street.

There was no street sign, no way to tell where I was. Downtown was burning off to my left, and I knew that was west of my position, but that wasn't much of a help. Even if the streets had been marked I wouldn't have known one from the other. They all looked the same to me.

I was completely lost.

I knew I had to find a car. Without that, I didn't stand a snowball's chance of making it home.

Halfway down the street I could see two zombies coming out of the shattered front doors of a convenience store. As I watched them cross the parking lot my breath formed thick clouds in front of me. I had been so wrapped up in the stress of escaping the warehouse and trying not to think about Marcus that I had forgotten how cold it was outside.

The two zombies were walking toward me, but they were still too far away for me to tell if they had seen me or not.

Another group of about seven or so was milling around in front of a small, two-story white-brick building about fifty yards away.

South of me there were several large Section 8 apartment buildings, and while I couldn't see any movement around them, I knew there would be more zombies there. North, south, and west were all closed to me.

Once again I was forced to go east, so I gathered myself up and started off at a trot.

There were zombies moving through the darkness on the other side of the empty lot not far from where I was. I saw a man against the white doors of a half-burned refrigerator, and then I saw more zombies coming out of the rubble near him.

With each passing moment their numbers grew, like ants coming up from a hive, until there were knots of them so thick in places they spanned the whole street.

I didn't even bother to pull my gun. There were so many of them it would have been futile to waste the ammunition.

I looked for a way out, and found it around the corner of a wrecked apartment building on the other side of the empty lot.

There were gaping holes in the walls, and when a small group of zombies moved towards me, they made a gap so that I could see all the way through the building. Beyond them it looked clear. I ran for the opening and came out on a wet, unlined street.

There was a drainage ditch at the end of the block and I ran there.

I ended up in the bushes at the base of the slope, knee deep in filthy brown water, with ropy vines laced with thorns biting into my face and arms.

But I didn't stop moving. I made the other side and scrambled up it on my hands and knees. I was covered in mud when I came over the other side, and as soon as I stopped moving, the cold returned with a bite.

A huge field of wet grass stretched out in front of me.

Off to my left I could see the firelight from downtown, and as it caught the water on the ground it made the grass sparkle like a sea of jewels.

The grass sloped gradually upward, and the crest of the hill was dominated by a line of dark elms. I walked up to the elms, hoping to stay under the cover of the trees while I went north, paralleling the drainage ditch; but what I saw instead was a road packed with a slowly shambling crowd of the infected.

I ran back into the elms and headed north.

A fast-mover came at me through the trees, moving just as fast as I was. I tried to change direction on him, but he was on me before I could get out of the way. He tried to tackle me, but I kept my feet and managed to push him down to his knees.

I lit him up with my pistol, but he was moving too fast for me to get a clean shot. My first shot hit him in the chin. My second and third shots grazed his cheek and ear. I used my last two bullets to put him down for good.

Then I ran through the trees until I hit pavement again. It was a small, unlined road, and on the other side of that was a small white church, dark at the windows and square as a country barn.

The zombies came out of the woods on both sides of it, and there were even more behind me. There weren't any more fast-movers, but there were a lot of the slow ones.

I was completely surrounded.

I was freezing too, wet all the way up to my waist. I looked for a hole to run through, but there wasn't one. I was trapped.

I holstered my weapon and pulled out my baton.

Slowly, deliberately, I searched the crowd for my first target.

"I love you, April," I whispered, and said a little prayer that it wasn't going to be my good-bye to her. "I love you, Andrew."

A zombie in a black shirt and ball cap closed on me. His teeth were slick with blood, poking through flaps of shredded skin where his lips had once been.

I drew the baton back and I was timing the stroke when the shot rang out.

The zombie slumped to the ground without a sound. There was a bullet hole in the side of his head that looked like a black flower.

I turned, stunned, toward the shot. Four black men with rifles were standing on the front steps of the church. One of them waved at me to hurry up, while the others sent a volley of bullets buzzing in the air around me.

Chapter 28

I ran for the porch, bullets whistling past my head.

The men on the porch were knocking down zombies all around me, giving me a clear shot right up to the door. I hit the steps at a full sprint and the man who was waving at me caught me and pulled me over to the door.

"I got him, Simon," he yelled to one of the other men. "Let's go."

A big guy in his early twenties was down on one knee at the leading edge of the porch, firing through the rails. He glanced back over his shoulder and gave me a hard look.

"There's too many of them out here to leave around," he said to the one who had grabbed me.

"I ain't staying out here," my guy said. "We got him, now let's go."

"Get going if you're going," the one named Simon said, and then he pointed at me with his chin. "Give the cop your gun if you're going."

The first man hesitated.

"Get going," Simon barked at him. "Hey cop, you know how to shoot one of those things?"

"Yeah," I said, and took the rifle from the first man. "I got it. How much ammo you got?"

"A whole damn church full," Simon said.

The first man hesitated, but I pushed him back gently towards the door and told him it was okay. "Are there more of you inside?" I asked.

He nodded.

"Go inside."

He slipped inside the church without a word. There was a green metal ammunition box on the porch behind where he had been standing, filled to the top with loaded magazines for the rifles.

I looked at the rifle in my hands and read Remington on the barrel. There was no shoulder harness and no scope, and the action still had clumps of packing grease at the corners.

I ejected the magazine, checked it, then stuffed it back in.

The others started firing. "Come on, damn it," Simon said to me. "Fucking help us out here."

I looked across the yard at the zombies closing in on us. The parking lot went right up to the front walk and then continued on around to the right side of the building. A white rail fence separated the parking lot from the road, and about a hundred feet or so beyond that was the line of black elms I had just run through. The zombies were coming in from all sides now.

"How many of them are there?" Simon asked me, his voice just a notch or two away from an animal's growl.

"A couple hundred at least," I said, taking a post to his left. "A lot more than this."

An older man standing off to Simon's right threw some magazines at my feet and then went back to firing. The three of them were unorganized. They shot at whatever crossed their path without thinking about maximizing their coverage, and a few of the zombies got in too close.

I walked down the length of the porch railing, firing at the ones who got through. I put four down in short order, and then made my back to the center where the three of them were firing.

I grabbed one of the men and pointed him toward the parking lot. "Focus on those over there," I said.

Then I grabbed the other guy and told him to get the ones coming from around back on the left side. Simon and I focused on the ones coming out of the elms.

Marcus once told me that I couldn't shoot my way out of a wet paper bag. He meant with a pistol. With a rifle, I was a completely different kind of shooter. I learned to shoot a rifle when I was a kid, deer hunting with Dad up in Minnesota, and it always felt like a perfect fit in my hands. Once I had the stock seated against my shoulder, it was a massacre.

I went through magazines in a hurry. The infected were falling all over the parking lot, and soon it was thick with their corpses. I even started knocking them down on the other side of the fence, while they were still out in the street.

The acrid smell of gun smoke filled up the porch, but still I kept on firing. I was hitting targets on both sides of the porch and didn't stop until the box of magazines was almost empty. I didn't even notice the others had stopped shooting.

When I finally stopped shooting, the yard and the street and the parking lot were stacked deep with bodies. A few zombies were still on their feet and moving slowly toward us, but the crowd had thinned down considerably.

"Get her," Simon said to the man at my left, pointing

at a young girl of maybe thirteen who was dragging her useless left leg toward the porch.

Simon loaded up another magazine and shot the last four zombies still walking the yard.

"Anybody got movement?" he asked, scanning the yard over the sights of his rifle.

"They's done on this side," said the man watching the parking lot.

"Over here, too," said the other man.

"Good." He swept a pile of brass off the porch with his toe. "You shoot real good," he said to me, but it wasn't exactly a compliment the way he said it. More like an accusation.

I could sense his hostility. The way he stared at me was more than just posturing. There was real hatred there. Not the kind of hatred one man has for another, but the kind of hatred men feel for symbols, for forces that control their lives and keep them down.

I watched his eyes, very much aware of the guns we all held and the unspoken something filling up the air around us.

I knew what he was doing. It was a gangbanger's game, to see if I would flinch. On the street, it's a way of establishing dominance. Once somebody makes eye contact, they hold it, and won't look away.

If you're a cop and you look away first, you're in trouble, because they know they own you.

I lowered my shoulders slightly and got ready for whatever was coming next. He stood square, trying to intimidate me. He was a good four inches taller than me, with a wide, flat nose and a couple of good-size gaps in his teeth. His flannel jacket made him look bulkier than he probably was, but I'd say he still had at least fifty pounds on me.

The other two men didn't get it. I knew what the stare meant, the rules of the game, but even I didn't know why we were doing it. Had he really bailed me out just to do this?

The moment dragged out uncomfortably, both of us waiting for the other to show some signs of weakness.

While we stood there, staring at each other, the church door opened, and I heard a very calm voice call out from the darkness, "It's time to come inside. Both of you."

Chapter 29

The door was open, but neither of us moved. We were still face-to-face, waiting for the other to flinch. I saw his eyes flick to my badge just for the thinnest fraction of a moment, and when our eyes met again, I could tell there was a lifetime of hate stored up there. That was the symbol he hated so much. I was every cop that had ever bullied him, made him feel small, fucked with him just for the hell of it.

"Simon," the voice from inside the church said. "Come inside."

Simon didn't want to leave. He wanted to put his hands around my neck and squeeze. But there was something that wouldn't let him do that, and I sensed it was that voice from the darkness.

At that point, I knew there wasn't going to be a fight, and Simon knew it too. He snorted at me like I was lucky and walked back inside the church.

The other two men followed Simon inside, leaving me alone on the threshold. It was dark inside the church, and all I could see were a lot of silhouettes standing between the pews.

Somebody coughed. Feet shuffled on the wooden floor. The voice said, "Officer, come inside please."

I took one last look at the yard full of dead bodies, remembering the last church I'd been in, and stepped inside. It was dark, but I could still see the faces closest to me. Simon was standing in the corner, giving me a smoldering, hateful look. The man who let me use his rifle was standing next to an older woman and two young children. The others stood in groups, watching me.

"Thank you," I said, not really knowing what else to say. "You people saved my life out there."

Simon said something under his breath and turned away.

"You're welcome," one of the other men said. It was the same voice I had heard through the doorway. "Come in. We don't have much here, but it's warm and dry, and you look like you've had quite a night."

A very distinct change came over the room when he spoke. The others made way for him, and even in the dark, I could see that he was their center, their leader.

We shook hands. His grip was powerful and confident, and I got a sense from just that handshake why the others looked up to him. He carried himself with natural, unassuming confidence, like one who always seems to be in charge, and accepts the responsibility as easily and with as much grace as another man might put on a coat.

I decided right away that I liked him. Simon had already made it clear that if it were up to him, I'd be a bleeding piece of hamburger out there in the elms, but this man was not that way. He welcomed me, and because these were his people, they welcomed me too.

I looked him over quickly while I shook his hand. He was an older black man, maybe five-seven or so, and about 150 pounds. He wore clean blue work pants with a sharp crease, a black belt, and a starched, light blue button-down shirt, fastened at the neck. His eyes danced with fiery intensity behind fragile, gold-rimmed glasses. His boots were brightly polished. I guessed he was in his sixties, with a good splash of gray at the temples, but it was hard to be sure because his body was thin and ropy with muscles.

"I'm Tiresias Maple," he said.

"Thank you, sir. I'm Eddie Hudson."

"Call me Tiresias," he said warmly. "Everybody here does."

"Are you the minister here, Tiresias?"

"No," he said. "No, unfortunately, the Reverend Joshua Jones died earlier this evening."

"Oh," I said, and then a long, uncomfortable moment followed. "I'm sorry."

"Please, don't be. You had no way of knowing. And besides, we're glad you're here. We've been inside since before nightfall and haven't heard anything about what's going on. The radio and TV have been off the air for a long time now."

I looked around at the others in the room. They were watching me expectantly, and I could tell they wanted good news. Better news than I could give them.

"It's bad out there," I said, because if I were in their shoes I'd want to know the truth. "There are fires burning all over the city, and the places that aren't burning are overrun with those zombie things."

"What about the army?" somebody asked.

"I don't know anything about the army. Maybe they've got troops on the way. I know we could use them. From what I can tell, most of the police officers and firefighters are dead. And I've heard this is happening all along the Gulf Coast, from Mexico to Miami. If that's true, other cities are probably hurting as bad as we are. That'll probably slow down the military response, too. They'll have to divide their resources over a huge area."

A woman in blue jeans and a black top asked me, "What about a safe area or something? Ain't somebody coming to get us?"

"I'm sorry," I said, "but what you see is what you get. I just came from Police Headquarters hoping to answer that very question, but it was overrun. If somebody had a plan, it's out the window now. There's no one left to take charge, and I haven't seen another police officer for hours."

"So what are we supposed to do?" somebody else asked.

"I don't know. Find a way to survive, I guess. From what little I've seen, you people are better off than almost everybody else." I looked around at their faces and tried not to think of the folks at the Lexington Baptist Church. These people didn't need to hear about that. "I guess you just hold what you got till something changes."

They turned quiet while they took all that in.

Tiresias finally broke the silence and said, "It looks like we'll be on our own for a good while still. The Lord helps those who help themselves, so it's time to help ourselves. I'd like everyone to continue fixing the damage and boarding the windows. When that's done, we'll begin the service."

The others went off, murmuring to each other about what I'd said.

"Officer Hudson," Tiresias said, "you're welcome here. There was another police officer here earlier. An Officer Gibbs. I'm sorry to say he's also passed on."

"Gibbs?" I had a classmate at the academy named Gibbs. A big, dumb guy who you couldn't help but love, even though, God help him, he could hardly tell if he was wearing his uniform frontward or backward. "Did you happen to catch his first name?"

"No, I'm sorry. He was in pretty bad shape when he came to us."

"What does it matter?" Simon said suddenly from the shadows. I hadn't noticed he was still standing there. "One cop's just like another. As long as he's dead, who cares?"

He came out of the shadows just enough for me to see his face, his eyes searching for a fight.

"Something you want to say to me?" I asked him.

"Tiresias, why are you gonna let him stay. After what that first cop done to us, how can you let this one stay?"

"That's enough, Simon."

"He don't care about us."

"I said, that's *enough.*"

Tiresias put a lot of emphasis on that last word, and it worked on Simon. He backed away, but the hate was still smoldering in his eyes.

Under different circumstances a look like that would have earned him a night in the jail, and probably a layover in the hospital too; but things had changed.

Tiresias told Simon to go and light the candles for the service.

"From now on," he said, "we worship in the light."

Simon slipped away without saying anything else, leaving me with Tiresias. I saw the blue spurt of a dozen matches, and soon the whole inside of the church began to glow with a yellow, flickering light.

I could see the others moving around inside, and some were even smiling. God help me, it was the first smile I had seen since before Marcus died, and it filled me with warmth.

"We've had the church blacked out since before nightfall," Tiresias said, and pointed to the boards on the windows. "Our thinking was that those persons out there are somehow attracted to light and sound. Anything that might indicate the presence of an uninfected person."

I nodded. "You're not worried about the light attracting them now?" I asked.

"Actually, I am," he said, taking off his glasses and breathing on them. He took a moment to polish them on his shirtsleeve, a gesture that reminded me more than a little of Ken Stoler. "But I think it's more important to give people the small signs they need that things will get better. These people have been through a lot, and they need something more than just huddling together in the dark."

"This is the service you talked about."

"Yes." He slipped his glasses back on. "I was hoping you would join us."

"I shouldn't," I said. "Ever since this started, I've been trying to make it back to my family. That's where I want to be."

"You're a young man, Officer Hudson. You must have a young family."

I nodded, and looked away. "I have a son. Andrew. He's six months old."

"That is young," Tiresias said, and to my surprise he chuckled. "I remember what that was like. I have two daughters myself. They're both grown."

"You must be worried about them."

"I am. One's in Dallas, the other in Atlanta. I'm very worried. I've said my prayers for them, though."

I had nowhere to go from there, nothing I could say to him. His problems weren't that different from my own, yet I didn't share his confidence. Prayers weren't enough for me. I needed to hold my child to put my mind at ease.

"You're welcome to stay," he said at last.

"Thank you," I said uncomfortably.

He took a moment to glance around the church. The inside was well lit, and the pews were filling up.

"I take it you're out of ammunition," he said

"I am," I said. He surprised me with that. "How'd you know?"

"I saw you holster your weapon earlier. I don't think you would have done something like that if you still had bullets left in your gun."

I nodded.

"That officer I told you about earlier," he said. "He was badly injured when he came to us. He was only able to fire a few shots before those people out there attacked him. His body is upstairs. Perhaps you'll stay for the service. Afterwards, you can take whatever ammunition you can find and then you can go to your family."

I didn't want to, but I realized it would be stupid to say no. He and his people had been good enough to take me in when I needed it most, and now they were giving me ammunition, too.

"Excellent," Tiresias said. "I'll start in just a moment."

"You? I thought you said you weren't the minister here."

"I'm not," he said. "I'm a bricklayer. Been doing it for more than fifty years. But I've been coming to this church for longer than that, and the folks here asked me to lead them in prayer after the Reverend Jones died. I had planned on waiting till morning to do that, but after what's happened, I think now is as good a time as any."

We shook hands again and I took a spot next to a pillar behind the last pew. My plan was to leave as soon as I could slip out and try not to be noticed. I figured the fewer questions they asked me, the easier it would be.

The place was alive with moving light. It made the place seem warmer, friendlier. People around me chatted with each other and exchanged greetings and it was almost surreal enough for me to think I had dreamed everything up to that point.

Almost.

The people milled around like Sunday morning until they saw Tiresias mount the pulpit.

Everyone took their seats.

That's when I slipped away. I stepped back into the shadows and made for the upstairs room near the front door, where Tiresias said I would find Gibbs's body.

I half expected every step to carry me over the edge of a cliff. It was like there was a big coiled snake moving slowly through my gut. I wanted to sit down and rest, to let the sick feeling inside me pass, but I knew I couldn't. I still had miles to go before that could happen.

I took the stairs slowly, one at a time, lugging my heavy, mud- and blood-stained boots up the steps like I was climbing a gallows, and from somewhere behind me, I could hear Tiresias leading the others in prayer.

Chapter 30

The upstairs room was really just a storage closet. They kept a few broken chairs and a cheap metal picnic table off in the corner, but the rest of it was empty.

Almost empty, anyway. There were eight corpses along the opposite wall beneath a blue window. The bodies were covered with white tablecloths and tied off with a small gauge rope.

They reminded me of the root balls of trees about to be planted.

There wasn't any sign of gore. There were no pools of congealed blood and no foul odors. It was all very clean and decent. The bodies were laid out on the floor, but it had been done with obvious respect.

Of course, Tiresias and his people had only been able to do so much to cover up the violence that had brought those bodies to that point. I saw a white hand and wrist, still wearing a watch and wedding ring, sticking out from under the sheet, like it was reaching for something.

I stopped in my tracks, waiting for the rest of the body to unfold itself and come after me. That didn't happen, though. The body was at rest.

Even still, there was something grotesque about the way that hand rested there, palm upwards on the floor, like it wanted something I couldn't give. I got the feeling from that mute gesture that it was reaching back for the life that had once moved it, even if that meant returning to this nightmare world of the necrosis virus.

It wanted even that.

I moved very slowly as I crossed the rest of the way to the bodies and worked back the sheets, one body at a time, until I found Gibbs's corpse. I pulled the sheet back far enough to uncover his gun belt, but I didn't want to look at his face. It made it easier, somehow, not to.

He had two full magazines in his belt pouch and I took them both. I slapped one in the gun, tucked the other into my belt, and then slid the sheet back over his body.

I kept meaning to turn around and go, but it was hard to look away. It was like watching the hands of a clock chase each other around the dial. Nothing ever seems to change, but all the while, something precious slips away.

I looked out the blue window at the unburied corpses in the parking lot, and I thought about what it all meant. The problem was so big, so incredibly vast.

I had a vision of myself standing in the middle of an immense, utterly featureless plain, the horizon impossibly distant in every direction. Wherever I turned there were miles and miles of nothingness. There was no sound, no taste, no reference of any kind. I was alone, and my questions had no answers. If I could have painted a picture of my personal hell, that featureless plain would have been it.

I heard footsteps.

They stopped somewhere behind me, and I turned to face them.

Simon was standing there, and he was holding a bat.

"What do you want?" I asked him.

He shrugged, but he made sure I saw the bat.

"Is that supposed to scare me? It doesn't, you know. After all, I'm not the one who brought a bat to a gun fight."

"You ain't gonna shoot me."

"You sound awfully sure of yourself."

"Yeah, well, I got good reason to sound sure of myself, because I'm gonna knock the fuck out of you if you take one step closer."

My pulse quickened, and my body tensed. This was familiar territory for me, the old game of who's got the biggest balls.

"What's wrong with you, Simon? Did somebody write you a ticket and hurt your feelings. Come on, fess up. I bet you've got warrants, don't you?"

"You think this is funny?"

"No, Simon, I don't. I think you're an asshole. That's about as far as I've taken it and that's about all I care to know. Now why don't you take your dumb ass downstairs before you get yourself hurt."

His eyes narrowed on me and I knew things were about to get really nasty.

When he took a step for me I drew my gun and pointed it right at his head. If he had been a little faster, he probably could have put the bat upside my head. But as it was, he stopped in his tracks.

My finger was twitching on the trigger, ready for him to make a move.

Wait for it, wait for it.

"Stop it. Both of you. Stop it."

It was Tiresias. He was behind Simon, standing at the top of the stairs. Simon didn't take his eyes off me. My gun didn't move.

"Simon," Tiresias said, his voice was softer the second time.

But neither one of us moved. Simon was fighting a battle with himself, and I watched it play out on his face. He desperately wanted to wrap that bat around my skull, but at the same time I knew Tiresias had a special power over him.

In the end, that power won out, and Simon let the business end of the bat fall to the floor with a thud.

Damn, that thing would have hurt.

"Simon," Tiresias said, gently, but very firmly. "Go downstairs."

Simon didn't say another word. He wrapped his fury up inside him and walked downstairs, leaving me with Tiresias.

When he was gone I said, "I wouldn't have shot him unless he made me."

Tiresias didn't say anything to that for a long moment. He took his small, gold-rimmed glasses out of his shirt pocket and slipped them on. In his powerful hands they looked like they might crumple.

He smiled at me and said, "I'm blind as a man can be without these things."

"I didn't start that," I said, pointing at the stairs. "I don't know what his problem is, but I didn't start it."

"He doesn't like the police."

"Was that it? Gosh, I couldn't tell."

"His feelings are misplaced, obviously, but tonight has been very hard on him."

"Yeah, well, it hasn't exactly been a cakewalk for me either."

"No, of course not. It's been hard on all of us. But it's been especially hard on Simon. He lost his mother tonight. She was a good woman, and a dear friend of mine."

"I'm sorry about that," I said. "But he acts like I'm the one who killed her. I never said a cross word to him before he tried to get me to fight on the porch."

"Things are rarely as simple as they ought to be," he said. "We carry so many things around inside us, so much baggage. Sometimes that baggage keeps us from changing when we need to."

"That may be," I said, "but it still doesn't answer why he hates me so much."

Tiresias paused over that for a moment. Finally, he said, "I brought Simon and his mother here as soon as I heard about what was happening. Simon's mother was a nurse. When the first wounded starting showing up here, she treated them as best she could. Your friend Officer Gibbs was one of those wounded. She worked on him for a long time, but in the end there was nothing she could do for him but let him slip into that coma-like state the infected have. At the time we still didn't understand what was happening with the people who did that. How they—came back. After he rose up he attacked her. That's how we lost her. Her body is over there with the others."

There was nothing I could say to that. It didn't make Simon any less of an asshole in my opinion, but at least it gave his hostility a context.

We stood there for a moment in silence before he said, "You must be eager to leave."

"Yes," I said.

"You said you have a six-month-old son, right?"

I nodded. "His name's Andrew."

"So young," he said, and whistled through his teeth. "Do you know where you'll meet your family?"

"I haven't got a clue. We didn't have time to make plans. I don't know how I'm going to find them. I've already been to my house once tonight, but they weren't there. Her car wasn't in the garage, so I guess they could be anywhere. I just don't know."

"And there's no place you can think of where she

might have gone? Your church maybe? Or another family's house?"

"No. It's just us."

"So where will you start looking for them?"

"You know, I don't have the foggiest idea. They could be anywhere. I suppose I'll go back to the house and start from there. Maybe they left me a note or something. Last time I was there I didn't really take the time to look around. First thing I need to do though is find a car."

He cracked a small smile. "I don't think you'll have a problem with that. You have friends, after all."

"I appreciate your optimism. But I think I've been kicked around a little too much tonight to share it. From where I'm standing, it looks like I'm going at it alone from here on out."

"That bothers you." It wasn't a question, just a dry observation.

"Don't you think that's enough?"

"Absolutely. Being alone is a terrifying thing. It's enough to scare any man, even one who is as equipped to take care of himself as a police officer."

I nodded uncomfortably. All I wanted to do was get out of there, find a car, and make my way back to my house.

I happened to glance back at the bodies and I noticed the hand still sticking out from underneath the sheet. Tiresias had said Gibbs was injured not too far away, and I figured that meant his patrol car had to be close by too.

"What about Gibbs's car?" I asked him. "Did you see where he left it?"

"Yes. But I'm afraid it won't be much use to you. When I found him he was climbing out of a culvert a few blocks over. His car was at the bottom of that culvert."

"Eddie," he said, and it startled me a little to hear him use my first name, "do you mind if I ask you a personal question?"

Here it comes. Leave the sermon early, the preacher grabs you by the ear later.

"No," I said warily. "Shoot."

"I've been thinking about everything I've seen tonight. Sitting in this church, there's not much else to do. Just sit and pray and think."

He walked over to the blue window and looked out, then ran his finger lightly across the sheet, respectfully, mindful of the heavy burden under it.

"So many people have died tonight," he said. "So many friends and strangers and people I'll never know. It boggles the mind. What I want to know, Eddie, is if you've tried to put some kind of value on it. Have you thought about what it means?"

His back was to me, which was good, for had he been looking at me he would have seen my mouth fall open. The man was in my head, saying the words that I had said to myself in the exact same spot where he was now standing. I was dumbfounded.

I thought about telling him about my vision, about the featureless land where answers had ceased to exist and that I had named my personal hell, but I held back. Somehow, I just couldn't put that in words.

Instead I simply said, "That's not an easy question to answer."

"No, it's not. But it occurs to me that those of us who live through tonight are going to have to try and put some kind of meaning to it. Those of us who live are going to be defined by this, changed by it in ways we can't even begin to imagine right now. You will have to raise a child in this new world. You have to put your thoughts in order. If not now, soon."

I thought about it, about putting my thoughts in

order, about what I might tell Andrew about this night, many years from now when he happened to ask what it was like, and it shamed me that I had nothing to say. There was a great big hole where the answer should have been. All I could think of was that I wasn't ready for something like this to happen, that it wasn't fair.

I had no idea how to put it all in one little neat package. The world had flipped upside down and left me hanging. There was absolutely nothing in my experience to prepare me for the new world Tiresias was talking about. Now that I was asked to articulate what I was feeling, all I could do was stammer around the issue.

"I don't have an answer for you, Tiresias. I just don't know what I think. I guess my gut reaction is that it just isn't fair. I saw one of the officers I used to work with die tonight. I watched him as he slipped into one of those things. He was a husband and a father, just like me. He loved his wife and his new baby as much as I love my family, and in the end, he couldn't even remember their names. He told me he didn't even remember what love felt like. That's the worst part of all this, I think. That's what really scares me about those things. It scares me that I could lose my mind that way. Die without any understanding. It makes me wonder what we did to deserve that kind of cruelty."

He nodded silently. I got ready for him to harangue me about God, and maybe give me the bit about Job and how we're just not equipped to understand the ways of God, but to my relief he simply turned and stared out the window.

When he turned back to me he said, "For me, tonight has been about salvation. For you, it seems to be about justice. We couch our thoughts in different language, but I think we're not too far off from each other. Justice and salvation, after all, are two sides of the same coin as far as God is concerned."

He turned and looked out the window again, and it seemed his mind was focusing on something that only he could see.

"I was standing here when I saw you come out of the trees," he said.

"I'm lucky you were there."

He tapped on the window thoughtfully. "You know, it occurs to me that the hardest part of the days and weeks and years to come is not going to be putting the conveniences of our old world back together, but reestablishing the bridges between those who survive. There's a lot of work ahead of us. A lot of community building."

"How do you mean?"

"I used to come home and watch the news. I would sit on my couch and stare at the TV and shake my head, wondering why we never seemed to get anywhere. Everything was the same. Always the same thing, night after night, year after year. I have the terrible feeling that what we're seeing out there is the failure of our community, that all of that death is simply the manifestation of our lack of place, a sense of who we are and what we mean to each other. Our cities have turned into a nightmare landscape of violence and apathy where personal responsibility is optional and our affection for one another withered to a ghost of its former self. I know as a police officer you have seen what I'm talking about. Perhaps you're better equipped than most to understand what I mean."

"People have always been that way though, haven't they? None of this is new, like you say. Isn't it man's nature to be self-serving and cruel. Brotherly love only goes so far as it's mutually advantageous."

"Nothing is impossible, Eddie." He said it with honest conviction, not irony. "People can change. Worlds can change. Christ's death destroyed a community, but his resurrection created a new world. Maybe that's our task. Have you thought about that? Have you considered that maybe this is the birth of a new world, that what happens next is a golden opportunity to change the nature of man in a fundamental way?"

"Those are brave words, Tiresias."

"New parents can't afford to be anything but brave, Eddie."

"You're right about that."

I stood there for a moment, ready to leave, but almost not wanting to.

"Do you have any idea where you'll go from here?"

"Not a clue," I said.

"You said you needed a car, right?"

"Yeah. I figured I would head east from here and try to find one in a traffic jam somewhere. That's worked for me once already."

"I think I can help you," he said. "Did you happen to see a maroon Pontiac in the parking lot when you were fighting on the porch?"

I shook my head.

Then he did something that completely floored me. He reached into his pocket and pulled out a set of car keys and put them in my hand. I stared at the keys, and then at him.

"I can't take your car, Tiresias."

"Yes, you can. I don't need it. The people you met downstairs, they are my family. That's where I'm going to start building my bridges. Now it's your turn to go home, start building the bridges from your end. Hopefully I'll meet you in the middle someplace."

His kindness shocked me like a punch in the gut. Had our positions been reversed, I'm sure I wouldn't have done the same thing for him, and it made me doubt if what he said was true. How many more people like me were out there? How many others had as far to go as I did?

His dream of building a world full of bridges was still a long way off—I knew that—but maybe it wasn't impossible either. Maybe it could be more than a pipe dream.

With the keys in my hand I walked down the stairs and out the front door of the church. I walked through a haze the whole way. If the others watched me leave, I wasn't aware of it. I wasn't even aware of the cold night air against my face as I walked across the parking lot, found Tiresias's car, and climbed inside.

Chapter 31

If there's any truth to that old saying that cleanliness is next to godliness, then Tiresias's '88 Pontiac Grand Am was the window to a godly soul.

I have been inside thousands of cars as a policeman, but never have I seen a car with 120,000 miles on it that looked as good as his did. There wasn't a speck of dust anywhere. No trash. No smell of stale smoke. No soda stains on the seats. It was perfectly clean.

I rubbed an appreciative hand across the dashboard and put it in gear. Gravel crunched beneath the tires as I pulled out of the parking lot. I tried hard not to run over any bodies.

I drove Tiresias's car through the cracked and broken streets of the east side, and for the longest time I saw nothing but blacked-out houses and moldering urban decay.

But even as I drove through those ruins, I felt my mind coming together, clearing. I still had a deep sense of urgency, a longing to get home that overpowered everything else I was feeling, but it was tempered now with the realization that things could make sense, that the world didn't have to stay upside down. It was only a sense. Still, the answers, the answer, eluded me. But I took comfort in the hope of an answer, for before, even that had seemed impossibly distant. Now that I was moving, distance didn't seem like such a massive obstacle.

I worked my way steadily northward from the church, and when I finally left the confines of the east side and turned onto a dark farm-to-market road that made a long loop all the way across the northern edge of San Antonio, I almost felt like I was floating.

Feeling better than I had all night I took the robbery detective's phone from my belt and tried April's cell again. The first time I just got static, but the second time it started to ring. I almost sensed that it would.

April picked up. "Eddie?" she said, her voice frayed around the edges. "Eddie, is that you?"

"It's me, sweetie. I'm coming home. I'm on the way there."

"Oh, thank God. Me too."

"Is Andrew okay?" I asked.

"He's crying. I'm taking him home to get the formula. He hasn't eaten all night."

"Okay," I said. "I'll meet you there."

"Eddie, don't hang up. Please."

"I'm not," I said. But we were speaking across oceans of static. "April, are you there? April."

More static, and then a moment of silence. I almost spoke her name again, but just then I heard her scream. It was a horrible, crippling sound.

"April," I said, my own voice cracking. "April!"

There was nothing left of the connection. I tried calling again and again and got nothing but static.

Panicked, I stomped on the gas and ran at top speed all the way back to my subdivision.

Because I was coming in from the east, I took the

Blackberry Lane entrance. I drove across the front lawn of somebody's house to get around a knot of traffic, and then I was rolling again.

From Blackberry I turned onto Rock Gate and started up towards my house. Once Rock Gate crosses Border Beacon it curves sharply to the right and starts a gradual uphill slope that continues all the way across the subdivision. Just around the curve, Rock Gate comes together with Starlight Crest, meeting at a forty-five-degree angle.

My plan was to go past Starlight Crest, turn onto Lullaby, and take that back to my house, but as I got into the intersection I saw a black SUV coming from my left.

At the same time I saw a car with only one headlight coming towards the intersection on the other side of Rock Gate. It was swerving drunkenly from one side of the street to the other, completely out of control. I stared at them both in turn, my mouth in the shape of an O. It had been hours since I'd seen another moving vehicle, and here were two of them. And they were on a collision course.

The black SUV and the car entered the intersection at the same time, and I cringed in anticipation of the impact.

There was an aching crunch of metal and breaking glass. The back end of the SUV popped up and slid sideways, its momentum sending it into a 150-foot-long neutral skid. Still going sideways, it bounced over a curb and into a lawn, where it crashed into a tree.

The car spun counterclockwise and ended up sideways in the intersection, its front end crumpled beyond recognition.

When I got to the intersection there was a fine yellow cloud of smoke and dust in the air and the car's horn was blaring continuously.

The SUV was nose down at the base of a tree, its back right tire still spinning uselessly in the air.

In the commotion it took me a second to register that the SUV was a Nissan Xterra.

I thought, *April.*

"April!" I yelled, and then, yelling her name over and over again, I jumped out of Tiresias's car and ran for her.

Chapter 32

I ran toward the car yelling April's name at the top of my lungs.

As I came up on the back end of the Xterra I heard the driver's side door open.

"April," I said.

I turned the corner to the driver's side and saw April standing there with my Springfield .45 in both hands, pointing it right at my face.

She fired as soon as she saw me and I heard the bullet whistle past my ear. I made a startled noise and jumped back behind the tailgate.

"April. What the hell?"

"Get away from my baby!" she said, shrieking it at the top of her lungs.

"April," I said. "April. It's me."

"Get away. Leave us alone!"

"April, sweetie, it's me. It's Eddie."

There was a really long pause before she finally said, "Eddie?"

"It's me, April. It's me." I didn't move from behind the car. "April, put the gun down, okay?"

"How do I know you're not one of those things?"

"Oh, for the love of Christ," I said under my breath. "You know it's me because we're having this freaking conversation."

"Don't yell at me."

"I'm not yelling." But then I caught myself and made my voice go as small and as nonthreatening as I could. "I'm not yelling. April, I know you're scared. I'm scared, too. Okay? But it's me. Eddie. Now please, April, put the gun down and let me show you."

I waited for her to speak. I could picture her there, her lips trembling, holding that huge gun in her shaking hands and fighting against her fear and every motherly instinct in her body to believe what she was hearing.

It didn't matter that she had almost killed me. The fact that she was willing to face down anything to protect our child made me so proud of her that I could have forgiven her anything at that moment.

"April?" I said quietly. From inside the car I could hear Andrew starting to cry. "April?"

"Eddie?"

"It's me."

I stood up slowly and inched over toward her side of the car. "April, I'm gonna step around the corner now, okay?"

"Okay."

Very slowly, I put my hand around the corner and waved it. When she didn't fire, I went farther, until I was completely around the corner, facing her. She stood there, shivering, tears running down her beautiful face, and so overcome by her emotion her whole mouth quivered with it.

I was looking straight down the barrel of the Springfield.

She looked me over, and her face gave way to recognition, and then to shock at the sight of me.

I didn't realize how bad I looked until just then. I was covered in mud and grime and God knows what else. I barely looked like her husband. No wonder she tried to shoot me.

Finally she said, "Oh, my God," and let the gun fall to her side.

"Are you guys okay?"

She covered her mouth with her hand, her body racking with convulsive sobs. "Eddie. Oh, my God, Eddie."

I reached out to pull her into my arms, but she put up her hand to stop me. Her eyes went huge, looking at something over my shoulder.

I turned and saw a woman climbing out of the car that had just hit her SUV. She had a nasty-looking wound on her arm that had to be from a bite, it was so torn up.

She stumbled sideways into the street, confused by the blaring horn and the dust in the air; but when she saw us, all the confusion vanished. Her lips pulled back, and she came for us with all the speed she could muster.

"Get Andrew," I told April. "We'll put him in my car."

April jumped into the backseat and worked the buckles on Andrew's car seat. While she was doing that, I was scanning the area, looking for trouble.

I found it in the next yard. Two zombies were lumbering into the street, headed our way, and a third was coming up fast behind them.

I fired twice, and both zombies went down. While April kept wrestling with Andrew's straps, I waited on the woman who had hit April's car. When she was in range, I dropped her with my best shot of the night.

"What's taking so long?"

"It's the straps," April said. "Something's stuck. The buckle won't come loose."

"Hurry, April," I said. The car horn and the gun shots were like a beacon for the zombies. I saw three more come out of a house across the street, and I could see more moving our way from down the street.

"You got it yet?" I yelled.

"No." Her hands were all over the car seat, trying to get Andrew out. Andrew picked up on the emotion and started screaming, not hurt, but very scared.

I shot the three zombies that had just entered the street and then jumped into the Xterra to help April. She was right. The straps were stuck somehow, and the buckle wouldn't give.

Out of the back window of the Xterra I could see more and more zombies. They were coming out of houses, between houses, out of everywhere at once.

A large, long group of twenty or so got between us and Tiresias's car, and I knew we were out of time.

"Here," I said, pushing April aside. "Let me get in there."

I put my foot on the seat next to Andrew's car seat and used all my weight to pull the strap toward me. When it finally let go I went tumbling backwards, into the front seat.

"Get him out," I said. But she was already doing that. She pulled him out of the seat and then we were standing in the front yard of a stranger's house, surrounded by a growing crowd.

I kept my breathing slow and under control. There was no way we could force our way through the crowd with Andrew in tow, and the only option was to stand and fight.

A woman in a white, floral nightgown was the closest. Most of her stomach had been eaten, and she walked hunched over so that the strands of skin that had once been her face dangled over her shoes like jelly fishing lures.

I closed the distance between us and put a bullet in her head. After that I burned through my two magazines in a hurry. Before I knew it, I had piles of corpses stacked up around the Xterra.

But for all my shooting, I didn't make a dent in their numbers.

I was facing April and Andrew when I fired my last bullet at a man who was wearing nothing but a ripped T-shirt. Poor Andrew's whole body flinched with the gun's report.

"We've got to get to my car," I said. "Where's the gun you had?"

"In the car."

I ran to the Xterra and rummaged through the front seat, but I couldn't find it. "Where?" I asked.

"It's there," she said.

I looked again, pushing Andrew's blanket and toys out of the way until I finally spotted it on the passenger-side floorboard.

I got control of the Springfield just in time to fire at a zombie a few feet from the car. When the bullet hit his forehead big chunks of the top of his head splattered onto the pebbled walkway behind him.

The Springfield was a serious weapon. It made the Glock look like a pellet gun in comparison. One shot was enough to make the zombie's head and feet trade places and send him tumbling into the grass behind him.

"Eddie!"

I jumped out of the Xterra, trying to find April in the crowd I had let get too close.

Three zombies had cornered her near a line of

bushes and she was slapping at them with her free hand, blocking Andrew from them with her body.

"Eddie!"

They towered over her, and as she turned to get away, one of the zombies managed to pull Andrew from her arms.

"Eddie!" she said, screaming it.

The zombie who had grabbed Andrew was an older woman in the process of losing her bathrobe. I hit her at a run, grabbing Andrew and yanking him away from her as I made contact.

The woman fell to the ground, but not before she swiped at Andrew's face. She missed, hitting him in the arm instead, and leaving a thin, two-inch-long cut on his bicep.

He yelped in pain.

"Fucking bitch," I said, and before she could get up I kicked her in the face with everything I had.

When I looked up April was nowhere to be seen. But there were zombies everywhere.

I backed up, and once I had a free lane through the crowd, ran for the street. From there, I could see April dodging for her life.

I yelled out to her, but I don't think she heard. The Springfield had five shots left, and I used them all. I shot my way through part of the crowd and ended up around the corner from where the accident had happened.

I still had Andrew in my arms, and he was holding on to my neck, screaming. The crowd followed us, surrounding us again.

The only weapon I had left was my baton, and I snapped it open with my free hand.

"You and me, buddy," I said to Andrew, and kissed his cheek. "You and me."

I tensed up, ready for the fight. I knew that I was

looking at the end, and I promised myself there'd be no escape without my son. I'd die before I gave him up, and if they took him from me anyway, then they could have me too.

"I love you, buddy," I said, and dug in.

That's when I heard a nasty series of thuds and the whine of a small-bore motor struggling to accelerate.

I watched in stunned silence as headlights momentarily backlit the crowd. A few turned to face the light, only to be mowed down by the front end of Tiresias's car.

The car careened through the crowd and went sideways into a skid that stopped barely ten feet from me.

April threw the door open.

"Hurry," she said, and I did.

I pushed my way into the car and we were rolling before I could even close the door.

"Are you okay?" she asked.

"Yeah, you?"

She nodded. "How is he?"

"One of them scratched him," I said.

"Oh, my God. Where?"

I showed her.

"Do you think—"

"I don't know," I said.

Chapter 33

Looking out the passenger window, I watched the houses of our neighborhood slip past like snapshots of a lost world. Some of the neighborhood seemed so peaceful, so normal, it was hard to believe anything had happened.

Other parts were less so.

A white-haired woman in a green dress was on her knees at the corner of our street, eating someone's arm. I closed my eyes.

Wrecked cars were everywhere. Wrecked people, too. Here and there they drifted into the street, watching us drive by with dead, empty eyes.

Andrew was in my arms, and I could smell him. Nothing intoxicates like the smell of your own baby. I pulled him close. His crying had given way to sobs and then to an unhappy silence. He was cold, wet, and hungry, but he sat still in my lap.

The cut on his arm filled the car with an uneasy silence. April and I both looked at it, and we both worried. I remembered Ken Stoler and Dr. Stiles both saying that the necrosis virus was transmitted through bodily fluids, or at least they believed that was how it was transmitted, and I prayed that none had passed to Andrew. Maybe a scratch could be just a scratch.

"Do you think it'll be okay?" April asked as she pulled up to the front of our house.

"I hope so," I said. But I didn't know.

There were zombies milling our way from both ends of the block. "We need to hurry, April. Let's get him inside and clean it. Then we'll go somewhere."

"Where?"

"I don't know. Somewhere out of the city."

We hurried inside. April stopped right inside the front door and cupped a hand over her mouth.

"Oh, my God."

"I know," I said, looking at the dead bodies I'd left spread throughout our home. "I was here earlier. Don't worry. I'll clean it."

April went to work on Andrew. She cleaned the wound half a dozen times at least, scrubbing it even though he screamed in protest, then changed him and got a couple of extra clothes for him to wear.

Meanwhile, I loaded up the formula, bottles, and bottled water. While we worked, April told me about her night.

"Right after you called that first time," she said, "I went around locking doors and windows. I had your guns with me, and Andrew and I were sitting on the couch. And then Mr. Cowper from across the street started banging on the door. I know I shouldn't have, but he looked normal, and he was looking right at me, through the window. I opened the door, and, oh, my God."

"What?"

"Part of his stomach was gone!" She said, and tried to choke the tears back. She tried to tell me again, but couldn't. All she could do was bend down and kiss

Andrew on his forehead and let the tears fall on his face.

"What did you do?" I asked.

It took her a moment, but she stood up straight, composed herself, and said, "I shot him."

Our eyes met, and I loved her more at that moment than ever before. She was strong. She was brave. She was beautiful in her contradictions, so gentle and loving with our child, so fiercely unrepentant in protecting him.

"Where did you guys go?"

"We went to Franklin Street after that. You know those new apartments they're building? We parked back there, up along the tree line. I listened to the radio until the stations went off the air. And then, after you called the second time, I kept trying to call you back. It must have taken two hours to get through."

I nodded. "Is he ready to go?"

"Yeah."

"Okay," I said. "Let me go see if it's safe. I don't have any more bullets, so we'll have to be quick."

She looked confused. "You're not going to take the shotgun?"

"You have it?" I asked.

"It's right there." She pointed to the couch. The shotgun was right there, between the pillows.

"Outstanding," I said.

I grabbed it, broke open the breach and checked the shells, and then we were off, rolling away from the curb before any of the zombies that had seen us drive up were close enough to be a threat.

"Where do you want to go?" she asked.

"Out of the city," I said. "Somewhere where it can be just us."

She knew the perfect place. She didn't tell me where, but she didn't have to. I could tell as we entered the Hill Country we were headed for the Roundtop Bed-and-Breakfast, where the two of us had spent our first night as husband and wife.

The place was empty.

It was a small, German-style frontier two-story with a view of miles and miles of cedar and oak trees. We found a room with a southern exposure, changed Andrew's diaper again, and put him down to sleep.

We watched him drift off to sleep and kept watching him for a long time after that.

Later, we stood arm in arm, staring out the windows that were painted by distant, wind-whipped fires, and watched the city burn. When morning came, a shimmering blood-red cloud loomed over the skyline like a brooding eye.

"Don't go back out there," she said, looking up at me with eyes as deep as the sea. "Please."

"I'm not going anywhere," I said, and squeezed her close.

Chapter 34

Six weeks later, I was back in a police car, looking down on a winding ribbon of road leading up the hillside to where I was working an overtime job. Road crews had been working around the clock to clean up debris from that night, and the ones I had been hired to protect were clearing abandoned cars off the roadway, using bulldozers to push them onto transports that hauled them away to someplace.

The bulldozers were silent now, and the road crews were enjoying a late-morning break.

I got out of the car and sat on the hood so I could see everything going on below me. A giant buzzard found a roost on top of a light pole not far away.

It was one of those glorious winter mornings, where everything seems touched by perfection. The sky was a vaulted ceiling of absolute blue. There were no clouds. From one horizon to the other, there was nothing to disturb the velvet of its touch. The Earth was bathed in a blue so startlingly cold and rich and immaculately clean that when I removed my sunglasses and felt the dry breeze of morning on my skin, I realized I was

whole, for the first time in a very long while. There had
been a housekeeping in my soul, and I felt like I was living the first well day after a very long sickness. I could
breathe again.

I watched the buzzard spread his massive black wings
and hold them open so the sun could warm his body.

"Me too," I whispered.

The weeks following the outbreak were the hardest
I've ever known. None of the days compared to the
frantic rush and desperate searching of that first night,
but they were hard nonetheless. It was the endless
readiness, the constant tension and expectation that
something bad was about to happen. It didn't take long
for exhaustion to set in, and when you passed people in
the street, or sat next to them at roll call briefings, you
could see that beaten-down look in their eyes.

April begged me not to go back to work. She said we
could go up into the mountains and disappear. The
military had succeeded in containing the outbreak to
the Gulf Coast states, she said. No one would ever need
to see us again if we went to the mountains of Montana.
She said the city was no place to trust with a child.

I think the thing that finally convinced her I should
go back to work was that there were no reports of rioting. It was an environment ripe for explosion, and yet
not one person put a match to the fuse. The outbreak
had left a weird sort of calm in its wake. April saw that
calm, and a glimmer of hope returned to her mind.

It helped too that Andrew made a full recovery.
Nothing remained of that night for him but a faint little
scar. Our worries that he might be infected never
amounted to more than sleepless nights.

In the end, she let me go back.

On my way to work that morning I stopped and
bought the local paper. It was the first issue since the
outbreak, and I had been eager to dive into it. I was

hungry for information—real information, not the stuff we had been living on from the word-of-mouth grapevine—and I skimmed the paper ravenously.

Most of what it said was a repeat of what I had already heard in briefings and from other people, but there were still some statistics there that I hadn't heard.

San Antonio had been a city of 1,200,000 people before that night, and now the best estimates put the population somewhere around 300,000. More than three fourths of the city had died.

And my department got hit hard. We went into the outbreak with just over 2,200 officers, and now there were less than 200 of us left.

The highest-ranking officer to make it through the outbreak was a lieutenant from Fiscal Services, and the only reason he made it through was because he was out on a fishing boat in Canyon Lake with his two teenage sons.

When he got back he found himself brevetted to chief.

After the fires were put out, the long, unbelievably complex task of putting the world back on it rails began. There were official meetings held in city hall and unofficial street meetings held in churches and out in the front lawns of people's homes. And slowly, the rubble started to clear.

People were organized. A census was taken. Power was turned on. All the pieces of the puzzle were turned around and studied and gradually a new picture began to emerge.

There was a massive, unspoken tide of emotion swelling up in everyone, a belief that this time around, we could do it right.

But while everyone believed we could make it better than it had been, not everyone agreed on how that should be done. The most vocal voice of them all was Ken Stoler.

Ken had lived through the night, and in the weeks following the outbreak, he had become a staunch advocate for the infected. He had an article in the paper, laying out his plan for containing the zombies, studying the necrosis virus, and finding a cure. His driving belief was that we, the uninfected, were obliged to save the infected from themselves. He even founded an organization to further that agenda. He called it People for the Ethical Treatment of Zombies, or PETZ.

Early on, his organization scored a major victory and got a court order prohibiting the military and the police from shooting the infected unless it was in self-defense or defense of a third party. It was a major headache for me and my fellow officers, and I'd be lying if I said we obeyed the injunction completely. Things happen in the fog of war. Especially in strange wars.

I didn't need to read Ken's article to know what it said. I had heard it all firsthand while I was working security at one of the numerous public meetings following the outbreak. Ken delivered his speech to an angry crowd, and I had to escort him off the stage.

When I got him to safety he turned to me and said, "Thanks, Eddie." He held out his hand. "No hard feelings?"

I punched him in the nose. "That's for stealing my truck, you asshole," I said, and left him sitting on his butt, staring up at me like a pouting child.

I closed my eyes and then slowly opened them. The city skyline was visible off in the distance, and my thoughts wandered back to Tiresias. He was out there somewhere, alive no doubt, and still waiting for me to make the connections, to build the bridges he had first extended to me. I was a long way from that, still, but I could feel the changes brewing inside of me.

I read on, going from one article to another, reading about adventures that weren't much different from my own. But I didn't get the enjoyment from the paper that I thought I was going to get.

In the end, I gently folded it up and tossed it back into the car. I didn't feel like reading anymore. There was no sense in stirring everything up again, I thought.

And besides, it's hard to read the paper when so many of your friends are dead.

But then I saw them. April and Andrew were coming up the road toward the first security gate. I radioed down and told the policeman there to let her through. Suddenly all the hard feelings washed away, and as I watched them drive up the hill, I felt good again.

April opened the car doors and got Andrew out. She pointed me out to him and tried to get him to wave to Daddy. I didn't get a wave, but his eyes lit up.

I walked toward them, and in that moment, my part of the world made sense. Andrew smiled at me, and I realized that the answer to everything, the one landmark on the featureless plain that was my private hell, was the smile on my baby's face.

Turn the page for an exciting preview of
Joe McKinney's terrifying follow-up to

DEAD CITY . . .

The dead are rising . . . and this time it's a worldwide
plague of ravenous flesh-eaters!

APOCALYPSE OF THE DEAD
by Joe McKinney

"A rising star on the horror scene."   —Fearnet.com

APOCALYPSE OF THE DEAD

Available November 2010

Wherever Pinnacle Books are sold

They asked him, then, whether to live or die was a matter of his own sovereign will and pleasure. He answered, certainly. In a word, it was Queequeg's conceit, that if a man made up his mind to live, mere sickness could not kill him: nothing but a whale, or a gale, or some violent, ungovernable, unintelligent destroyer of that sort.

—Herman Melville

Chapter 1

Down there in the ruins it was low tide. Galveston Bay had receded, leaving the wreckage of South Houston's refineries and trailer parks up to their waists in black water. Moving over the destruction at eight hundred feet in a Schweizer 300, the thropping of the helicopter's rotors echoing in his ears, Michael Barnes scanned the flooded ruins for movement. The Schweizer was little more than a pair of lawn chairs strapped to an engine, but its wide-open bubble cockpit offered an unobstructed view of what had been, before Hurricane Mardel ripped the skin off the city, a vast cluster of tankers and docks and refineries and arterial bayous, the breadbasket of America's domestic oil and gas industry. Now the world below Michael Barnes's helicopter looked like a junkyard that had tumbled down a staircase.

Flying over the flooded city, Barnes remembered what it was like after the storm, all those bodies floating in the streets, how they had bloated and baked in the sun. He remembered the chemical fires from the South Houston refineries turning the sky an angry red. A green, iridescent chemical scum had coated the flood-waters, making it shimmer like it was alive. That mixture of rotting flesh and chemicals had produced a stench that even now had the power to raise the bile in his throat.

What he didn't know—what nobody knew, at the time—was the awful alchemy that was taking place beneath the floodwaters, where a new virus was forming, one capable of turning the living into something that was neither living nor dead, but somewhere in between.

Before the storm, Barnes had been a helicopter pilot for the Houston Police Department. Grounded by the weather, he'd been temporarily reassigned to East Houston, down around the Galena Park area, where the seasonal floods were traditionally the worst. The morning after the storm, he'd climbed into a bass boat with four other officers and started looking for survivors.

Everywhere he looked, people moved and acted like they'd suddenly been transported to the face of the moon. Their clothes were torn to rags, their faces glazed over with exhaustion and confusion. Barnes and his men didn't recognize the first zombies they encountered, because they looked like everybody else. They moved like drunks. They waded through the trash-strewn water, stumbling toward the rescue boats, their hands outstretched like they were begging to be pulled aboard.

The city turned into a slaughterhouse. Cops, fire-fighters, National Guardsmen, and Red Cross volunteers went in thinking they'd be saving lives but emerged as zombies, spreading the infection throughout the city. Barnes considered himself lucky to have escaped. When the military sealed off the Gulf Coast, they'd trapped hundreds of thousands of uninfected people inside the wall with the zombies. Barnes emerged with his life and his freedom; nearly two million weren't so lucky.

And with the rest of America in an unstoppable economic nosedive after the death of its domestic oil, gas, and chemical industries, he considered himself lucky to get a job with the newly formed Quarantine Authority, a branch of the Office of Homeland Security that was assigned to protect the wall that stood between the infected and the rest of the world.

But all that was two years ago. It felt like another lifetime.

Today, his job was a routine sweep with the Coast Guard. Earlier that morning, a surveillance plane had spotted a small group of survivors—known as Unincorporated Civilian Casualties by the politicians in Washington, but simply as "uncles" by the flyboys in the Quarantine Authority—working to wrest a wrecked shrimp boat loose from a tangle of cables and nets and overgrown vegetation. Most of the boats left in the Houston Ship Channel were half-sunken wrecks. And what hadn't sunk was hopelessly, intractably mired in muck and garbage. There was no chance at all that a handful of uncles could get a boat loose from all that mess and make a run for it. And even if they could, they'd never be able to beat the blockade of Coast Guard cutters waiting just off shore. They'd be blasted out of the water before they lost sight of land. But the Quarantine Authority's mission was to make sure nobody escaped from the zone, and so the order had gone out, as it had numerous times before, to mobilize and neutralize as necessary.

Now, along with three other pilots from the Quarantine Authority, Barnes was slowly moving south toward the Houston Ship Channel. Once there, they'd rendezvous with the boys from the Coast Guard's Helicopter Interdiction Tactical Squadron, known as HITRON, and act as forward observers while the H-Boys took care of any survivors who might be trying to escape to the Gulf of Mexico.

"Good Gawd, would you look at them?" said Ernie Faulks, one of the Quarantine Authority pilots off to Barnes's right. In the old days, Faulks had made his living flying helicopters back and forth from the oil rigs just offshore. He was an irredeemable redneck, but cool under pressure, especially in bad weather.

Barnes glanced up from the ruins below and saw a string of seven orange-and-white Coast Guard helicopters closing on their position. Even from a distance, Barnes could pick out the silhouettes of the HH-60 Jayhawks and the HH-65 Dolphins.

"You know what those babies are?" said Paul Hartle, a former HPD pilot and Barnes's preferred flanker. "Those are chariots of the gods, my friend. Ain't a helicopter made that can hold a candle to those bad boys."

"I'd love to fly one of them things," answered Faulks. "I bet they're faster than your sister, Hartle. Sure are prettier."

"Fuck you, Faulks."

Faulks made kissy noises at him.

"All right guys, kill the chatter," Barnes said.

Technically, he was supposed to write up the guys when they cussed on the radio, but he let it slide. A little friendly kidding was good for morale. And besides, as pilots, Barnes and the others were seen as hotshots within the Quarantine Authority. They were held to different standards, given special privileges, looked up to by the common guys on the wall. Being pilots, they had to do more, take bigger risks. It was why all these guys loved flying, why they kept coming back.

But in every profession there is a hierarchy, and while Barnes and his fellow Quarantine Authority pilots had a firm grip on the upper rungs of the status ladder, the very top rung was owned by the H-Boys from the Coast Guard's HITRON Squadron. Originally created to stop drug runners in high-speed cigarette boats off the Florida coast, the H-Boys now did double duty patrolling the quarantine zone's coastline. They flew the finest helicopters in the military, and their gun crews had enough ordnance at their disposal to turn anything on the water into splinters and chum. The pilots in the Quarantine Authority worshiped them, wanted to be them when they grew up. It was the Quarantine Authority Air Corp, in fact, that had come up with the H-Boys' nickname.

"Papa Bear calling Quarter Four-One."

Quarter Four-One was Barnes's call sign. Papa Bear was Coast Guard Captain Frank Hays on board the P-3 Orion that was circling overhead.

"Quarter Four-One, go ahead, sir."

"I'd like to welcome you and your men to the show, Officer Barnes. Now, all elements, stand by to Susie, Susie, Susie."

"Mama Bear Six-One, roger Susie."

Barnes scanned the line of orange-and-white helicopters until he saw one to the far right dipping its rotors side to side. That was Mama Bear, Lt. Commander Wayne Evans, the senior officer in the squadron and the quarterback for this mission. Once the sweep got under way, he would be the link between the individual helicopters and Papa Bear up in the P-3 Orion. Barnes had worked with Evans before and knew the man had a talent for keeping a cool head and an even cooler tone of voice on the radio when things got sticky.

"This is Echo Four-Three, roger Susie."

"Delta One-Six, roger Susie."

"This is Bravo Two-Five, roger Susie."

The pattern continued down the line of Coast Guard helicopters, each one answering up with their call sign and the code word "Susie," which was the signal for the sweep to begin.

When they'd all answered up, Mama Bear said, "Quarter Four-One, you and your men drop to three hundred feet and recon the quadrants north of here. Sound off if you spot any uncles."

"Yes, sir," Barnes answered.

He gave the orders for his team to drop altitude and spread out over the area. They had done this many times before and they all knew the drill. And they all knew that the order to sound off if they spotted any uncles was superfluous. The HITRON boys had the finest heat-sensing equipment in the world. Their cameras would spot any bodies down there long before Barnes and his men could. What Barnes and the others were expected to do was identify whether or not the bodies spotted were uncles or zombies. The HITRON boys would only get involved if they had uncles.

But telling the difference under the current conditions wasn't going to be easy. They had maybe thirty minutes of usable daylight left, and there was a spreading shadow over the ruins that gave everything, even at three hundred feet, a monochromatic grayness.

Barnes recognized the ghostly outlines of Sheldon Road beneath the water. Its length was dotted with tanker trucks and pickups that, even at low tide, were a good five or six feet beneath the surface. He looked east, across a long line of metal-roofed warehouses that shimmered with the reddish-bronze glare of sunset. From frequent flyovers, Barnes knew that at low tide the water was only about two or three feet deep on the opposite side of those warehouses. If they were going to find uncles, that's where they'd be.

Within moments his instincts proved true. Boats and cranes and even a few larger tankers had been spread by the tides across the flooded swamp that had once been a huge tract of mobile homes. In and among the debris and stands of marsh grass he spotted a large number of people threading their way toward three medium-sized shrimp boats waiting just offshore. One of them already had its engines going. Barnes could see puffs of black smoke roiling up from beneath the waterline.

Several faces turned up to track his movement over their location. He felt like he could see the desperation in their expressions, and he turned away. He didn't like doing this, but it was necessary.

"Quarter Four-One, I've got uncles east of the warehouses."

There was a pause before Mama Bear answered up. "Quarter Four-One, roger that. You sure they're uncles?"

Barnes could hear the indignation in the man's voice. Though they were all on the same team, the H-Boys knew they were the all-stars. Barnes was sure the man was cussing to himself that a Quarantine Authority pilot in a Schweizer POS had spotted their objective before his boys did.

Barnes enjoyed making his reply. "Oh, I'm sure, Mama Bear. I estimate between forty and sixty uncles. Looks like they've got themselves three shrimp boats, too."

There was a pause. *Must be on the private line to Papa Bear*, Barnes thought.

Finally, Mama Bear answered. "Roger that, Quarter Four-One. Go ahead and give 'em Mona."

Come again, thought Barnes.

"Uh, Quarter Four-One, I didn't copy. You said to give 'em Mona?"

"Roger."

"Mama Bear, did you copy they got three shrimp boats in the water?"

"Roger your three shrimp boats, Quarter Four-One. Echo Four-Three and Delta One-Six will fall in behind in case you need assistance. Now give 'em Mona."

Give 'em Mona was the strategy most commonly employed by Quarantine Authority personnel when they spotted uncles trying to breach the wall. The expression came from the amplified zombie moans the Quarantine Authority personnel played over their PA systems. The moans carried for tremendous distances, attracting any zombies that might be in the area. Usually, the moans were enough to send the uncles into hiding.

But this isn't a bunch of uncles throwing rocks at troops up on the wall, Barnes thought. *Those people are a viable threat. They have boats. They have boats in the water, for Christ's sake. You guys are underestimating the situation.*

Barnes reached forward to the control panel in front of the passenger seat and flipped the PA system power switch. Instantly, the air filled with a low, mournful moan that Barnes could feel in his chest and his gut.

He hated hearing that noise. He squeezed his eyes shut and tried to block out the images of bodies festooned in the branches of fallen pecan trees, of people screaming for help in flooded attics, of his brother Jack getting pulled under the water by a nest of zombies they'd wandered into when they were less than two miles from safety. But it was no use. Sometimes the images were too powerful, too vivid, and when he opened his eyes, he had tears running down his face.

Barnes didn't even hear the first shots. He heard a loud plunking sound, like a rock dropping into water next to his ear, and when he looked over his shoulder, he saw a bullet hole in the fuselage.

Missed my head by six inches, he realized.

He heard another sound below him. Glancing down, he saw what appeared to be a faint laser beam between his shins. The bullet had pierced the lower section of the fuselage and entered the supports right below his seat. He had daylight pouring through the bullet hole.

"Quarter Four-One, they got a shooter on the ground!" Barnes heard the panic in his voice but couldn't fight it.

"Take it easy," Mama Bear answered.

More shots from below. Barnes could see the man doing the shooting, the bursts of white-orange light erupting from the muzzle of what appeared to be an AK-47.

"I'm hit," Barnes said.

Instinctively, he pulled back on the stick and started to climb. He couldn't see the Coast Guard Jayhawk that had moved into position above and behind him, but he heard the pilot's angry shouts as he turned his aircraft to one side, narrowly avoiding the collision.

"Goddamn it, watch yourself, Quarter Four-One!" the pilot said.

Barnes's Adam's apple pumped up and down in his throat as he fought to get himself back under control. He scanned the airspace around him, then made a quick instrument check. Everything appeared to be holding steady.

Out of the corner of his eye, Barnes saw the Coast Guard Jayhawk rotate into position over the uncles below. Barnes could see several uncles shooting now, while farther off, people were jumping into the water and trying to climb aboard the shrimp boats.

"Kill that Mona, Quarter Four-One," shouted one of the H-Boy pilots.

"Roger," Barnes answered.

He leaned forward and killed the PA switch. But as he did, he saw a flash of movement that grabbed his attention. A man was kneeling in the shadows between a wrecked fishing boat and what appeared to be the rusted-out pilothouse from a tugboat. He had a long, skinny metal tube over his shoulder and he appeared to be zeroing in on the Jayhawk to Barnes's right.

Barnes recognized it as an RPG and thought, *Where in the hell did the uncles get an RPG? That's impossible. Isn't it?*

Barnes glanced to his right and saw that the Jayhawk had rotated away from the shooters so that its gun crews could bring their 7.62-mm machine guns to bear on the targets.

"That guy's got an RPG," Barnes heard himself say. "Heads-up, Delta One-Six. That guy's got an RPG. Clear out. Repeat, clear out!"

"Where?" the other pilot asked. "Where? What's he standing next to?"

"Right there!" Barnes shouted futilely. He was pointing at the man, unable to find the words to describe his position amid all the rubble. It all looked the same.

"Where, damn it?"

But by then the man had fired. Barnes watched in horror as the rocket snaked up from the ground and slammed into the back of the Jayhawk, just forward of the rear rotor. The Jayhawk shuddered, like a man carrying a heavy pack that had shifted suddenly, and then the helicopter started spewing thick black smoke.

"Delta One-Six, I'm hit!"

"Fucker has an RPG!" shouted the other H-Boy pilot. He was moving his Jayhawk higher and orbiting counterclockwise to put his gun crews in position.

"Delta One-Six, she's not responding."

"Come on, Coleman," said the other Jayhawk pilot. "Pull your PCLs off-line."

"I'm losing it!"

Delta One-Six made two full rotations, wrapping itself in a black haze as it drifted toward a partially capsized superfreighter. As Barnes watched, the Jayhawk clipped the very top of the superstructure and hitched forward toward the ground in a dive. One of its gunners was holding on to his machine gun with one hand, the rest of him hanging out the door like a windsock in a stiff breeze. The pilot tried to level off the aircraft right before they hit, but only managed to snap the helicopter's spine on impact.

A moment later, a thin plume of black smoke rose up from the wreck.

Then the radio exploded with activity. "He's down, Echo Four-Three. Delta One-Six is down."

"Get him some help over there. You got one moving!"

It was true. Barnes saw the pilot stumble out of the cockpit, his white helmet smoking. The man threw his helmet off, and he fell into the water. When he bobbed back up to the surface he was holding a pistol in his hand.

"Oh, shit, Echo Four-Three, we got problems. I got infected moving into the area."

"What direction?" asked Mama Bear.

"From the ten. I got a visual on thirteen of them."

"Uh, Mama Bear," said Faulks. "Ya'll got a whole lot more than that. I got a visual on about forty or fifty over here at your two o'clock."

"You want me to go down and extract your man?" Barnes asked.

"Negative, Quarter Four-One," Mama Bear said. "Echo Three-Four, give me your status."

"One second," said the pilot. "We're about to smoke out this RPG."

A moment later, a steady stream of tracer rounds erupted from the Jayhawk's gunners, slamming into the little pocket of debris beneath the tugboat's pilothouse.

The shooting went on until the pilothouse collapsed.

"Echo Three-Four, RPG neutralized."

"Your boy's in deep shit over here, guys," said Faulks.

Barnes rotated so he could see the downed pilot. The man was standing in the middle of a ring of zombies. The way he was standing, it was obvious he'd broken one of his legs, but the man fought bravely, placing his shots carefully, not rushing them.

"You guys gonna help him?" Faulks said.

"Roger that, Echo Three-four."

The Jayhawk and the three other Dolphins moved into position, but Barnes could tell it was too late for the man on the ground even before the H-Boys started shooting. The man was pulled down below a sheet of corrugated tin by one of the zombies, and a moment later the water turned to blood where he had been standing.

"Echo Three-Four to Mama Bear, Delta One-Six has been compromised."

A pause.

"Roger that, Echo Three-Four. Status report."

Instinctively, Barnes swept the area, taking it all in. He saw the smoking helicopter, the zombies advancing through an endless plain of maritime debris, the uncles scrambling to escape the zombies, jumping into the channel and swimming for the boats. One of the boats had already made it a good fifty yards from the bank.

Echo Three-Four completed his status report. There was another pause while Mama Bear conferred with Papa Bear, and then Mama Bear gave the order that turned Barnes's stomach.

"Smoke 'em all," said Mama Bear. "Disable those boats and neutralize any targets in the water."

A moment later, the air was alive with tracer rounds.

Barnes watched as the machine guns chewed up people and zombies and boats, and something inside him went numb.

*   *   *

Three miles to the east, on a small shrimp boat chugging quietly away from the darkened coastline, Robert Connelly heard the guns and saw the smoke columns rising up into the darkening sky.

"You okay, Bobby?" he said to his son.

The boy nodded into his shoulder and Robert hugged him.

Robert turned and looked over the faces of the forty refugees who had commandeered this boat with him. Several of them coughed. Half of them were sick with one kind of funk or another. Their faces were gray and gaunt, their eyes dull and languid in the darkness. They were all too tired, he realized, to understand just how lucky they were. The others had insisted on going to the main docks just above San Jacinto State Park, claiming there'd be more places to hide there. But Robert and his people had refused to go that route. They decided to take their chances, alone, down around Scott Bay. And now, as he listened to the explosions and the gunfire, it looked like that gamble was paying off.

He listened to the water lapping against the hull, to the steady droning thrum of the engines. He felt the wind buffeting his face.

He could feel the anxiety and the frustration and two years of living like an animal among the Houston ruins lifting from him. He took a deep breath, and though his chest hurt, it felt good to breathe air that didn't taste like death and stale sweat and chemicals.

He squeezed Bobby again.

"I think we're gonna make it," he said.

Chapter 2

"Bobby?"

A hard thud against the door.

"Bobby, let me see you. Bobby?"

Robert Connelly looked through a yellowed, grimy window, trying to catch a glimpse of his boy out there. He saw a few of the infected staggering around in the dark, trying to keep their balance as the boat pitched on the dark waves.

A hand crashed through the window and Robert stepped out of reach. The zombie groped for him, slicing its arm on the glass stuck in the frame. There was a time when seeing the zombie's arm cut to ribbons like that would have made him vomit, all that blood. Now the arm was just something to avoid.

Robert got as close as he dared to the broken window. "Bobby, are you out there? Bobby?" Sometimes the infected remembered their names, responded to them. He had seen it happen before.

He waited.

There was another thud against the door and this time something cracked.

"Bobby?"

He heard the infected moaning, the engines straining at three-quarters speed. The waves slapped against the hull.

He stepped over to the controls and looked out across the water. Far ahead, shimmering lights snaked across the horizon, sometimes visible, sometimes not, depending on the pitch of the bow over the waves. He thought for sure it was Florida. They had almost made it.

The thought took him back almost two years, to those lawless days after Hurricane Mardell. He remembered the rioting in the streets, the terrified confusion as nearly four million people scrambled to safety. Bloated, decaying corpses floated through the flooded streets. Starvation was rampant. Sanitation and medical services were nonexistent. Helicopters circled overhead for a few days after Mardell, picking up whomever they could, but there were so few helicopters, and so many to be rescued.

And then the infected rose up from the ruins.

At first, Robert believed they were bands of looters fighting with the authorities. He didn't believe the reports of cannibalism. Paranoid hysteria, he called it. But then he saw the infected trying to get into the elementary school gym where he and Bobby and about a hundred others had been living. After that, he knew they were dealing with something more than looters.

He took Bobby on a desperate three-day trek north, and they made it as far as the quarantine walls, where they were turned back by soldiers and police standing behind barricades.

"We're going to survive this," he told his son. "I will keep you safe. I promise."

He had said those words while they were sitting on the roof of a house less than half a mile from the wall, sharing a can of green beans they'd salvaged from the kitchen pantry. There was no silverware, none that they trusted the look of anyway, and they had to scoop out the food with their fingers. In the distance, they could see helicopter gunships sprinting over the walls. It was late evening, near dark, and they could hear the sporadic crackle of gunfire erupting all around them.

"It doesn't matter, Dad."

Robert Connelly looked at his son. The boy's shoulders were drooped forward, the muscles in his face slack, like somebody had let the air out of him. "Bobby," he said, "why would you say something like that? Of course it matters."

There were two green beans floating in the bottom of the can. Robert offered them to Bobby.

The boy shook his head.

"There's no point."

"Bobby, please. It matters to me."

The boy pointed at the wall. "Look at that, Dad. Look at those walls. Look at all those helicopters, all those soldiers. Think how fast they put all this up. They're not ever going to let us go. They want us to die in here."

Robert hardly knew what to say. Bobby was only thirteen years old, too young to think his life was valueless.

But he'd already noticed there were no gates in the quarantine wall.

He hoped they'd simply missed them.

They hadn't.

For two years, Robert kept them alive, fighting the infected, rarely sleeping, scavenging for every meal. The struggle had carved a fierce resilience into his grain, a belief that his will alone was enough to sustain them against the cozy, narcotic warmth of nihilism.

With a small band of like-minded refugees, he found a serviceable boat in the flooded debris field of the

Houston Ship Channel. There wasn't a sailor among them, and yet they'd dodged the helicopters and slipped through the Coast Guard blockade undetected. For a glorious moment that first night, holding his boy, he'd believed they were really going to make it.

Now, he knew better.

One of the forty refugees on board the *Sugar Jane* was infected, and that first night, while they were at sea, he turned.

Robert Connelly was the only one left. He'd made a promise to his son and he'd almost kept it. He'd sought to escape the criminal injustice his government wrought upon him by locking him up inside the quarantine zone, and he'd almost succeeded.

But almost only counts in horseshoes and hand grenades, he thought, smiling faintly at the memory of one of his father's favorite expressions. And now the *Sugar Jane* was a plague bomb bound for some unsuspecting shore.

But what was the sense in worrying about it? It didn't matter anymore.

Not without the boy it didn't.

Not to Robert Connelly.

There was another thud against the door, and it splintered. A shard of plywood skidded across the deck, landing near his feet. Bloody fingers tore at the hole in the door. A face appeared at the widening crack, the cheeks and lips shredded to a pulp, the small, dark teeth broken and streaked with blood. The moaning became a fierce, stuttering growl.

That might be Bobby there; it was hard to tell. But it didn't matter.

Robert looked over the controls. The boat would run itself. And it looked like they had enough fuel to finish the voyage. There was nothing left to do here. He stood as straight as the rolling deck of the boat allowed and prepared to run for it.

There was a hammer on the chair beside him.

He picked it up. Tested its heft.

It would do.

The door exploded open.

Bobby and two others stood there. Bobby's right hand was nearly gone. So, too, were his ears and nose and most of his right cheek.

"Ah, Jesus, Bobby," Robert said, grimacing at the wreckage of his son.

They stumbled forward.

Robert moved past Bobby and swung at the lead zombie, dropping it with a well-placed strike to the temple.

The other closed the gap too quickly, and Robert had to kick it in the gut to create distance. He raised the hammer and was rushing forward to plant it into the thing's forehead when Bobby grabbed his shoulder and clamped down with a bite that made Robert howl in pain.

He knocked the boy to the deck and swung again at the second zombie. The claw end of the hammer caught the zombie in the top of the head and it dropped to the deck.

Bobby was on him again.

He grabbed the boy and turned him around and hugged him from behind, determined not to let go. A group of zombies was bottlenecking at the door. Robert knew he had only a few minutes of fight left in him. He charged the knot of zombies at the door and somehow managed to push them back. Hands and arms crowded his face, but he wasn't worried about escaping their bites. Not at this point. All that mattered was getting on top of the cabin and up into the rigging.

Bobby struggled against his hold, but Robert managed to get his left arm across Bobby's chest and over his right shoulder, pinning the boy's arms. With an adult, it wouldn't have been possible. But with a boy, and especially with a boy who had existed at a near-starvation level for two years, Robert managed fairly well.

The zombies clawed at him. They tore his cheeks and arms and neck with their fingernails. One of them took a bite out of his calf. But they couldn't hold him.

He was breathing hard by the time he reached the top. He could feel his body growing weak. The infection felt like somebody was jamming a lit cigarette through his veins. But he reached the top of the rigging, and once he was there, he slipped a small length of rope from his back pocket and looped it around Bobby's left hand, then around his own.

"It's all right," he whispered into Bobby's ear. "Don't you worry. We're together now and nothing else matters."

In the distance, he could see the bobbing string of lights that marked the Florida coast. Fireworks exploded above the horizon.

It was the Fourth of July.

"It's beautiful, isn't it?"

The zombie, his child, struggled against him. It wouldn't be long now. He felt so weak, so sleepy. Soon, nothing else would matter.

They were together. And that was enough.

"That's what counts," he said. "I love you, Bobby."

Chapter 3

It was a cloudy, humid morning. Some of the prisoners were trying to sleep. Others were gazing vacantly out of the bus windows as it made its way southward through the heart of Sarasota, Florida's coastal district. Billy Kline had his head against the wire mesh covering the windows, watching the others as they swayed in their seats to the motion of the bus. Beside him, Tommy Patmore was absently pulling at the loose threads of his work pants. The mood was subdued, quiet, each man lost to his own thoughts.

A few of the guys had their windows down, but not even the occasional draft of sea air that managed to find its way into the bus could cover up the smell. Their work clothes were little more than heavy-duty orange hospital scrubs with SARASOTA COUNTY JAIL stenciled across the back, and though they were supposedly washed after every use, they nonetheless stank of mildew and sweat and something less definable that Billy Kline had only now identified.

It was the rank odor of despair.

He'd been thinking a lot about despair lately. There

were times when he felt it as a physically immediate
and distinct sensation, like the burning itch between
your toes after a few days of taking communal showers;
or the painful swelling in your bowels that came with
your first few meals; or rolling over at night and seeing
the man in the cot next to you enveloped in a living
haze of scabies. But there were other times when it was
more tenuous, like when you heard the resignation in
your mother's voice when she said good-bye at the end
of your ten-minute Tuesday night phone call; or when
you seethed with a cold, mute rage every time some
bored guard emptied everything you owned onto his
desk from a paper grocery sack and picked through it
like he was looking for a pistachio kernel in a pile full
of shells.

He felt so much rage.

Billy was twenty-five, halfway through an eight-month
sentence for selling stolen property to undercover officers. Before that, he had done two months for car burglary, charges dismissed. And the year before that, he'd
done three months, again for car burglary, and again
with the charges ultimately dismissed. There had been
other visits, too.

But this time was different.

This latest round of trouble had finally pissed his
mom off to the point where she no longer asked for ex-
planations or feigned credulity when he provided them
unsolicited.

This time, he had finally hit bottom.

Beside him, Tommy Patmore sucked in a deep
breath.

Billy leaned over and whispered, "You're gonna un-
ravel those pants you keep picking at 'em."

A murmur.

"What'd you say?"

"Be quiet."

Tommy glanced furtively around the bus. No one was paying any attention to them.

Billy followed Tommy's gaze and frowned. "What's wrong with you?"

One more look around.

"Ray Bob Walker came to see me this morning before we left. They asked me if I wanted to join."

Billy sighed inwardly. He'd been dreading this.

"And? What'd you say?"

Tommy looked at him. It was enough.

"Ah, Tommy, you gotta be shitting me. What were you thinking?"

"Be quiet, Billy. They'll hear you."

"Fuck them. Tommy, I told you those Aryan Brotherhood assholes will get you killed. Is that what you want? You know what those guys do. What the fuck's wrong with you?"

"Be quiet," Tommy said. "They'll hear you."

He looked around the bus again. Billy looked, too. He saw a lot of bald heads: a mixture of blacks and Mexicans and white guys. The Mexicans and the white guys all had prison tats on their necks. The white guys came in two body types. You had the big guys, stout, meaty, biker types. They tended to be the older ones, doing time for robbery or check kiting. Then you had the lean ones, wiry, wild-eyed. They were the loud ones, the meth heads, the fighters, the ones with something to prove.

Tommy is going to fit in well with the younger ones, Billy thought. He had the body type. He had the same desperate air about him, an urgent need to fit in somewhere, anywhere. But then, all the young white guys who joined the Aryan Brotherhood started out that way. They were all angry, frustrated, a little frightened to find themselves alone in a world that demanded so much and yet seemed to promise so little in return. The

Aryan Brotherhood offered safety. It offered direction. It offered a society that gave its members rank and made them something special within their own little world. It offered an "us" and a "them." For someone like Tommy Patmore, the appeal was irresistible.

But they hadn't looked twice at Billy. With a last name like Kline, they all assumed Billy was Jewish. But if he was, his family had neglected to tell him about it. And yet his name was enough to brand him a Jew in the eyes of his fellow prisoners. It made him a sort of nonentity, a prisoner like the rest, yet distinct enough that he didn't fall inside any of the racial lines that sharply divide all U.S. jails and prisons. At six-one and a hundred and ninety pounds, he was big enough and tough enough to stand in the no-man's land between the gangs, but it was a precarious existence. He was always watching the man behind him, because that man could turn on him at a moment's notice, and maintaining that nearly constant state of vigilance wore Billy down, exhausted him.

That was the big reason why he hated to see Tommy Patmore get sucked into the gangs. He liked Tommy. Now, Tommy was one more individual he'd have to watch out for.

"Just do me a favor, would you?" Billy said. "Do your time smart. If they try to talk you into hurting somebody, get the hell out. The last thing you want to do is spend the rest of your life in a state pen someplace."

Tommy swallowed the lump in his throat. Then he looked down at his hands folded in his lap.

That was all Billy needed to see.

"Ah, Tommy, you are one dumb son of a bitch. What did you agree to do?"

"Please don't say anything."

"What are you going to do? Tell me."

Tommy looked around, then folded down the waistband of his pants, exposing a five-inch-long piece of tin that had been hammered into a crude shank, some duct tape wrapped around the blunt end as a handle.

"They haven't told me who yet."

"Ah, Tommy. For Christ's sake."

"Don't say anything, Billy. Please."

"I won't," Billy said.

He looked away in disgust.

In his mind, he tried to wash his hands of Tommy Patmore, though it wasn't as easy as it should have been.

They were pulling into Centennial Park. The Gulf of Mexico stretched out before them like a flat green sheet of cold pea soup. Gulls circled over the water, filling the morning air with noise. The smell of the ocean was thick and pungent and pleasant. Billy closed his eyes and breathed in deeply. For a moment, he imagined that all his problems were somewhere else.

But it was the last quiet moment he would ever know.

The driver parked the bus in the middle of a nearly empty parking lot, and things started to happen quickly after that.

Billy shuffled off the bus with the others.

A few of the men stretched.

A guard came by and collected their SID sheets, the 3 x 5 index cards that contained all their personal information and that they had to present to the guards every time they moved from one place to the next.

Billy and three of the others were pulled off the line and brought over to the equipment stand.

A guard handed Billy a canvas sack with a strap meant to go over one shoulder like an Indian papoose and a sawed-off broom handle with a dull, bent spike shoved into one end.

"Collection detail," the guard said. "You're with Carnot. Over there."

Deputy Carnot, who the prisoners called Deputy Care-not because he didn't seem to give a shit about anything except talking on his cell phone, waved his men over and pointed them toward a large plain of grass south of the parking lot. He didn't even have to stop talking on the phone. Billy and the other members of the collection detail had all done this before. They knew the drill. Fan out. Fill your bag. Empty it into the garbage sacks brought up by the runners.

Billy worked steadily for the better part of an hour, going up and down the grassy expanse of Centennial Park, spearing trash, while the others went around emptying garbage cans into sacks and carting them off to a Dumpster that had been brought in for their use. It was easy work, mindless, and in his head he was drifting.

All that morning, the wind off the Gulf had been trying to clear the clouds from the sky, and it was finally starting to succeed. It was getting hot. Billy walked over to where Deputy Carnot was sitting in a lawn chair next to a yellow watercooler, talking on his cell phone.

"Hey, boss, you mind if I get a drink?"

Carnot gave him a frown and a dismissive wave of his hand. *I don't give a shit. Do what you need to do and lemme alone.*

It sounded like he was talking to his girlfriend. Billy shook his head and smiled. Then he filled a paper snow cone cup with water and leaned on his trash spike while he drank it down in one quick gulp. It felt good going down, cold and clean.

He leaned down again for another drink, and that's when he saw it.

He froze.

About a hundred feet away, DeShawn James, one of the younger black guys on the work crew, was wrestling with a heavy trash can, trying to pull it out of a wooden bin so he could empty it. Behind him, hugging a line of shrubs and coming up fast, was Tommy Patmore.

Billy could see the tin shank glinting in Tommy's right hand.

Damn it, Tommy. You are one dumb son of a bitch.

Billy glanced at Carnot. The man was oblivious, still talking on his phone. No one else seemed to have noticed Tommy making his move either, and that was good.

Billy filled his cup, stood, and looked away, anywhere but at what Tommy was doing.

And that's when he saw the man coming down the sidewalk toward him. His right arm was dark with dried blood, but he was walking normally, which is why Billy didn't clue in right away that he was looking at a zombie. Like everybody else, he had seen the news footage from Texas. He had seen the infected wading through the flooded streets of Houston, their movements jerky and uncoordinated. He had seen the fighting in San Antonio and Austin and Dallas. He had read about them in magazines and seen the public service announcements on TV, telling you what to do if you should ever encounter one of the infected. But none of that occurred to him just then. All he saw was a man who didn't look right but who sent a shiver down his spine just the same.

It wasn't until he saw the man's milky eyes that everything clicked.

And then he knew what he was looking at.

"Hey, boss," he said.

Carnot rolled his eyes up at Billy. *What the fuck do you want?*

Billy pointed at the approaching zombie with a nod of his chin.

Carnot looked over his shoulder, then did a double take. "Holy shit," he said. He stood up and backed away from his lawn chair, still holding the cell phone to his ear.

The zombie stepped off the sidewalk and onto the grass. It raised its arms, its hands outstretched and clutching for them in a gesture of supplication that Billy found strangely funny.

But he stopped laughing when the zombie started to moan. When you do nothing but sit around the common room of a jail pod all day, you watch a lot of TV. He had heard that moan before, on the news. Once, he'd seen a news spot where hundreds of the things had been moving down a San Antonio street. The things had been packed in tightly. And even with the volume turned down and the other guys talking and laughing and making asses of themselves all around him, he could still feel the gooseflesh popping up on his arms. But seeing it on TV was nothing like hearing it in person. The real thing took his breath away.

"Shoot it," he said to Carnot.

But Carnot just stood there, the phone still stuck to the side of his face.

"Hang up the fucking phone and shoot," Billy said.

Carnot groaned. Then he seemed to find himself. He looked at the phone like he was surprised it was still there. Then he said, "Babe, I gotta go."

He flipped the phone closed and slid it into his gun belt.

Then he pulled his gun.

"Sir, you need to stop."

"He's not gonna stop," Billy said.

"Shut up," Carnot snapped.

He raised his gun and pointed it at the zombie's chest.

"Stop, police!" Carnot shouted.

The man lumbered forward.

"Jesus, Carnot, he's not gonna stop. Fucking shoot him already."

"Stop," Carnot said. But his voice was barely a whisper. He lowered his gun, raised it again.

"Oh, for Christ's sake," Billy said. He stepped around Carnot with his trash spike raised like a javelin and jammed it into the zombie's temple.

The zombie didn't go down. It stayed on its feet and even turned a little toward Billy, its hands coming up to clutch at him. Grunting with the effort, Billy held on to the spike and worked it around inside the wound until the zombie's arms dropped down to its sides and it sagged to the ground. Billy guided it down onto its back and then yanked his spike free.

"Holy shit," Carnot said. "What the hell did you do?"

Your job, you idiot.

But he didn't say that. His gaze went right past Carnot to the parking lot. Three more zombies were limping toward them. They looked different than the one Billy had just put down. They were shabbier. Their clothes were gray, filthy rags. Their faces were gaunt, smeared with blood. They looked like the zombies he had seen on the news, the ones inside the quarantine zone.

He heard moaning to his right and looked that way.

"What the hell?" he said.

There were two zombies there, a man and a young boy, their wrists tied together.

"Hey, boss," he said. "We're gonna need that pistol."

"Yeah," Carnot said.

But the deputy was shaking so badly he could barely point his gun at the approaching zombies, all of whom had started to moan loudly. The sound carried with disturbing clarity across the park. It seemed to be coming from everywhere at once.

"We have to get to high ground," Billy said.

Carnot nodded, but didn't move.

"Come on," Billy said.

He grabbed the deputy by the shoulder and pulled him toward the bus. There was enough of a gap between the zombies that Billy thought they'd be able to make it at a brisk walk, but they hadn't gone more than a few steps when one of the prisoners tumbled out of the bus doors and landed on his back in the parking lot. It looked like his throat had been torn out. One of the guards climbed down after him, his face and the front of his uniform soaked through with a reddish-brown stain.

"Get on your radio," Billy said to Carnot. "Call for help."

Carnot reached down to his belt and felt for where the radio should have been, but wasn't. He looked back at the water cooler. Billy followed his gaze and saw the radio in the grass next to the lawn chair.

"For Christ's sake," Billy said.

One of the other prisoners was coming across the grass toward them. Most of his face was gone. Billy stared at the man. He'd heard the infected could ignore pain that would put an uninfected person over into unconsciousness. There were recorded instances of the infected walking around with their intestines hanging out of their bellies. But Billy hadn't really believed those things until now. That man, his face had literally been chewed off. And he was still coming.

Billy looked around for a place to take cover. The news had said to seek the high ground, if possible. There was a gap between the approaching zombies and through it he saw a car parked off by itself.

"There," he said to Carnot. "That car over there. Come on."

They ran for it, Billy pulling Carnot along behind him. The car was a fairly new Buick in decent shape. It was empty, and Billy was glad for that. He jumped onto the roof, turned, and pulled Carnot up next to him. Then they got on the roof and stood side by side, watching the zombies getting closer.

"You're gonna have to shoot," Billy said.

Carnot raised his weapon. Billy watched him take aim at a man in running shorts and the remnants of a bloodstained white T-shirt.

"Shoot him," Billy said.

Carnot fired. The bullet smacked into the man's shoulder and spun him around, but it didn't drop him. He turned back toward them and came on again.

"Head shots, damn it," Billy said.

"I'm trying," Carnot said. His voice was trembling.

He fired three more times and managed only one hit.

Within moments they were surrounded. Mangled hands clutched at their feet. The moaning was deafening. Carnot was shaking badly now. He was firing wildly, completely missing zombies that were less than three feet from the tip of his gun. Billy, meanwhile, was kicking at hands and spearing at faces, making his movements count.

He got one of the zombies in the forehead and the man slumped forward onto his knees, his face pressed against the back driver's-side window by the bodies pushing in from behind him. One of the zombies in the back managed to ramp up over the fallen zombie's back and came up onto the roof.

Billy sidestepped around the zombie's outstretched arms and pushed him down onto the trunk.

He heard a click.

Carnot was standing there, pointing his empty Glock at the zombies below him. The slide was locked back in the empty position.

"Goddamn it. Reload!"

Carnot pointed the empty pistol at another zombie and tried to pull the trigger.

"Reload your fucking—"

But Billy didn't get a chance to finish. Carnot vanished. It was like Wile E. Coyote in those old Road Runner cartoons. One second he was there; the next he was gone, his feet pulled out from underneath him. The back of Carnot's head smacked against the edge of the roof with a sickening crunch and then they pulled him down to the ground.

As Billy watched, they swarmed Carnot, tearing at him with their teeth and their fingers.

His screams lasted only a moment.

Billy didn't waste time watching Carnot twitching in his death throes. Instead, he jumped to the ground and ran for it. A few of the zombies tried to follow, but they were slow. Billy was able to weave through them easily. Once he created some distance, he stopped, caught his breath, and looked for an escape route.

There were, he guessed, maybe sixty or seventy of the zombies walking across the park. Most were close by, already in the parking lot. A few were crossing the street into the hotels and green belts opposite the park. In the distance, he could hear police sirens getting closer.

"Never thought I'd be happy to hear that," he muttered.

Out of the corner of his eye he saw movement, a splash of orange coming around a line of shrubs.

It was Tommy Patmore. His arms and his stomach and his thighs were soaked with blood, but he didn't look infected. He looked shell-shocked, confused. The shank was still in his hand.

From behind Tommy, one of the other prisoners was coming up fast. He was limping, a bad bite wound just below his knee, but he was still moving with frightening speed.

A fast mover, Billy thought. The articles he'd read had mentioned how some of the zombies, the ones who were in really good physical condition before they became infected, sometimes managed to maintain a measure of their former physical prowess when they turned. But the same article had also said that it took longer for those people to turn. They'd only been out about two hours. How had this happened so fast?

He shouted, "Tommy, look out!" and ran for his friend.

He got there just as the fast mover was closing on Tommy, and he jammed his trash spike into the zombie's ear. The zombie fought like a big fish on a hook, but it eventually went down.

Billy pulled his spike out of the zombie's head and turned to Tommy.

"Are you okay? Did you get bit?"

Tommy's mouth was working like he was chewing gum, but he wasn't making words.

"Tommy, answer me."

"I . . . I killed him. I did it."

He was crying, his body shaking all over.

"What? Who?"

"DeShawn James. They wanted me . . . They told me to . . . I stabbed him in the belly and then I stopped, you know, I . . . I had changed my mind. I didn't want to hurt him. I didn't. But then he started fighting me."

Tommy glanced down at the shank in his hand like he didn't know what it was.

He said, "I didn't want to. God, there was so much blood."

"Yeah, well, you did. Now it's time to cowboy the fuck

up and deal with it. We're in a world of shit here, Tommy. Are you bit anyplace?"

"Bit?"

"Oh, for Christ's sake, Tommy. Are you hurt?"

"No."

"Good. We got to get to someplace safe." He scanned the buildings across the street. The hotel would be no good. Zombies were already walking up to the covered carport at the main entrance. But farther south, he saw a place that looked promising, a few low structures behind a large pink stucco wall. "Over there," he said. "Come on. Stay close."

And together, they ran for it.

Chapter 4

Houston, Texas: July 5th, 3:15 A.M.

I saw my first zombie from the window of a registered charter bus on the Gibbs-Sprawl Road as we entered the quarantine zone around San Antonio.

That was eight months ago.

She was weirdly sexless, not anything like what I expected. I remember she was standing barefoot in the weeds that had grown up at the edge of the road since the city was abandoned, and her greasy, stringy hair hung down over her face like a wet curtain. Her body was thin and rickety looking. She was wearing a baglike, bloodstained hospital gown, and to me she looked like an emaciated crack whore. She never even looked up, not even as our bus rolled on by. She just stood there, hugging herself with her bone-skinny arms in the cloud of dust our bus had kicked up. I wasn't disgusted like I thought I would be. I just felt sad.

But, like I said, that was eight months ago. I've seen a lot of zombies since then, a lot of death. I've studied them. I've gotten closer than I would have liked at times. Eventually—hopefully—all of these notebooks will get turned into some kind of cohesive whole, some narrative of the zombie outbreak that has brought our great nation from superpower status to the level of a ticking time bomb for the rest of the world, and in that narrative I'll try to find a reason for it all.

If there is one.

Somehow I doubt there is.

I'm growing more and more convinced that there aren't reasons to explain this world we live in. Not good ones anyway.

Maybe that's what makes catastrophes so horrible—the lack of a reason. I mean in a teleological sense. Our brains are wired to see the world in terms of cause and effect. Even the atheists among us find some small measure of comfort knowing that there's a reason things are so bad.

These days, I find myself more interested in the zombies themselves than I am with the traditional things with which a historian and commentator should be concerned. Xenophon, Plutarch, Sallust, Suetonius, Geoffrey of Monmouth, Raphael Holinshed, Francesco Guicciardini, Edward Gibbon—those great chroniclers in the history of historians—they all sought to cast a wide net, giving equal attention to personal agenda and facts. I would like to cast a wide net, too. And I have plenty of opinions. The economic impact of the outbreak at home and abroad, the political flare-ups, the big, empty speeches on the floor of the U.N. and on the White House lawn—all those things have their place in a history with any claim to completeness. But I find it hard to give a rat's ass about them. The politicians aren't out here on the street dying with the rest of us. They're all stashed away in some secure, undisclosed location, waiting it out. And their eloquent speeches don't tell the part of the story that needs telling.

I read Eddie Hudson's book and a dozen others just like it. I know what they described—all the shambling corpselike people flooding the streets, attacking every living thing they could find. Well, I've seen what happens after almost two years. The infected aren't dead. And like all living things, they've changed, adapted. The ones who have survived since the first days of the outbreak—and granted, there aren't many of them—have become something different. And yet, for all that, they are still dangerous; they are still unpredictable. They still attack. They're like alcoholics who can't help coming back to the bottle. Even if they don't want to.

That's the side of this thing I want to talk about.

July 5th, 5:40 A.M.

We've got about twenty minutes until takeoff, and I wanted to jot down a few notes about the quarantine zone. Sometimes I find it hard to wrap my mind around how big it is. The logistical scope of the project is simply staggering.

Back in its heyday, the U.S. Customs and Border Protection Agency patrolled the 2,000 miles of borderland between the United States and Mexico. Of the agency's 11,000 agents, more than 9,500 of them worked along that 2,000-mile stretch of desert. They hunted drug dealers and illegal aliens with a huge array of tools, everything from satellite imagery and publicly accessible webcams to helicopters, horses, and plain old-fashioned shoe leather. Even still, the border had more holes in it than a fishing net.

In comparison, the Gulf Region Quarantine Authority only has a wall of some 1,100 miles to patrol. The wall stretches from Gulfport, Mississippi, to Brownsville, Texas, paralleling the freeway system wherever possible to aid in the supply and reinforcement of problem areas. The GRQA keeps this stretch of metal fencing and sentry towers and barbed wire secure with just over 10,000 agents, most of them former CBP and National Guardsmen and cops. They are aided at sea by the U.S. Coast Guard and in Mexico by federal troops.

Yet despite their numerical advantage over the old U.S. Customs and Border Protection Agency, their job is infinitely harder. Nobody in the old CBP thought too much of it that a steady stream of illegals got through the border every day. They

*just shrugged and went on with life. But the GRQA can't af-
ford to even a single zombie through their line. That would
spell disaster. The pressure is high; the price of failure is apoca-
lyptic.*

*Their job terrifies me. These guys are frequently posted out-
side of major metropolitan areas where the zombie populations
are thickest. Day and night, they have to listen to that constant
moaning. They have to stand by and listen to the plaintive
cries for help from the Unincorporated Civilian Casualties, the
Gulf Region Quarantine Authority's official designation for
the people who were unable to make it out of the quarantine
zone before the walls were put up and were sealed inside with
the zombies. Hearing all that noise for just a few weeks is de-
moralizing. I can't imagine what it would be like to hear it
every single day for months and years at a time.*

*Even worse, I can't imagine what it would be like to grow
used to hearing it.*

*It is little wonder that so many of the GRQA go AWOL at
least once or twice a year. Or that they are never punished for it
when they do. Most don't even get their pay docked.*

*And it's no wonder that the leading cause of death among
GRQA agents is suicide.*

*Actually, I'm surprised it doesn't happen more often than it
does . . .*

From the copilot's chair of a Schweizer 300 helicopter, Ben Richardson looked out across the flooded
ruins of southeast Houston. They were at two hundred
feet, skimming over what had once been wide-open cattle-
grazing land. It was under twenty feet of water these
days. Here and there, he could see the top of an oil der-
rick just below the surface. Dead trees poked skeletal
fingers up through the water. Every once in a while,
they'd pass over a perfectly round metal island, the re-

mains of oil tanks. Dawn was spreading over the
flooded landscape, dappling the water with reds and
yellows and liquid pools of copper.

"Looks pretty, don't it?" Michael Barnes said.

"Amazing," Richardson said. They were talking
through the intercom system built into their flight hel-
mets, but even then they had to nearly yell at each other
to hear over the noise the little helicopter made.

"All those colors you see . . ."

"Yeah?"

"That's oil in the water. Most of this area is so thick
with it you'll be able to see a film over the water come
midday."

Nice, Richardson thought.

This area had once been the hub of the oil and gas
industry in the United States. Now, all of it was gone. It
was no wonder that gas had gone to more than twelve
dollars a gallon in the last two years.

"You see many people down in this area?" Richardson asked.

"You talking about uncles or zombies?"

"Either."

"You see dead bodies every once in a while. You
know, floaters. Hardly ever seen anybody alive, though.
The water's too deep."

Richardson stole a sideways glance at Michael Barnes,
the Gulf Region Quarantine Authority pilot who had
been assigned to fly him around for the next two weeks.
Barnes was a former Houston Police officer, and he still
looked the part. He wore a blue flight suit with a black
tactical vest over that, his sidearm worn in a jackass rig
under his left armpit. He was thirty-eight, tall, lean. He
never seemed to smile.

Richardson had a knack for understanding people.
It was why he was so good at writing about how people
dealt with disasters. But Barnes was a tough nut to

crack. He answered all of Richardson's questions, even the personal ones, with plainspoken ease. But even still, Richardson sensed a hard grain of meanness in the man that was like a warning not to get too close.

"Hang tight," Barnes said. "I'm gonna swing us around and head north toward downtown. I want to show it to you while it's still at high tide so you can see the Hand."

"What's the Hand?"

"That's what we call the shape made by the flood-plain. Due to elevation and runoff and the tides and all that stuff, the outline of the flooded areas changes throughout the day. If you catch it during high tide, the waters look like an outstretched hand about to grab downtown."

"You're joking?" Richardson said.

"Nope. You'll see it right away."

"How come I've never heard that before?"

Barnes shrugged. "The powers that be don't like to make a big deal of it. We have a bad enough time with treasure hunters trying to sneak in. I guess they figure it would make our job even harder if we become some kind of tourist attraction."

Richardson nodded.

After a moment, Richardson said, "I was going to ask you about the treasure hunters. What do you think makes people want to risk sneaking in through the quarantine? Is there really that much worth stealing in here?"

"I guess so. You think about it, really, there's proba-bly a fortune down there. I mean, all our banks and mu-seums and jewelry stores and all that. Those places weren't cleaned out before the storms, and as far as I know they weren't cleaned out afterward. Not with the infected roaming the streets. And with the economy being what it is, can you really blame people for wanting to risk busting the quarantine for some potentially huge profits?"

"No, I guess not."

"Hell, even in good times, just the rumor of treasure is enough for some folks."

Richardson looked down again. They were passing over some kind of refinery now, pipes and trucks and mangled debris visible through the water.

"You're not thinking of going in with some of the treasure hunters, are you?"

Richardson smiled sheepishly. He was never very good at concealing what he was thinking.

"The thought had occurred to me."

"Well, don't think about it too hard," Barnes said. "I mean, you're a nice guy and all, but if I see you trying to come through the quarantine wall some night, I'll shoot you in the head, same as anybody else."

He said it breezily enough, but there was still something there that made it pretty plain he wasn't joking.

"Point taken," Richardson said.

The helicopter's engine hiccupped and they lost altitude momentarily as Barnes wrestled with the controls.

Richardson's stomach went halfway up his throat.

"What the hell was that?"

"Nothing to it," Barnes said. His voice was glassy smooth. "These old Schweizers, they're finicky."

"Are we okay?"

"Yeah, we're fine. Don't worry about it."

Richardson looked doubtful. The helicopter ride was scarier than he thought it would be, and it occurred to him that it wouldn't take more than a strong wind to hurl the thing to the ground.

"Where'd these bullet holes come from?"

Barnes glanced at the holes. "The uncles."

"They shoot at you?"

"Sometimes."

Richardson groaned. "That doesn't make me feel any better."

"It's no big deal," Barnes said. "Here, look down over there. I want you to see this. Whenever I come through here, I always try find some dolphins."

"Dolphins?"

Barnes pointed through the cockpit bubble to the water below. Richardson leaned over to see. They were flying over what had once been I-45, the street lamps and overhead road signs just poking up through the water. Barnes dropped the altitude even lower and cut their airspeed to a crawl. From a height of some sixty feet or so, Richardson could look through the fairly clear water and see the cars and debris down at road level.

"You see 'em?" Barnes said.

Richardson scanned the water for a long moment before he saw what Barnes was trying to show him. There were dolphins down there, three of them. They were headed northbound, toward downtown, paralleling the freeway below them. Richardson guessed the water was between fifteen and twenty feet deep, just deep enough for the animals to skim over the roofs of the sunken cars and still stay submerged. They almost looked like motorcycles zipping through traffic.

"That's amazing."

"Yeah," Barnes agreed. "There aren't many perks to this job, but that's one of 'em."

Richardson watched the dolphins until they finally turned off and swam into the deeper water east of town. They were getting closer to Houston proper now and seeing larger and larger buildings, the ground-level floors flooded to the ceilings.

Richardson crinkled his nose. "Hey, you smell that?"

Barnes looked aft and cursed under his breath.

Richardson turned around in his seat, as much as his seat belt would allow, and saw a long, thick cloud of brown smoke trailing out behind them.

"Holy shit, are we on fire?"

"No, we're not on fire," Barnes said. He sounded annoyed. "The smoke is brown. We're burning oil. The smoke from a fire would be dark black."

Barnes turned back to his controls and started checking gauges.

"Are we going down?"

"We're fine," he said, a bit peevishly. "Just keep quiet and don't touch anything."

Barnes keyed his radio and said, "Quarter Four-One to Dispatch."

"Go ahead, Quarter Four-One," said a woman's voice.

"Quarter Four-One, we're losing oil pressure. I'm smoking pretty bad. I'm gonna try to get us back to Katy Field."

There was a pause on the dispatcher's end that Richardson didn't much like.

"Ten-four," the dispatcher said at last. "What's your location, Quarter Four-One?"

"Quarter Four-One, we're over Bay Area Boulevard and El Camino Real. You have any other units in the area?"

"Negative, Quarter Four-One."

There was a pause on Barnes's end that Richardson liked even less than the dispatcher's.

"Ten-four," Barnes said.

"Quarter Four-One, be advised. I have Katy Field standing by for your approach."

"Ten-four," Barnes said.

Richardson watched Barnes's hands flying over the controls. He had no idea what the pilot was doing, but he could tell plain enough that they were in some serious trouble.

"Officer Barnes?"

"Shut up."

Several tense moments went by. Barnes continued to work the controls. A terrible acid fear spread through Richardson's gut as the engine continued to sputter and smoke. Despite Barnes's best efforts, they were losing altitude and their airspeed was slipping.

The engine sputtered once more and smoke began to pour into the cockpit. Warning lights lit up all across the control panel.

"Quarter Four-One, we're going down. Repeat, we're going down. Coming up on El Dorado and Galveston Road."

Richardson didn't hear a reply. The helicopter shook beneath him, and the next moment they were going down way too fast, coming up on a large grouping of trees and some overhead power lines.

"Hang on," Barnes said.

They hit the water with a hard smack that knocked the air from Richardson's lungs and threw his whole world forward like he was caught on the crest of a wave. The blades of the helicopter's props struck the water with a series of loud slaps before they snapped completely free of the fuselage. The control panel sparked and for a moment there was so much smoke that Richardson couldn't see.

Then water started to pour over his legs.

He screamed.

He felt hands groping at his chest. He tried batting them away, but couldn't. "Stop it," Barnes ordered him. "I'm trying to get you loose."

And a moment later, Richardson felt himself coming out of his seat, strong arms pulling him across the cockpit of the helicopter and into cold water that came up to his waist. He coughed and tried to rub the acrid smoke from his eyes. The water in his mouth tasted nasty, oily.

"Are you okay?" Barnes asked.

Gradually, Richardson's vision cleared. He looked at the officer and nodded.

Barnes turned on the helicopter and then punched it. "Fucking piece of shit," he said. "Goddamn worthless fucking piece of shit."

Richardson was still too stunned to take in the fact that he had just lived through a helicopter crash. It was all he could do to stand on his own two feet.

Barnes, meanwhile, was digging through the cockpit for the emergency kit and his AR-15. He came up with an orange backpack and two rifles. He came over to Richardson and stuck one of the rifles into his hands.

"You know how to use that?"

Richardson took hold of the rifle, gripping it like they'd taught him in the army twenty years earlier.

He nodded.

"Good," Barnes said. "Because we're about to have company."

Only then did Richardson get a sense of their surroundings. They had landed in what looked like a grocery store parking lot. He could see the tops of cars and trucks just rising above the water. Off to their right was a subdivision, the houses sagging in on themselves, empty black holes where the windows and doors had been.

There was movement all around them.

The noise of the crash, he thought. *It'll be like a beacon for the infected.*

Ragged shapes that hardly looked like people anymore stumbled into the water from the subdivision, filling the air with the sounds of their splashing and their moaning.

He looked down at the gun in his hands, then at Barnes.

"Let's move out," Barnes said. "We're on the clock now."

Chapter 5

Art Waller was eighty-four years old and suffering from the classic one-two punch of gastrointestinal nuisances that nature so generously doles out to the elderly: a fixed hiatus hernia and a peptic ulcer.

Add to that two bad knees, a back that screamed at him every time he had to reach below his thighs, and a palsied shake that he was pretty sure was the advance calling card of Parkinson's, and his life was basically an object lesson in misery.

Still, for all that, right now, he had no intention of giving it up.

He turned slightly. Just enough to see that the thing behind him was still gaining.

Art needed a walker to get around. The tennis balls on its legs softened the noise, but the contraption still clanked each time he put his weight on it.

Clank clank. Clank clank.

He was creeping along, but it was as fast as he could go.

He chanced another look at his pursuer. There, on

the sidewalk, less than ten feet behind him now, was one of the infected. It shouldn't be here. They were supposed to be quarantined. He had seen them on TV and they had said they were all locked up behind the wall. It shouldn't be here.

But it was. And it was about to catch him.

The zombie used to be a nurse here at the Springfield Adult Living Village, but she was nothing but a mess now, no legs. They'd been torn off below her thigh. Now, she was pulling herself along on her belly with raw, bloody, mostly fingerless stubs that had once been her hands, leaving a thick blackish-red snail trail behind her.

And she was getting closer.

He gasped. The sound came up inside him like the rattle of dried beans in a coffee can. He was ashamed at the weakness he heard there, angry at himself. Damn it, he'd fought in Korea. Now, this miserable body of his was moving like the hour hand on a clock.

And that zombie behind him, she was the minute hand.

It was a slow-motion pursuit, but she was going to catch him. It was just a matter of time.

Clank clank. Clank clank.

He tried a few doors, but it was the Fourth of July weekend and there was almost nobody left here at the Village. Just a skeleton crew of staff and a few residents.

He tried another door.

"Help me," he cried. "Please."

Behind him, the thing crawling on the sidewalk began to moan.

The sound of it unhinged something inside him. Union troops, he remembered, waiting on one knee in some cornfield someplace, their rifles ready at their cheeks, told stories of hearing the Confederates coming toward them, the rebel yell echoing off the surrounding hillsides. It did something to you deep in your bowels, they said, rattled you.

This was infinitely worse.

He tried to go faster.

Clank clank. Clank clank.

Just ahead, there was a hallway. He could hear voices. A man's deep voice. A woman's laughter.

The man's voice again.

Ed Moore, he thought. *The retired U.S. Deputy Marshal.*

"Help me," he said. "Ed?"

He put everything he had into it.

Clank clank. Clank clank.

Ed Moore had moved to Florida back in February because he liked the weather. For eleven years after his retirement from the U.S. Marshals Service, he'd lived in Amarillo, the Texas panhandle, where the winters were an endless parade of icy sleet and gray skies and wind that never stopped howling. Compared to that, Florida, with its comfy little villas nestled among the bougainvillea and palm trees and the live-in staff who wandered the place in their golf carts, was an absolute paradise.

The woman, Julie Carnes, was new to the Springfield community. She'd moved in at the end of June. She'd caught his attention right off, slender, a pretty face. Not handsome, but pretty. Still wore her hair long. He liked that. He leaned against the doorway to her private cottage and tipped his cowboy hat to her through the screen door. Ed said he thought it was time he introduced himself.

She was knitting something. She folded the needles together and rested them on the lap of her white dress.

He was wearing loose, faded blue jeans, black boots, a clean white shirt open at the neck. He doffed his cowboy hat to her as he entered, exposing a thick, uncombed tangle of white hair before sliding the hat back onto his head. There was a weatherworn look about him, like he should be trailing a cloud of dust.

She said, "You the resident cowboy?"

He smiled. He didn't mind smiling. He still had all his own teeth. "You're just like I figured," he said.

"Oh? And what did you figure?"

"Well, I figured I'd found somebody I could talk to."

"How do you know you can talk to me?"

"Well," he said, "I ain't never seen you in purple. I hate purple on a woman. All the women around here, they wear purple like it's some kind of uniform."

"You mean an old-lady uniform? I'm seventy-five years old, Mr. Moore. I don't need a uniform for people to know I'm an old crone."

"You ain't a crone," he said. "You wanna know the truth? I think you're about the best-looking woman in this place. I mean that. I'm talking about the staff, too. And by the way, you can call me Ed."

She nodded. There was a lull.

"So, you're here by yourself?" she said.

"For the last six years."

"You've been here six years?"

"I've been here since February. I've been on my own six years."

"Ah," she said. "Two years for me."

"You get lonely?"

She shrugged. "Sometimes. A girl can knit only so many scarves. Why, you asking me out?"

"Jerry Jeff Walker's gonna be in Tampa next Friday."

She laughed. "I knew it. A cowboy. The hat isn't just for show, is it?"

"Been wearing it all my life. Don't see any reason to give it up now."

"You mean now that you're not a marshal anymore?"

"How'd you know about that?"

She looked down at her knitting needles, fidgeted with them. "I asked around about you," she said. He thought he saw a blush, but that might have been the light.

Encouraged, he said, "They'd don't have cowboys where you come from?"

"I'm from Monroeville, Pennsylvania. They got George Romero, and that's about it."

"Ah."

"You like living here?" she asked.

"It's okay. Actually, to tell you the truth, not as much as I thought I would. I don't play golf, and I don't read like I planned on doing. Most of these other guys here, they sit around all day and watch the news and talk about how much better things were when Ronald Reagan was in office. It makes me wanna pull my hair out."

"So what do you do?" she asked. "Sit around with them and wait for something to happen?"

"Well, I had kinda thought that something just did happen."

She blushed that time. He was sure of it.

He was about to ask her if she wanted to come back to his place for a drink when they heard panting outside the door.

"Help me," came a man's voice. "Ed?"

Julie looked at Ed. He frowned. He went to the screen door and poked his head out, a silhouette standing there in the sunshine.

"Art? What's wrong there, buddy?"

"The nurse," he panted. "Out there. She's infected. Oh, Jesus, after me. Ed . . . please help me."

"Hold on there, Art. I'll help you." He turned to Julie. "You mind if I bring him in here?"

"Of course not," she said, and rose from her chair and started clearing skeins of yarn and magazines from a couch in the living room.

They sat Art down on the couch, the two of them lowering him onto his seat even as he went on frantically babbling about something going on outside in the hallway.

"What happened to him?" Julie asked.

Ed shook his head.

"Out there," Art said. He was gasping. "She's out there."

"Who's out there?"

"The nurse. She doesn't have any legs."

"What?"

"Ed," Julie said. She looked frightened.

"I'll go check it out. You stay here with him."

He slid out the door and stood there for a moment, looking around, then headed off in the direction from which Art Waller had come.

The hallway was empty, quiet, checker boarded with patches of sunlight and shadow, but Ed could still feel the hairs standing up on the back of his neck. Something felt wrong.

Back in 1992, he'd gone into a house in Hugo, Oklahoma, with an arrest warrant for a militant white supremacy nut accused of a church bombing that killed two black women. The house had looked empty, but Ed wasn't so sure. All his internal alarms were blaring. He'd stepped into a back bedroom, and something told him to stop. Looking down, he saw a tripwire under his foot that led up the doorjamb to a shotgun mounted in the ceiling. Another inch and they'd have been cleaning him up off the floor with a sponge and some hot, soapy water.

He had that same feeling now. Moving slowly, he stepped up to the corner of the hallway and looked around. He saw a long, dark smear of blood on the sidewalk. The trail turned in to a room a few doors up the walk. He glanced behind him and saw Julie standing in the doorway, watching him. He motioned her back inside. Then he set off toward the blood trail.

The door was propped open and inside he saw two paramedics and Art Waller's legless nurse feeding on the body of a supine woman, her torso ripped open like a canoe. The body shook and twitched as the zombies tore into her.

Ed nearly vomited.

Three blood-smeared faces looked up at him.

Ed backed away.

One of the zombies, a tall, slender kid in his twenties whose only injury seemed to be a small but festering wound on his shoulder, got to his feet.

The next moment he was running at Ed.

Fast mover, Ed thought. But before he could react, the thing had closed the distance between them. The zombie raised its hands for Ed, and Ed sidestepped him, coming up behind him and pushing him headlong as he swept his feet out from under him.

The zombie crashed headfirst into a bougainvillea bush and got wrapped up inside its dense inner branches.

When Ed turned back to the cottage, the second paramedic was already on his feet and limping more slowly than the first toward him. The legless nurse was dragging herself toward him on her belly.

He stepped out of the doorway and almost ran down the hallway to Julie's cottage, but he stopped when he realized the zombies would follow him.

He couldn't lead them straight to Julie and Art.

He looked around for a way out.

The first zombie, the fast mover, was pulling himself out of the tangled bougainvillea. The second one step-ped out of the doorway. And now he could hear their moans. The sound carried through the courtyard and it made his blood run cold.

Without a plan, he took off running across the court-yard, away from Julie's cottage.

They were still behind him, but he had a pretty good lead. A few quick turns and he lost them somewhere near the path that led down to Tamiami Road and Cen-tennial Park.

And that's when he heard voices.

One voice, actually. A woman's. "It was such a lovely wedding," he heard her say. "Your Daddy was so proud. I remember watching the two of you come down that aisle, you holding on to his arm, just smiling ear to ear. I think it was the only time I ever saw him cry."

Ed followed the woman's voice. It belonged to Bar-bie Denkins, whose husband had died thirty years ear-lier and left her obscenely rich. The woman was in her late eighties now and thoroughly senile, Alzheimer's. Her cottage door was standing open. There was blood on the door frame. Inside, her quarters were packed with unopened boxes of sporting goods and picture frames and vegetable juicers and miracle cleaning products, all of it sold to her by unscrupulous telemar-keters she was too starved for attention to hang up on.

Off in a far corner of the room, a zombie was bump-ing into boxes, trying to fight its way to where Barbie Denkins sat, chattering happily away.

"You didn't want those red flowers on your cake," Barbie said. "But I went ahead and did it just the same, and it was a better cake for it. You tell me it wasn't."

The zombie saw Ed and turned his way.

Beside Ed, next to the door, was an umbrella and a wooden Louisville Slugger baseball bat.

He picked up the bat.

The zombie stepped around a row of boxes, its head leaning to one side at an unnatural-looking angle. One of its cheeks had been torn open so that the mouth was elongated, the bloodstained rows of its teeth visible all the way back to the molars.

It moaned as it raised its hands at him.

Ed took a step forward and swung for the fence, planting the sweet spot of the bat on the side of the zombie's head.

The thing went tumbling backward against the wall, then landed in a heap on the floor.

It didn't move.

There was a pain in Ed's left shoulder and he worked it around in the socket. The joints were protesting the sudden exertion.

"Stay here," he said to Barbie.

Outside her door, the first of the two paramedics was coming around the corner about fifty feet away.

The second one wouldn't be far behind.

He flexed his shoulder once again and raised the bat for another blow. He'd take care of these two, then go back inside and get Barbie.

Piece of cake.

GREAT BOOKS, GREAT SAVINGS!

When You Visit Our Website:
www.kensingtonbooks.com
You Can Save Money Off The Retail Price
Of Any Book You Purchase!

- **All Your Favorite Kensington Authors**
- **New Releases & Timeless Classics**
- **Overnight Shipping Available**
- **eBooks Available For Many Titles**
- **All Major Credit Cards Accepted**

Visit Us Today To Start Saving!
www.kensingtonbooks.com

All Orders Are Subject To Availability.
Shipping and Handling Charges Apply.
Offers and Prices Subject To Change Without Notice.

Feel the Seduction Of
Pinnacle Horror

When Darkness Falls
Grab One of These
Pinnacle Horrors

Scare Up One of These
Pinnacle Horrors